TENGU

THE
MOUNTAIN
GOBLIN

JOHN DONOHUE

TENGU

THE
MOUNTAIN
GOBLIN

YMAA Publication Center
Boston, Mass. USA

YMAA Publication Center, Inc.
Main Office
PO Box 480
Wolfeboro, NH 03894
1-800-669-8892 • www.ymaa.com • ymaa@aol.com

Cover Design: Axie Breen

ISBN-13: 978-1-59439-125-5 (cloth cover)
ISBN-10: 1-59439-125-4 (cloth cover)

ISBN-13: 978-1-59439-123-1 (paper cover)
ISBN-10: 1-59439-123-8 (paper cover)

POD 1108

Publisher's Cataloging in Publication

Donohue, John J., 1956-

Tengu : the mountain goblin / John Donohue. -- 1st ed. -- Boston, Mass. : YMAA Publication Center, c2008.

p. ; cm.

ISBN: 978-1-59439-125-5 (cloth); 978-1-59439-123-1 (pbk.)

1. Burke, Connor (Fictitious character) 2. Terrorists--Fiction. 3. Martial artists--Fiction. 4. Martial arts fiction. 5. Suspense fiction. I. Title.

PS3604.O565 T46 2008   2008936440
813/.6--dc22   0810

To my sisters and brothers
Patricia, Anne, Peter, Matthew, Mary, and Christopher:

First companions on the way.

Prologue

DEMONS

A famous physicist once said that it's impossible to examine the world objectively: The very act of looking disturbs the gossamer filaments that bind the universe together and, as a result, they vibrate with unanticipated harmonics. Our mere existence changes everything.

We move through life thinking that the distinction between ourselves and others, between ourselves and the world, is absolute. The Zen masters know better. We are linked in ways that are both intimate and fearsome.

I have come to believe that this is so. I don't think I could ever have anticipated the events that would have brought me somewhere far from my home, facing death beside the one person I most admired in the world. Looking back, it is as if we were drawn to that place by a chain that, for all its invisibility, was stronger than the steel of the sword that my master taught me to wield.

Our progress through this world sets the sea of molecules in motion. Like tide or wind, our very passage through the world creates unseen patterns in the fabric of life. They churn and swirl. Some fade away into quiet; others spawn into things of a size and monstrous intensity we could never imagine.

These, ultimately are the demons that haunt us. They are not some force from out there—they are creatures of our own making. They grow, sometimes without our awareness, spinning off into the darkness, until the day their orbit brings us once more into collision.

The old teachers were men alive to the currents that swirled around them. Human storm cells themselves, they churned through life with an intensity that de-stabilized the system. And they knew this. So they searched the darkness, aching to divine the pattern of the cyclones that moved, just beyond the limen of consciousness. The power they sensed was something to harness, something to defend against. Something to fear.

The *sensei*, students of both motion and stillness, know that the quest for mastery and control creates new currents, new powers, and new challenges.

These challenges become tests that some survive. But all too often, only the bystanders remain to tell the story.

Yet, the melancholy dignity they have passed on to those who follow in their footsteps is this: together, we can face the looming force in the darkness and not flinch.

1

BURN

The snow burned. It had fallen and frozen into granules overnight, an early dusting of white that hissed across rocks, coiling in the wind like a snake.

Higashi's normally well-manicured hands were red and raw. He slipped as he scrambled across the stone bridge and cursed himself under his breath for being foolish enough to come out here. It was so unlike him to take the risk. He typically lived a life of tight control in a carefully constructed world of his own. But there was a fascination for him in actually seeing this subject, an intense fixation on this man, because Higashi's discovery of him was important in ways no one else had suspected. Now his city shoes gave him no purchase on the icy patches, smooth and uncaring, of the pathway. He could feel the cold working through the thin soles, drawing the warmth from his feet, making him clumsy.

He was not a field agent. He spent his days reviewing logs of phone and e-mail intercepts, a vast blizzard of paper spewed out by the intelligence service's computers. He sifted through fragments of conversations; small pieces of life caught and held up for inspection, pulsing with ghostly implications. Higashi's brain stored and dissected facts, seeking the threads of a connecting web so faint and fine that too heavy a touch could snap it. And when he twisted and turned the data, playing the light just so, a pattern was sometimes revealed. Then, alone in his analyst's cubicle, he would sigh. When he did, the noise of satisfaction, so loud in the hushed scrubbed air of the office, made him glance about guiltily, afraid that his small expression of triumph would be enough to make the web dance with alarm.

Usually he moved slowly, with the cool circumspection of a man who lived most vividly in his head. But, as a man whose subjects were typically beyond Japan's borders, he also grew obsessed with the possibility of this time seeing the suspect with his own eyes.

But there was more to this ambition than he cared to admit. His life was spent working tiny shards of information, hint and innuendo, teasing them into some sort of meaning, a mosaic of blurred boundaries and indeterminate shapes. His father, while he had lived, had hoped for a son who could do more. The old samurai adage that to know and to act were one and the same thing rang through Higashi's childhood. His father, who had early detected a dreamy remoteness in his son, hoped that the rigorous training of the judo *dojo* would pound some sense into the boy.

Even years later, Higashi would shudder involuntarily at the memories of body heat and the scent of sweat, the sound of bodies being pounded flat. It was a world of danger, where people came at you with moves as unpredictable as they were unrelenting. Higashi dreaded it. His father, on the other hand, was a short, squat man in a worn *gi*, who would shuffle onto the tatami mat with the subdued swagger of a man at home in a brutal element. He could not understand his son, and the young Higashi realized with a sinking feeling that he could never meet the expectations of his sire.

The slight and hesitant Higashi was easy prey for the other boys in the class. He went through the motions, learned the moves, but was never able to marshal the fierce, tight explosion of effort that led to success on the judo mats. And in Japan, the nail that sticks up gets banged down. Higashi's time in the judo *dojo* became an exercise in futility and humiliation. Eventually, even his father came to realize it. Higashi never forgot the ill-concealed look of disappointment on his father's face.

Higashi worked hard to compensate. His obvious intelligence permitted him to distinguish himself in his studies. If his father could never quite fathom his bookish son, he could at least take pride in his academic success. But Higashi's penchant for living in his head often made him tone deaf to the nuance of social relations that were so important in getting ahead in corporate Japan. Eventually, and only through his father's connections, he landed a job as an analyst in the security agency.

And now he was on the cusp of being able to discover something remarkable. It was rare that the pieces all fit together, and he yearned to see it with his own eyes. It was a validation of his skill and an opportunity to prove himself. It was something that all the field agents had missed. All the young, tough men who had the same confident swagger as his father. The compelling reason that had ultimately spurred him to leave the safety of his desk was bigger than ambition, more potent than intellectual curiosity. All too often it was the operations agents, not the analysts, who got the credit. In their dismissive attitude toward the analysts, Higashi relived his childhood humiliation. He burned with resentment that he could never be like them, and yet hungered for their recognition. Now, he believed this one safe sojourn into the field would show them—show them all—that he was worth their respect.

Higashi didn't breathe a word of his plans to anyone.

The notice of a special Winter Training event—a *Kangeiko*—was flashed across Higashi's computer screen by the customized search protocol he'd written. Special winter training was common in January and February all over Japan. Martial artists in white uniforms would practice barefoot in the snow, faces ruddy in the wind and bodies steaming with effort. The very thought of it made Higashi shudder. He was not a man accustomed to extremes. But this special event's listing held a name that ultimately pulled him out of the office, onto the train, and into the wooded hills of a rural temple.

The grounds of the temple should have been soothing to someone like Higashi. They were rustic, yet orderly. A weathered *torii* marked the entrance to the precincts. Traditional wooden buildings were set among the trees and a large flagstoned plaza was cradled in the bowl created by surrounding hills. The wind whipped through the gray tree branches. Pines clung to the slopes, dark blotches against the frosty hues of winter.

He had shuffled into the temple grounds with the small crowd of spectators to watch the demonstration of the ko-ryu, the old styles of martial arts. Higashi was nondescript: slight, with his belly starting to swell into the soft middle age of a desk man. His clothes were respectable, but worn looking, his black hair shaggy and unkempt. His small hands were clean and the nails kept fastidiously short. He was a man out of his element. But he wasn't there because of his affinity for the martial arts. Far from it, he was there to put a face to the name of the man he had studied in secret for so long.

Higashi edged closer to the ropes that separated the crowd from the martial arts masters, mouth slightly open with the effort of solidifying the essence of what he knew into the person who stood before him. A lumpy form, bundled in the traditional clothes of old Japan, Higashi's subject was surprisingly agile for a man his age. Higashi saw the man's focused expression, the force of breath that pushed, steam-like into the air, and the whir and snap of ancient swordplay as the old master went through his routine.

Higashi was not a man attuned to others. But even someone more sensitive would have been hard pressed to note the minute surge in awareness on the part of the old swordsman. His eyes were slitted with concentration, shielded by high cheekbones and brow. They flickered once toward Higashi as they registered the vibrations of acute interest coming from the nondescript man in the dark overcoat. Then the whirring arc of steel claimed the old master's whole attention once more.

There were other demonstrations after this, and Higashi wandered the grounds of the temple, partly in an attempt to keep warm, but also hoping to catch a glimpse of his quarry once more. The afternoon sky began to fade to gray with the approach of evening. Higashi was increasingly alone as his shoes crunched along the gravel pathways, lost in thought about the old man, reviewing what he knew, rehearsing the presentation he would make to his superiors.

He looked up with a start at the harsh call of a crow. Alone on the hillside, he could hear the wind and the dry clacking of tree branches. He turned around quickly, sure that someone was on the path behind him. But he saw no one. He focused his attention back down the slope. Hidden by the curve of the land, karate students were exercising in the distant courtyard. He could hear the bark of their cadences bouncing along the hills. And when he looked down the curving path as it dipped into a hollow, the trees seemed to close ranks, crowding in on the trail and blurring its boundaries in the waning light.

He stuck his cold hands in his coat pockets, hurrying back the way he had come, his report forgotten. The brilliance of his investigative triumph seemed suddenly unreal and unimportant. He was now just a man, alone on a winter hillside, cold, and suddenly jumpy. He walked quickly toward the temple, activity masking a growing unease. A more experienced man would have heeded the visceral message his body was sending. A field agent would have known that fear, like cunning, springs from a primitive reflex for self-preservation. Higashi the analyst knew little of cunning. He was learning more about fear.

Lost in his reverie, he had gone far up the slopes. The hills were networked with paths that meandered by scenic overlooks and small clearings. In these spaces, tiny, ancient dolmens listed sadly off their uprights, like forgotten, exhausted travelers. Higashi, lost, walked faster, his head swiveling, eyes hungry for a familiar landmark. He was convinced that he heard footsteps in the woods behind him. But when he looked, there was nothing, just the looming trunks of trees, the wind, and the distant chorus of *kiai* from the karate students in the valley. He felt the hair on the back of his neck rise and he fled down the hill.

His face was slick with sweat. The path dipped down into a dark place. A small rocky streambed glinted with ice. He hurried across a small stone bridge, looking down to keep his footing. He slipped and fell anyway, righted himself and then hurried across the icy place, casting another terrified look behind him.

He ran headlong into the trap.

The old man emerged from the trees along the path, his robes one of many archaic shades living in the hollow of the hills. He stared at Higashi with a fire that halted the younger man in his tracks.

"Who are you?" the old voice hissed.

"Sumimasen," Higashi apologized, ducking his head and spinning around to flee.

"Yame!" the old voice ordered. Higashi felt powerless to withstand the command. Like a man caught in a nightmare, Higashi turned to face the old master. He trembled in fear and cold.

"I must know," the old one croaked, and removed a weapon from under his robes. It was a *suruchin*, a fine chain with a small weight at either end. He held the loops of the chain in his left hand and spun a short length in a tight circle with his right. The chain made a deep whirring sound in the cold air. Higashi was shocked into movement by the sound of the chain. He jerked forward in despair, hands held out like claws.

The chain whipped out, and the weight smashed into the ridge of bone where the nose met the brow. Higashi grunted and sunk to his knees, stunned and bleeding. The old man rewound the chain and watched Higashi impassively. Then the chain snicked out again, smashing into the younger man's cheek. Higashi could taste the blood in his mouth. He spit out a fragment of tooth. In shock, all he could think was how cold and hard was the ground on which he knelt, as cold as the old eyes that bore into him.

He cried out involuntarily as the old man swarmed toward him, but his cry was mixed in with the echo of the *kiai*, the shouts of the karate trainees in the courtyard. Higashi held up his hands defensively. They were beaten away. He tried to rise, but was slammed into the ground and had the wind knocked out of him. He lay stunned and disbelieving, his eyes wide, retreating into innocence. He regretted coming. He yearned for the safety of his cubicle, the ordered ranks of files under his control. He closed his eyes in the hope that, when he opened them, the old man would be gone. Like a bad dream.

When the fine chain looped around Higashi's neck, his eyes jerked open. He was dragged into the woods. He kicked feebly and tried to choke out a protest against the relentless and irresistible force. But no one heard.

Higashi recognized this man in an elemental way. He had the same hard eyes as those judoka from so long ago, the sheer physical presence of his father. It sparked a brief flare of resentment and resistance. Higashi knew what the old one was up to: his contacts abroad and the skills he was selling.

By the time he was finished with the interrogation, the old one knew what he wanted. He worked the nerve points with a casual brutality, his short, hard fingers jabbing, grinding, bringing fire to the last moments of Higashi's life. The analyst gasped and burned, largely powerless to resist the heat of questioning. But even then,

Higashi's mind whirred with a fading spurt of dispassionate analysis. His last coherent thought was that he was glad he had made a complete copy of the file and mailed it to his father. As if to say, here, this is what I've done, finally.

It was the one secret he was able to keep from his murderer. One final triumph on the rocky slope that Higashi's failing senses confused with a judo mat.

In the end, the old one simply snapped Higashi's neck, backing away with an odd fastidiousness as Higashi's muscles spasmed and then relaxed, a stain of urine spreading under the corpse.

The old man melted into the trees, his compact form moving silently through the gloom. In the distance, the *karateka* called together. Their voices echoed in the twilight, bouncing in cadence around the hills, strong, united, and purposeful. Alone in the forest, Higashi's body steamed slightly in the cold air, his eyes open to the sky. The trees creaked in the wind, branches rubbing together and making small noises like hurt animals. Far away, a crow called in distant protest of the coming dark.

2

ZANSHIN

Rain whipped against the high windows of the training hall—hard pellets cast by an angry hand. Inside, students knelt along the hardwood floor of the *dojo*. The room was silent except for the distant noise of wind and weather and the dry rasp of Yamashita's feet as he moved to the place of honor at the head of the room.

He moved with a fluid certainty, settling down into the formal sitting posture known as *seiza* with the soft inevitability of snowfall. Yamashita Rinsuke had been my *sensei*, my teacher, for twelve years, and I had seen him do remarkable things, but the simple spectacle of everyday actions was enough to show me that I was in the presence of a master.

In the martial arts, the really good teachers cultivate in their students an acute sensitivity to various stimuli. Your nerve endings are teased and jolted, your reflex actions made more subtle, and, for some of us, the result is a change in the ways we see the world and exist within it. The true masters are both brutal and refined, compassionate torturers, and guides who lead you to places where you will stand alone, confronting age-old fears that snarl in the abyss.

Once you've gone into that void and come through to the other side, it changes you. You glimpse it sometimes in people who've had a similar experience. I see it in my teacher's face in his rare unguarded moments. And I see it in the mirror. It doesn't make us better than other people, just different.

This day for a fleeting second, as he knelt, I saw something else in Yamashita's expression. It puzzled me. I knew he was displeased with the progress of the afternoon's class, but I didn't think that was what I had detected. My teacher wore a mask during class time—his shaved head swiveled on a thick neck and his eyes were dark holes in a face that regarded his students with silent comment. I've come to be the same way. This afternoon I thought I saw something unusual behind his eyes. It lasted a micro-second, almost like a gap in concentration—what they call *tsuki* in the martial arts—an elusive scent wafted away on a breeze, forever out of reach. Maybe I was imagining things; I know from experience that Yamashita's focus is impeccable. I let the thought go and settled myself, ready for whatever came next.

Lately, Yamashita let me guide the classes. Senior students often do this in the martial arts, but this was a new development for my teacher. His *dojo* was an exclusive one—you didn't get past the door without already having earned a few different black belts and carrying some strong recommendations from people Yamashita knew and trusted. He demanded a great deal from his pupils and they asked for a great deal back, so having his senior student lead the training had not been the practice in the past.

But things change. Some time ago, I had knelt before my teacher and received the ceremonial tokens of my status as *menkyo-kaiden*. It's the highest level of rank Yamashita awards and I'm the only one of his students who has lasted long enough to get it. And it was not just that I had endured the training. I had been tested. I had faced the fear of a fight to the death and had survived. I mean that literally. As I had bent to bow to him during the ceremony, an old wound burned down my back, the reminder of a slashing sword cut and an experience that had taught me that true commitment—to the art, to life—came with a price. Sometimes I wonder whether it was a challenge I could meet again.

Now as I teach, he watches the students as they move through their exercises. He watches me, as well. His gaze is hard and he misses nothing. I watch too, working to correct and guide, but my ability pales besides that of my *sensei*. It's not that I'm not good, just that he is so much better.

I was working with a new group of students, trying to get them to grasp the subtle difference between what we do in Yamashita's *dojo* and what they had been used to in other schools. They were only half listening, and I thought I knew why. I don't look the part of a *sensei*. For one thing, students seem much more willing to believe in an Asian instructor. There's a type of reverse discrimination going on here. Deep down, many martial artists got started in their disciplines because of a fascination with the Mystic Arts of the Far East, and they're still expecting their teachers to be little Asian men with wispy beards in flowing robes. I'm a bit of a disappointment to them. Not only am I not Japanese, I'm not even physically imposing. Average height. Dark hair. Blue eyes. My nose has been broken a few times. Years ago a distant relative from the Old Country told me that I had "a face like a Dublin pig," and things haven't changed much since then. And I was not Yamashita.

But Yamashita's *dojo* is a place where you get what you need, not what you want. He himself is a bit of a surprise. Asian, but not wispy. He's a dense howitzer shell of a human being. He prowls the practice floor like the burly predator that he is. He speaks in an elegant, curt manner with a precise pronunciation that many of his more senior students unconsciously begin to mimic. His hands are broad and the fingers thick, his forearms corded with the strange muscles of the swordsman. So I didn't feel bad that the novices thought I was decidedly second-string. Standing next to my teacher, most people are.

These new students were from various aikido schools and, while it's a nice art, like most systems of fighting it conditions you to do some things extremely well and to do other things not at all. They were all *yudansha*—black belts—and were skilled at the techniques of their system. Some came from the mainline aikido schools that were still connected to the founder's family. A few were from the harder variants promulgated by disciples who founded their own styles of the art. They all had the fluid movement and propensity for direction shifts and other disorienting moves that would let them dominate an opponent. Executed well, these techniques are effective. But the process of learning them, of repeating the same pattern over and over, of dealing with a choreographed response and a looked for result, creates a type of mind-set that Yamashita detests.

People, as my master has taught me and my experience has proven, are unpredictable. Our techniques are grounded in the commonalities of movement and possibility inherent in the human form, but there are always surprises out there. No matter what you expect to happen, you need to stay open to the possibility that things may not turn out exactly as you planned. It's a commonplace insight, but one that needs to be absorbed deep into your muscles, because to overlook it is to court disaster.

I had worked with the students on some variants of a very basic technique they knew as *ikkyo*. It's a defense to an attack that can come in different forms—a grab or a strike—but that ends with the attacker immobilized through an evasive maneuver that unbalances and distracts the opponent, leading him to a point where the joints are manipulated into an angle that violates normal human kinesiology and he's subdued. With students at this level of proficiency, the action is smooth and fast. Partners flow in a blur, swirling into the inevitable success of the technique. It's great, as long as the attacker cooperates.

But what if he doesn't?

I knew only too well that a desperate opponent will do the unexpected. The white scars I have on my hands are a fading reminder of a skilled lunatic who almost took my life. The fear and pain of that battle sometimes returns unbidden late at night and I am haunted by the memory of rain and death on a wooded mountain.

I was trying to impress upon the trainees the importance of real focus and a more elusive quality called *zanshin*. It means "remaining mind," and different teachers use the phrase in different ways. For Yamashita, *zanshin* is the quality that preserves you from losing sight of the unpredictability of life—and of your opponent. We train long and hard to focus on an attack or a technique—to give it everything we've got. But the effect of *zanshin* is the development of an awareness that is both inside and outside the moment. Commitment with flexibility. Balance while flustered. Creativity in chaos.

When my students started to flow into their *ikkyo* routine, I continually encouraged them to stay grounded in the technique, but not to lose themselves in it. It sounded contradictory even to me. The point I was trying to drive home was that they shouldn't be so confident in what they did. They needed to stay alive to the possibility that the opponent would not respond as they had come to expect, that the opponent wouldn't lose focus or balance, or flinch from the distracting *atemi* blow that was intended to set up the technique. It was hard to get through to them. They were more confident in themselves than they were in my ability to show them something new.

Yamashita finally called the group to order, seeing that alone I couldn't get the point across.

He regarded the class. They sat quietly; a few mopped sweat off their brows with the heavy sleeves of their *keikogi*. Many of them had just gotten the dark blue practice tops Yamashita has us wear. They are dyed a deep indigo and when new, the coloring comes off on the skin. I watched the students and smiled inwardly as they created faint blue smudges on their faces. It was a rite of passage we all experienced during our first months here.

Outside, a gust of wind pushed against the building—you could feel the subtle change in air pressure. Winter was upon us. Yamashita's head swiveled to take in the sitting row of novices. His thick hands lay in his lap, palms up and fingers curled slightly, dangerous looking even in rest. He spoke quietly and you had to strain to hear him over the sound of the rain on the roof.

"When we train," he said, "we must strive to go . . . beyond ourselves. To see more than what lies on the surface. So." He gestured with one hand and rose to his feet. He stood in the *hanmi* ready posture familiar to these *aikidoka*. "Familiar technique is a good friend, *neh*?" He flowed in a swift pantomime of the actions in the *ikkyo* technique. Immobilization of the attack with the left hand—a hip twist to off-balance the attacker—the distracting blow—then the finish, as smooth and certain as the downward flow of a current. He finished and looked at us. "But if you lose yourself in the technique, you . . . " he brightened as he came up with the finishing phrase, " . . . lose yourself. Do you understand?" Some heads nodded hesitantly. Others frowned to show him that they were thinking.

Yamashita looked about and sighed. "Sometimes what appears to be our friend can be our enemy. To be so certain that a technique will succeed is to court disaster." He looked eagerly about at the class. They had all been training for years in various *dojo*. Maybe that was the problem. Some schools were tougher than others, but they were all schools. People tended to cooperate with one another. It cuts down on injury and made sure that everyone could make practice again next week. But it wasn't real fighting. The whole point in real fighting is to make sure that the other guy doesn't make practice next week, or maybe ever again. And that's a hard lesson to teach someone.

"So," he concluded and gestured to me. I stood up with an inward sigh. Serving as my teacher's demonstration partner is a regular part of what I do, but it does induce high degrees of wear and tear and I'm not getting any younger. But today I got a reprieve. Yamashita gestured again to another student, a *godan*—fifth degree black belt—in aikido who had some of the most fluid moves we had seen that day.

"*Ikkyo*," he ordered. He didn't bother to identify who was attacker and who was defender. We were all experienced enough to know that the junior member always defends. Which meant that I would attack. We set ourselves and I looked for a brief moment at Yamashita, trying to figure out what exactly he wanted out of me for this demonstration.

He looked right back at me and his glance was the same cold, severe look he gave everyone on the *dojo* floor. "Take the middle way, Burke," he told me.

My teacher is not someone who believes in making things easy.

The whole thing works like this: The attacker reaches out with his right hand and grabs the collar of the defender. So I did, and the *godan* flowed right into the routine. He grabbed my wrist with his left hand while swiveling his hips so as to pull me forward and off balance. Then his right hand came around to smack me in the head and distract me, which should have set me up for the technique.

It's based on a simple premise: it's difficult to stay balanced and centered when threats are coming from either side of you simultaneously. The conventional wisdom is that you either opt to stay upright or block the strike, but you don't do both. At least most people don't.

But Yamashita has trained me to different expectations. I had learned by personal experience that there are people who can defend against things simultaneously. So you'd better learn to deal with it. Which was the whole point I was supposed to drive home to the *godan*.

He grabbed me and did the hip shift. I just extended my right arm through him, following his movement. His *atemi* shot out quick and crisp, a blur on the periphery of my left side. It was a good serious blow and I would have seen stars if it had connected. I liked that about the guy—he was doing this as hard as he could and had enough respect to know that I was capable of dealing with it. It was a shame what I had to do next.

The whole point of the demonstration was to reveal how inadequate his technique was. It's a hard thing to do to someone who's probably got over a decade invested in the move and the system that spawned it. But Yamashita is not in the illusion business. He believes in the underlying unity of everything that's effective and exhorts us to meld functionality with esthetics. Sometimes the result is as graceful as the swoop of a bird. Sometimes you are as subtle as a train wreck, but always your opponent should be the one left in the rubble.

The *godan* was used to dominating people through superior grace and technique. He wasn't used to someone like me. He shifted to draw me off-balance and I drove in to join him. The hand he tried to immobilize loosened its hold on his collar and sought his neck instead. His diversionary strike was hard and fast, but I slammed it away with my left forearm, and I saw the quick wince of pain tighten the skin around his eyes.

That flash was all I needed. I struck him a few times—a chop to the neck, a wicked elbow jab to the solar plexus. It happened too fast for me to bother to register. Then I was behind him, and I strung him out and dumped him hard on the floor. In the real world, you give the shoulders a little English as they go down—it makes the head bounce when it hits. But he was new to Yamashita's school and I tempered my throw with a touch of mercy.

He could fall pretty well, but the thud still echoed in the room. Outside in the murk, thunder rolled in mocking imitation. I came around to the *godan*'s side and looked in his eyes to make sure he was okay. They focused on me all right, and the look on his face was not pretty. I gave a mental shrug and helped him up. To survive in this *dojo*, you must learn to let go of some pride—no hard feelings, just hard training.

Yamashita glided up to us. "So. To assume a technique will work is to provide your enemy with a weapon to use against you. I have made Burke do this thing," my teacher turned to look at the class, making sure that the point he wanted to make was heard. Many of them were eyeing me warily. "In time, you will come to know him. His technique is . . . " he waved a hand as if to show what had just taken place, "as you see. But he sometimes holds back and does not push hard enough."

His students, I thought, *or himself?*

"Burke is a humane man," Yamashita continued. "It is a great gift. But each of us needs to balance mercy with . . . efficiency. The proportions are mixed differently in each of us. And we struggle for balance. Listen to him. Train well. Ultimately, you will find him a good teacher." Then he looked at me, his eyes dark and glittery in the lights, like the flash of stormy weather that was held at bay by the *dojo* walls.

"You must push them, Burke," he told me.

"Yes, *Sensei*," I bowed.

By the time class had ended, night had arrived. The rain came in waves, the distant drumming echoed in the murky night. Yamashita and I went up to the loft portion of the *dojo* where he had his living quarters. The training floor below was dark, and the soft lights from upstairs gave you a sense of warmth and comfort.

My *sensei* left me in the sitting area. I heard water running as he filled a pot. "I will make something hot to drink," he called to me from the kitchen. "I have a new blend you will like." I smiled to myself. Coffee was one of Yamashita's obsessions. He was like a mad alchemist and fussed over the process of brewing with all the attention and precision he brought to life in general.

"Where's it from this time?" I called. Last Christmas, I signed him up for monthly deliveries of something they called "new kaffe." So far, we'd sampled the produce of Jamaica, Madagascar, and a variety of other places that Yamashita delighted in pinpointing with the aid of a huge hardbound *National Geographic* atlas. He sits with the atlas splayed across his lap, stubby fingers tracing the contours of the countries in question. At those times, he looks like a happy child.

"Peru," he answered when he finally came in. He set a square wooden tray down and poured me a cup. It was an act of courtesy and hospitality on his part. I had come to look forward to the ritual. My teacher would invite me up. We would drink coffee, letting the smell and the steam wash against our faces. And I would see another side to this complex man.

I looked at his cup. There was a tea bag in it. "You're not joining me, *Sensei*?" It was unusual.

He smiled tightly. "This evening, Burke, I have a desire for something soothing." He picked up a spoon and fished the bag out. I could smell the mint.

"Is something wrong, *Sensei*?" I remembered the transient glimpse of trouble I had seen earlier in his usually stoic face.

Yamashita sipped at his cup, his eyes almost closed. He set the cup down and sat back, hands on his stomach. Then he looked at me. "I wonder, Professor," he replied, pointedly ignoring my question, "how the *godan* felt about the lesson you gave him?"

I shrugged. "He probably wasn't too happy. But you were right. It needed to be done."

"So," he said and sipped at his tea again. "As a teacher, it is difficult to know when a student is ready to hear something, *neh*?" I nodded in agreement. "This is perhaps one of the hardest things to gauge." He held up a thick hand and balled it into a fist. "When to give," he opened the fingers of his hand toward me, "and when to withhold," the fist formed again.

"How do you know when the time is right?" I asked my teacher.

He smiled. "Sometimes, you sense it. Or see it in a student's movements." He looked at me for affirmation. I nodded. We had both experienced this with trainees. Then Yamashita smiled. "Other times, you guess."

"Do you think he was ready for that lesson?"

"Time will answer that question," he said. Then he grew solemn. "Time . . . " he said, and appeared ready to go on, but the phone interrupted him. I got up and went to answer it.

"Hello?"

"You makee lice?" a screechy voice demanded.

"What!" I said, momentarily flustered. Yamashita looked up inquiringly at the tone of my voice.

"Yeah," the voice continued, "I'm interested in kung-fu lessons." Then the evil cackling started.

"You idiot," I told my brother Micky.

The voice on the phone became normal, more recognizable. "Yeah, well, I tried your apartment and got no answer. I figured you'd be there."

"What's up?"

"You comin' tomorrow?" Micky asked. It was his wife Deirdre's birthday and the entire family would descend on his house like a cloud of Mayo locust.

"Wouldn't miss it," I told him. "Why?"

"No reason," he told me pleasantly. Which was a lie. Micky was a cop and when he asked questions, it was for a reason. His conversation had all the subtlety of a chain saw. I promised I'd be there and we hung up.

"Your brother the detective?" Yamashita said. His eyes glittered in the lamplight. I nodded. "He wishes to see you," he stated in reply. It was not a question. He sat there quietly, watching me.

I lingered over the last of the coffee, but Yamashita never picked up the thread of the conversation that had been interrupted by Micky's call. I knew my teacher well enough to know that it wasn't that he had forgotten, rather that he did not wish to pursue it right now. My *sensei* doles out knowledge on a timetable known only to himself. I had learned to accept it. I finished my drink and then I said goodnight. None the wiser about what was disturbing him, I returned home tired, but uneasy. Off in the distance, muted thunder rolled across the heavens and the air pulsed with an energy that, although unseen, made the skin along my shoulders and neck tingle in trepidation.

3

HARD END

First Sergeant Warren Cooke had been thinking that he wished he had more tape. This was the middle of his third tour with the Special Forces and in his experience it was the little things that tripped you up. Careful preparation could mean the difference between bringing your people home safe or in pieces.

He knew deep down that the team he had been training was almost ready to go operational. Almost. And that nagged at him. When the orders came down to get the team saddled up, he was surprised, but obeyed. He was, after all, a soldier. But he still worried.

He had taped his equipment down and secured his pants legs and sleeves so that there would be as little noise as possible when he moved through the underbrush. In an operation of this type, noise was your enemy. Battle rattle was as dangerous as any bad guy. He had been checking his people out as well. They had tried to emulate his actions, but needed a bit more practice. He wished he had more tape.

His A-Team had been working with the Filipino Special Forces for months now. It was the sort of training assignment that was nothing new for Special Forces troopers, but the rules of engagement in a post-9/11 world had made the work more interesting. Typically, you worked with the locals on things that were second nature in the Special Forces: stealth and fire discipline, careful planning, and cold precise execution in even the hottest of free-fire zones. Depending on where you were, the raw material you worked with varied greatly. In the Philippines, the soldiers Cooke worked with were bright and motivated, which was half the battle. There were rumors that their senior officers sold off some supplies on the black market, but that had little impact on Cooke and his daily job. The Filipinos were relatively small men, wearing jungle pattern camo and baseball hats that made them look like eager teenagers. But Cooke had to concede; they had the potential to develop into an effective fighting force. If they survived the mission.

The new rules of engagement meant that the A-Team members now had more opportunity to work directly with their Filipino counterparts in anti-terrorist operations. From Cooke's perspective, this was a good thing. He had worked too long and hard with these troops to see them wasted. His presence might help them live long enough to learn their trade. Besides, whatever his reluctance, he knew that they would have to face the test of fire sometime— you could do all the practice drills you wanted but there was no substitute for what you could learn in actual combat. And, in cases where targets were confirmed terrorist elements—what they called CTEs—Cooke and the other SF troopers were authorized to use deadly force at their discretion.

So Cooke and two other Americans from the First Special Forces Group—Abruzessi and Barnes—were going along on this operation. Technically, they were observers and advisors, but any time he went into the field, he did so with the expectation that he'd be in a firefight. He had a silenced nine-millimeter automatic strapped to his leg, a combat knife on his harness, and three concussion grenades. A twelve-gauge combat shotgun hung, muzzle down, from his back, and an M-4 carbine with a folding sock was clipped to his front. It was the older model, with a rate of fire selections for single fire and short bursts. Cooke liked it that way. He knew troopers in Afghanistan with the newer, fully-auto option on the M-4 and they said it tended to overheat. Cooke liked to stick with what worked. His load was completed with ten, thirty-round magazines of ammunition, a radio transmitter that fed into an earplug, chemical sticks that glowed when twisted, and field dressings that made his harness pouches and the pockets of his fatigues bulge. A soft camelback canteen hung down his spine. Each time you went into an operation, the gear you carried seemed to multiply exponentially. It took a while to figure out what you really needed and how to stow it. Invariably, you ended up not using something or wishing you had something else. The trick was to strike a happy medium.

This operation had two objectives: the disruption of a terrorist cell affiliated with Abu Sayeff, and the collection of any intelligence regarding plans and personnel. But the data snatch was decidedly secondary. The Philippine government was looking for a dramatic strike against Muslim insurgents. This op was as much about PR value as it was about anything else. Filipino intelligence had been sniffing around a remote farmhouse on the northern Mindanao coast. Over the last few months, they'd verified its use as a center for local terrorist training. When a tip came in regarding a meeting that was to draw in the heads of local cells, the opportunity was too good to pass up.

Yet, tonight's mission made him uneasy. The planning felt rushed, particularly with the team just beginning to get its act together. Cooke had raised the issue of a delay to get some better intel, but he was ignored; they were going in anyway. The situation was a bit more fluid than Cooke was comfortable with, but very little was perfect in his world. He sighed.

Cooke was a soldier, however, and he kept the feeling off his face and out of his voice. The strike force had offloaded from trucks, and while the Filipinos checked their gear, he went over procedure one more time. "Okay," Cooke began, gesturing to the two other Green Berets, Abruzessi and Barnes, and unfolding a map. "Here's the target. It's three clicks down this artery from the main road. It sits on about two cleared acres. Three hundred meters north of the building is the river, which is navigable right down to the coast. Activity is equally divided between the road and the dock there. You can see the ocean from the dock—approximately eighty meters. We can expect them to have a boat moored there tonight." Joe Abruzessi—Joey Z—nodded along with the narrative. Barnes didn't move anything but his eyes.

"We've got three insertion points. Joey, you're with the squad approaching from upriver, heading to this point . . . " his finger came down on the map and Abruzessi picked up the narrative.

"I got the GPS coordinates as well as visuals. Once there, we move inland to cover the eastern flank of the clearing and the boat dock."

"Me and the other team approach from the west and do the same on the other flank," Barnes added.

"I come in from the south and set up as a blocking force where the road enters the clearing," Cooke said. In his mind, he could envisage it—a large V with the point flattened and its broad opening toward the river. The farmhouse sat in the middle of the V. "Your people with LGs clear on their role?"

Barnes and Joey Z nodded. The LGs—long guns—were the snipers. Barnes' squad was to eliminate the boat crew. Abruzessi's was to cover the route down to the dock. The idea was to have Cooke's people secure the building and provide any retreating terrorists with the idea that they could escape via the river. But escape would only come in one of two ways. Any armed resistance was to be met with lethal force. Those who surrendered would face a hard season of interrogation by the Philippine Secret Service. Cooke didn't think either option was too great.

"Okay," Cooke said. "My main concern here is fire discipline." It wasn't an indictment against the Filipinos. The plain fact of the matter was that any time you got a bunch of young, aggressive men together and armed them with high velocity firearms, they posed as great a danger to each other as to the enemy. "We'll sweep in from the south. I'm hoping we can get in there before they know what's happening. But keep your heads down. Walls will not provide cover—rounds will go right through them and keep going. If the bad guys move toward the docks, make sure your people keep within the planned fields of fire.

"We've got command affirmation on CTE status, so our presence in the field is a go," Cooke continued. "Fifteen to twenty people in the building. All bad actors. Lieutenant Aguilar is in nominal command of the op. He's been outstanding during his training with us. Basically, we do this with them by the numbers, and try to keep them from making major mistakes, but we can take whatever action we determine is necessary if the wheels come off."

"Outstanding," Abruzessi said. "This is much better than Columbia." It was his first tour with the First SFG, which had its primary field of operations in Asia. The three men looked at each other and silently agreed. They had all been shot at more than once. It was nice to be able to shoot back.

The two elements that made Cooke uneasy on any operation were the insertion and the extraction. Target approach was always a challenge; the slightest thing could give you away. Extraction had a different dynamic and was often more hairy, but this night they were in a nominally friendly environment and he wasn't too worried about that. His focus was on the approach. He and the Filipino Special Forces' troopers moved with exquisite care as they made their way through the forest that surrounded the farmhouse.

You never took the road. That was rule number one. The Filipino Lieutenant Aguilar had kept his group together fifty meters in from one side of the dirt road that led north from the main highway. The bush was alive with noise. Tree leaves rustled in the breeze, small animals scurried about in the underbrush, insects whirred and hummed, and the careful passage of nine heavily armed men was swallowed up in the night noise of a tropical forest.

At one point, the buzz of a small motorbike froze them in their tracks. They could hear it getting louder as it made its way toward them down the dirt road, the beam of light from its headlamp bouncing among the trees. The soldiers sank silently to the ground in a smooth ripple. Cooke watched their reaction with approval. The sound of the motorbike faded as it approached the main road. Cooke hoped the blocking force there snapped the rider up without too much fuss.

The soldiers waited, breathing quietly in the moist darkness. No sound from the main road. *Good.* Aguilar motioned the advance, and it began again. They were using night vision goggles, and they were familiar enough with them to move without too much of the exaggerated head movements that people tended to use when they first wore them. It made navigation easier, but when the point man came back to report the building in sight, Cooke and Aguilar flipped their goggles up to confer.

"We are set, Sergeant," Aguilar breathed, avoiding the sibilant tones of a whisper. Cooke nodded, even though it was doubtful Aguilar could see him. Aside from the darkness, Cooke's skin was dark brown and covered with face paint to decrease the sheen of perspiration that might catch light. Cooke had a fleeting thought, *this is a long way from Detroit,* but he pushed it aside and waited for Aguilar to continue.

The young officer flipped a cover off a luminous watch face. The other teams were to report in sometime in the next twenty minutes or so. The squad knelt in a defensive arc, keeping good noise discipline. Cooke nodded again in satisfaction. They had developed the knack of the good soldier; they knew how to wait in silence.

He felt the sweat sliding down the curve in his back. He sipped quietly from his camelback and listened impassively as a mosquito whined by his ear. The troops were equally still, and he liked the fact that they seemed contained and ready. After a while, he heard the squelch of the radio in his earpiece. One squelch for Alpha. The east force was in place. Not ten seconds latter, two squelches on the radio told them Bravo had arrived on the other side of the V.

A soft touch on his shoulder from Aguilar warned Cooke that his troopers were on the move. They crept to the edge of the clearing, flankers out. They all scanned intently with their night goggles, looking in the washed out green for the bright optical signatures that would reveal sentries. They waited and watched for movement.

The building was constructed of some sort of adobe, big enough for multiple rooms. A veranda faced them, and their view of the door was partially blocked by the overhanging tin roof. They would have to be careful with the approach; the wooden floor of the veranda could give them away. Windows spilled light out into the night. Cooke could hear the sound of a generator from the rear of the building. It sounded like a diesel engine to him and he sniffed the air, almost imagining he could detect the exhaust's odor. He had grown up in the city, and diesel always smelled like home. He let the fleeting thought fade away and stayed focused on the here and now. He swept the target, looking, feeling. He sampled the air for the telltale smell of a sentry's tobacco. But nothing registered. Mostly, he smelled the rich dirt smell of decaying things, his own sweat, and the faint scent of oiled metal.

Aguilar pulled them back from the edge of the clearing and into a circle. Cooke looked at him without saying anything. There was enough ambient light this close to the clearing for him to see.

The young Filipino spoke to his men in a quiet, calm voice, giving final orders: "You two men around the building to cut the generator on my command. Sergeant Bantay, take Gumato and Inclan to the front door to blow it. The rest of the squad—line up to pile in the entrance while the targets are still stunned by the explosion." Aguilar glanced at Cooke only once, and the older American nodded slightly in encouragement. Aguilar squelched his transmitter four times, sending the agreed signal for the assault to Alpha and Bravo.

Aguilar's team slipped across the clearing. Two men whipped around the corner, going for the generator. Cooke could hear voices inside. This was the moment of greatest risk—the moment before the assault, when the team was outside the building, exposed in the clearing. They waited for the interior to be plunged into darkness. Cooke could feel his heart beating faintly. The Filipino troopers were crouched and ready, waiting. Cooke wished they'd pull the plug on that generator. Aguilar was whispering into his microphone. Cooke came up to him. "What?"

"The generator is in a locked shed. They cannot get in."

Shit. The aerial surveillance photos hadn't been angled enough to reveal that sort of detail. It's always the little things. "They'll have to blow it," Cooke told the Lieutenant. The message was relayed. As the others waited, the soldiers charged with assaulting the door inched slowly toward it, easing across the veranda.

The old wooden floorboard creaked faintly and Cooke winced. One of the soldiers on the veranda jerked to a halt, over-reacting, and a piece of hardware on his harness clinked. They all froze for a moment. It seemed so loud out here, but surely it would go unnoticed by the people inside. Seconds ticked by. Slowly, they resumed their approach. One soldier moved to either flank of the heavy wooden entrance. The Filipino sergeant approached to place small shaped charges at the hinge points.

It all unraveled in an instant. The sound of approaching voices and footsteps from inside the building triggered a push of adrenaline through Cooke's body. He crouched, breathing deeply to focus his mind through the rush. He brought his rifle to bear on the door as it was flung open, throwing light across the crouching attack force. Cooke closed his eyes because the wash of light through his night goggles would be intense. A shout of alarm, and someone fired a quick burst. Then the door slammed shut. He couldn't be sure who had fired, but Cooke heard a yelp of pain. He yanked his goggles up and alerted the other two teams. "We're spotted." Bantay was laying face up, his torso in the dirt and his legs on the veranda. Aguilar was calling for his medic and simultaneously ordering the blowing of the generator. The other troopers were poised, waiting.

Cooke knew combat viscerally, and everything in him urged movement. This is where lack of experience showed. Aguilar and his men were good, but they had been caught off-guard and now hesitated. Right now, every second that bled away meant that their enemy would be better prepared for the assault. Cooke's nerves screamed with urgency. He had to get his men moving.

Cooke grabbed Bantay by his harness and hauled him out of the way. Aguilar was fumbling for the detonator, dropped somewhere in the dark. Cooke grabbed him by the shoulder. "No time!" he grunted, swinging his shotgun around and blowing the hinges off the door with two quick blasts.

The blast seemed to shock the troopers back into action. They rocketed through the door like a human torrent. Cooke heard the generator finally cut out and the assault force poured into the farmhouse, leading with their rifles and shouting for the occupants to get down.

The rule was simple: anyone inside holding a weapon was shot. Anyone not immediately compliant with a shouted order to lie down was shot. Muzzle blast was bright in the confines of the farmhouse. A man with an AK-47 screamed at them and loosed off a volley, turning to run even before he stopped firing. A trooper caught him with a tightly spaced pattern—three shots stitched up the side from hip to chest. The terrorists were stumbling over one another, some trying to escape, others lunging for cover. They were disoriented in the dark, and the room was cluttered with overturned chairs.

Good training made the difference. Despite the rocky start, the Filipinos recovered well. The soldiers worked the perimeters, moving quickly with a maximum of force to keep up the shock value. They swept through the three rooms with precision, progress punctuated by the crack and flash of rifle fire. They encountered some resistance toward the back of the building, and Cooke could hear the report of weapons toward the river. A few stray rounds whacked by his head, powder flying off the walls of the farmhouse, but by the time Cooke reached the back of the building, it was all over.

The words crackled over his headset as the other teams reported. "Alpha. Clear." Cooke stepped out of the back of the house and approached a body that lay sprawled in the grass, his M-4 at the ready. "Bravo. Clear." Cooke kicked a handgun away from an outstretched hand and nudged the body over. "Charlie. Clear." Aguilar's voice sounded both excited and relieved. The lights came back on in the house as someone restarted the generator. Cooke pushed up his night goggles. The man lay in the oblong patch of light that reached out from the back doorway. Dirt was smudged on the man's face, caked on his lips and nostrils by the blood.

The dead man had been clutching something in one hand, as if protecting it in his last moments. Cooke squatted, picked the videocassette up, and wondered what it contained that was so important. Aguilar approached him.

"The trucks are here, Sergeant Cooke." The American could see the spill of light from the vehicle-mounted flood lamps. The Filipino forces dragged the dead out of the farmhouse and lay them in rows. Specialists who had arrived with the trucks began to examine the building and its contents. Someone snapped a picture of the dead bodies. The prisoners lay face down while plastic cuffs were yanked tight around wrists. Their mouths were taped shut. *There's my tape*, Cooke thought idly. The prisoners were hooded and manhandled into the trucks.

Aguilar gestured at the building. "All secured. We're policing the building now. Our intel was good—there was a meeting of some sort here. They were watching something on a TV screen."

Cooke held the black oblong videocassette gingerly and showed it to Aguilar. There was Arabic writing on the white label, but it had a dark smear across it. "Probably make some interesting viewing," the American said. Aguilar nodded, but was more focused on policing the area and seeing to his men. Cooke scanned the area: sprawled bodies in the grass, the wet-eyed, hunched prisoners being trucked away. He smelled blood and cordite and his own sweat. Cooke wondered again what was on the videotape, what had been so important that his team had been rushed into action, but he was used to a world where not all his questions got answered. Most days, it was enough to get through an op in one piece. *Mission accomplished*, he thought. He straightened up and turned the tape over to one of the specialists working the scene. Then Cooke put it out of his mind and went to see how the wounded sergeant was doing.

4

FAMILIARS

I sold my car when they did away with my job at Dorian University. With a life-long and inadvertent genius, I had managed to alienate both upper administration and the faculty there. The two groups were usually at each other's throat, engaged in an academic blood feud whose mythic origins were by now irrelevant. The struggle gave meaning and shape to their lives, however. They would fight about anything—or nothing, for that matter. It was a refreshing change of pace for them to share a common object of contempt. Or it would have been if I hadn't been that object.

Academia is an odd place. Stately buildings and ivy, wrought iron fences, and libraries fragrant with the smell of old books. Young people scurry to and from class, fresh, energetic, and naive. But in the long halls and narrow offices, those who work there fester in the dark like overeducated viral agents. Wet-eyed professors with obscure, irrelevant specialties and inferiority complexes browbeat students. Administrators, buffeted by faculty contempt and general inefficiency, sink into venal scheming. Any college campus is a circus, complete with color, entertainment, and the occasional glimpse of something really amazing. At Dorian University, the circus had a large number of clowns and a truly impressive freak show.

I'm bitter, of course. I had worked there as an adjunct for years, the lone specialist in East Asia teaching for a History Department that uncovered the past while vigorously trying to hide its own inadequacies. The individual members of the department had not aged well. They were choleric, flushed with self-importance, and obsessed with the onset of hypertension and other scary hints of mortality. It was possible that the spring of intellectual inquiry had, at one time, flowed in the History Department. I had only known it as the academic equivalent of a salt pan.

A friend had managed to get me an administrative position with the new Asian Studies Institute at Dorian, but it hadn't lasted long. The faculty weren't crazy about me. I worked dutifully at my desk all day, Monday through Friday. But my years with Yamashita have changed me. I used to think of myself as an academic pursuing a research interest in the Asian martial arts. I have come to realize instead that I am a martial artist with an advanced degree. It provided me with a sense of distance from my colleagues at Dorian. I couldn't share the university-wide fascination with minutia and self-importance. The *dojo* has taught me that there are more vital things in the world than convoluted social science fads or the latest campus vendetta. People there found me utterly incomprehensible. And, ultimately, the mad dictator who was Dorian's president decided to sacrifice me in some administrative gambit I still wasn't too clear about. Not that it mattered. I was back to part-time teaching, cobbling together a living in a way that was depressingly familiar.

All of which helped to explain why I was late for Micky's party. Long Island, where we both grew up and he still lived, was the Land of the Car. Those condemned to the netherworld of mass transit did not fare well. On that fish-shaped island, three railroad spines stretch from New York City to points east, but they are designed like pistons to ram huge numbers of commuters into and out of Manhattan during the workweek, nothing more. It makes other complex forms of travel difficult.

But I persevered. I got off the train and stood for a moment on the raised platform, looking down on suburbia. The South Shore of Long Island is flat. You can look out into the hazy distance and see row after row of rooftops, their shingles glittering through the trees. Water towers pop up at intervals in the landscape, pale blue towers standing watch over strip malls and playgrounds. I walked down the concrete steps and into the streets of Micky's neighborhood.

It was familiar territory. We had grown up in a place much like this one: ranches and cape cods and split level homes lined up like so many dominoes in the developments that scrolled out along the flat, swampy terrain. Belts of scrubby woods separated the neighborhoods. Occasional shallow reservoirs that caught the runoff from the blacktopped streets were set like muddy blue jewels along the railroad line that linked the towns to Manhattan. As you rode the train east out of the city, the flash of green and blue in the window—patches of trees and water—lasted longer and longer as you traveled east through Nassau County. It created the illusion that the area hadn't been overdeveloped. But it was just that: an illusion.

You could flee Metropolis by train and pass town after town where the details varied, but not by much. The differences were so subtle that more than one commuter who fell asleep on the way home and woke with a start somewhere along the line couldn't tell from looking out the window which community was which. It was why the seasoned commuters had the litany of towns memorized, so that the call of Rockville Centre, Baldwin, Freeport, Merrick, Bellmore, and so on was a hypnotist's instruction, a subliminal cadence count that prodded you awake when it was time to get off at your stop.

My walk was a step back into the past. Aboveground pools hulked in yards, sealed up for the winter with chemically aromatic blue plastic covers. Piles of leaves humped along the roadside and kids threw themselves into them, oblivious to dire parental warnings about what lay, wet and slimy, below the surface. I passed the local school, and way out on the playing fields red-faced kids were playing touch football on tired looking grass: I saw someone hook the runner's coat and swing him to the ground. The sky was clear, and high up you could see the jet contrails leading into Kennedy airport. Some days, I miss it all.

Cars were parked along all the available curb space near Micky's house. There were three or four in the driveway, packed in tight, with the last one jutting out onto the sidewalk. I walked up the path to the front door. It was a cold day, and the glass in the storm door was fogged up from all the people inside. I could hear the kids screaming in the backyard, despite the stockade fence Micky employed in a vain attempt at kid control.

Inside, there were people all over the place. I have two brothers and three sisters and they all seem bent on providing the world with as many young Burkes as is possible. I kissed my sisters Irene, Mary, and Kate hello and gave my mom a hug. My dad's been dead for a while now, but I never come to these things and don't imagine that I catch sight of him out of the corner of my eye. Sometimes I watch my mother sitting at gatherings like this and, in her unguarded moments, I imagine I see the brief light in her eyes, and I know she is feeling the same. Then there is a subtle sagging in her form as the illusion fades. I held on to her then, for a minute, feeling the bird-like fragility of her form.

But her eyes were clear and sharp, when she asked, "How have you been?" She worries.

I grinned and shrugged. "Good, Mom. It's working out." My mother has concerns about my career prospects. She was elated when I got the job at the university and was more upset than I was when I got canned. I think she worries that my youngest brother

Jimmy will never leave her house and is terrified at the thought that I might return there as well.

I made reassuring small talk with her, letting her know I was keeping busy. I used to assure her I was staying out of trouble, but she talks to Micky and there's no sense in lying to her. She'd find out anyway.

Deirdre was in the kitchen. She's got high cheekbones and almond-shaped eyes, and it makes her seem as if she looks at the world with a great deal of skepticism. She married my brother Micky, so the appearance probably has some basis in reality. Dee is a product of the same Irish-American stew as the rest of us. She was smart enough to know life doesn't always live up to our expectations, but deep down she was good enough never to entirely surrender the hope.

"Hey, Dee," I said, giving her a peck on the cheek and a bouquet of flowers.

"Aww," she said, "you didn't have to do that. . . . " She was pleased, but I could also see her eyes working. Dee worries about me, too. She's convinced I'm living on the edge of destitution. I had no doubt that she and my mother would force a shopping bag of leftovers on me when I went home. I could see myself staggering down a train platform in Brooklyn, loaded down with excess rolls, meats, and other surprises. It was somewhat embarrassing. Connor Burke: scholar, martial artist, bagman.

"Michael," she called out the window into the backyard.

"Wha!" a voice demanded.

"Connor's here," Dee called with a heavy Long Island accent. When she said my name, it sounded like 'Kahna.' Her kids said it the same way. Dee jerked her head toward the backyard. "Go see him. I'm gonna get a vase for these."

The backyard was where the men and children hid from women, the controlling elements in their lives. Even in the cold,

Micky was out there, hovering over a barbecue. He wasn't alone. Our brother Tommy was huffing across the yard, clutching a football while three small children clung, screaming, to his legs. They were having the time of their lives, but Tommy, never in the best of shape, looked like he was going to die. Off in the far corner of the yard, some older Burke kids were murmuring to each other and pressing the toes of their sneakers against the thin sheet of ice that had formed on a shallow puddle. They looked like prisoners planning the Big Break.

I came out the door and Micky glanced at me. "Finally," he said. "Now we can eat." Micky is whipcord thin with a patch of white in his dark reddish-brown hair. He has a military mustache that bristles with energy. As a homicide cop he's seen lots of things, the kind most of us don't want to know about. It tends to make him cranky. The two of us have always been different in many ways. But when you peel us down to the core, the surface differences fall away and are unimportant. We'd been together, smelling blood, and lived through it. So when we look at each other, the recognition of experiences shared is like a current arcing through space and making a connection.

But we don't talk much about that. Micky squinted at me, then bent down, opened the lid on a big orange cooler, and handed me a bottle of beer. He picked up his own bottle and clicked the neck against mine. "Confusion to our enemies," he said and took a sip.

"Why should we be alone?" I replied.

Micky's partner Art came through the sliding glass door that led to the den. He smiled at me. Art is bigger than my brother and his hair is a lighter, sandy sort of red. But he has the same cop mustache. And the same cop eyes.

"Deirdre wants to know how much longer, Mick," Art said.

Micky poked the meat with a finger. "Gimme five minutes and we're set."

Art nodded at that. He started to head back to the house, then turned. "You talk to Connor about that thing yet?"

My sister Irene's husband Nick came into the yard just then. Micky jerked his head in Nick's direction. "Not now," he told Art.

"There's a thing?" I asked.

"Oh yeah," Art said. "Right up your alley."

"Art . . . " Micky warned him. Then he looked at me. "After dinner. We'll talk about the thing."

"And what a thing it is," Art said over his shoulder as he headed back into the house.

"I love it when you guys get technical," I said to my brother.

Nick rooted around in the cooler and pulled out a beer, too. He looked at us with bright, expectant eyes, waiting to be let in on things. We changed the subject.

We had eaten and the light outside was fading. I always feel a bit overstuffed and sluggish after a family feed like this. But the kids hadn't slowed down at all. They had gobbled down their meals and bolted for the yard, leaving paper plates piled haphazardly in the trash and a trail of potato chip crumbs that stretched from one end of the house to another. Twilight deepened and in the strengthening invisibility of night, they hooted like animals from far off jungles.

The den is Micky's lair. It's littered with old furniture and bad decorations. My brother paneled it himself, and in spots the wooden sheets of fake walnut are coming away from the furring strips. There's a neat little space with a desk and a small file cabinet in one corner. On the wall to one side of the desk, there's a framed collection of family pictures: my folks on the day they were married; all of us kids at the beach, squinting into the sun shining from behind the photographer. My dad, cocky and smooth-faced, posing outside a tent in Korea. He's wearing a sidearm and a set of faded fatigues. His billed cap is pushed way back on his head. He looks young and thin and his ears seem big. He wouldn't be that thin again until just before the cancer finally got him.

I sighed to myself, and Micky came up behind me and heard.

He handed me a beer, and in a rare moment of vulnerability, put his arm around my shoulders. We stood there for a hair's breadth, sharing Dad, before he used the motion to turn me around to lead me to a seat. Art was with him. I looked at them expectantly, but Micky seemed like he didn't want to talk business. Whatever it was.

Micky gestured at the picture. "Remember what Dad used to say about the Marine Corps?" he asked.

"Sure," I said. "Two things. 'Best thing I ever did other than marry your mother . . . '"

"And?"

"And 'Don't ever join,'" I finished.

"Smart man," Art concluded approvingly.

"The Service . . . " Micky said with poignant reminiscence. "It's a whole other world."

Now I knew my brother had in fact served a tour with the Marines in his younger years. It was both a source of exasperation and pride to our dad. He hadn't relaxed until Micky came home. And in short order Dad began to worry again: Micky was, after all, home.

"You gotta watch out," Art said, keeping this odd little conversation rolling.

Who knew where we were heading? "Come on," I said, "you were both in the military."

"We were idiots," Micky said.

"Speak for yourself," Art said. "I knew just what I was doing . . . though I did come away with a strong desire to never go camping again."

My brother snorted and drank some beer. Both men smirked in remembrance of things that I, a lifelong civilian, would never know.

I held up a hand. "Boys. Please. I can swear that I have no desire to enlist."

"Enlist?" Art asked. "You're too old."

"Too weird," Micky added.

"So what are we talking about?" I asked. I paused and added with emphasis, "Is it . . . the thing?" It was hard to keep the sarcasm out of my voice.

Art got up and made sure the door was shut. It has a habit of popping open at odd moments. Micky's carpentry is effective but rarely precise.

My brother eyed his partner. Art came back to his seat and sat forward, cradling his beer bottle in his hands. "Okay. Look. I got this call about you."

"I didn't do it," I grinned. But neither man smiled back.

"Seems your fame is spreading, Connor," Micky snickered. "Someone wants to know whether you're the real deal."

I sighed. I've been in the paper a few times over the last couple of years. I get some mail from martial artists who yearn to know "what it's like to put your skills to the ultimate test." That's the way one guy put it. Some people confuse real life with a movie. I hate to break the news to them: being on the sharp end of events is scary and exhausting. There's no sound track. No guarantee of a satisfying ending. When I think back, and I try not to, I'm left with a jumble of memories; my mouth so dry I couldn't swallow, the feel of another human being's waning heat. There's the smell of blood and the crackle of radios when the ambulances arrive, as well as the flush of guilt, relief, and surprise. Finally, I recall the desire to sleep forever.

I looked at my brother and his partner, then held my hand out. "Come on. What's up?"

Art licked his lips. "I got a semi-official inquiry about you. Guy I knew years ago in the service named Baker." He looked at Micky and said, "He re-upped and made a career out of it."

Micky shrugged and made a face that said we all screw our lives up in unique ways.

"This Baker sounds like a real hard-charger," Micky continued. "You know, Special Forces stuff: parachutes, scuba gear, sneaking around, cutting throats . . . " He looked up at Art. "Like someone else I know."

His partner shrugged. "Yeah, well, I was young and foolish once, too."

I sat forward. Special Forces? This was a part of Art's life that I knew nothing about. Micky saw the look on my face and laughed tightly.

Art shot him a dirty look, and continued. "Baker loved all that crap. After I mustered out, I lost touch. But you hear things . . . he's been involved in all kinds of stuff."

Micky looked at me. "Like the martial arts."

"Aha," I said, ever alert to a clue.

"Aha," Art echoed.

"They did some sort of basic hand-to-hand training when I was in the Marines," Micky said.

I nodded. "Basically judo and jujutsu, from what I've read."

"Yeah," Art added. "That and the more subtle techniques like jump on the enemy's head once you knock him down." He reminisced for a minute. "Simple, yet effective."

"So what's Baker want?" I asked, trying to get them back on track.

Art fished a note out of his pocket. "He's involved with some new unarmed system fighting they're teaching." He looked at the small piece of scrap paper. "It's based at Fort Bragg at something called CERG."

"Let me guess, "I said, "the Center for Effective . . . " I trailed off, at a loss for inspiration, but sure that I was on the right track. The military loves acronyms.

"Close, but no cigar. It's the Combat Effectiveness Research Group."

"Seems important, yet extremely vague," Micky said. "Now I'm sure this is something related to our government."

Art gave his partner a look, then faced me. "Anyway, Baker's always on the prowl for new ideas and techniques . . . "

"New blood," I suggested.

"Fresh meat," Micky corrected.

" . . . and he had read a bit about you. He made the connection between you and Micky, then between Micky and me, and was making some inquiries about you."

"What did you tell him?"

Art held up a finger, "Well, we both spoke with him. I said you were an academic, a writer of fine, yet obscure tomes . . . "

"I said you had a knack for pissing people off and getting into trouble," my brother continued.

Art nodded thoughtfully at the comment. "It's true, you know, Connor." He put a hand on my shoulder. "And I say that as a friend."

I shrugged his hand off and smiled. "Will you cut that out?" I looked at Micky. "What else did you say?"

For once, my brother's face lost its usual sarcastic look. We both had light blue eyes and the same smirky facial expressions that had outraged countless nuns in our bumpy progress through parochial school. But it was gone now and he was very quiet and very serious.

"I told him," Micky said in a careful voice, "that I had seen you do some remarkable things in some tough situations."

Art added, "I told Baker I thought that you were the real deal."

"Hmm," I said, momentarily surprised at them both.

Then Micky reverted to type. "We also told him you needed a job."

"He said he'd contact you," Art supplied. "He may have a proposition."

I didn't know what to say to that.

Art, however, did. He sat back and took a long sip of his beer. "Baker's a wild man, Connor. Keep your eyes open. But look on the bright side."

Micky and I looked at Art skeptically.

"Your mother will be so pleased," he told the two of us, beaming.

5

BLADE SONG

The video footage was flat, and it obscured the subtlety of angle and timing. The old teacher regretted that. But the audience wasn't trained to appreciate subtlety and the outcome was clear enough. That was all that mattered.

They watched it without comment, which was unusual. They were garrulous as a rule, excitable, and given to flowery discussion. The small old Japanese man in the corner was just the opposite. Words leaked from him in a cadence that was shaped by patience, the slow drip of insight squeezed out drop by drop only by the force of necessity. He felt no need for speech, certainly not here. The image on the television screen spoke for him.

The group's mission had not moved him, but their timing had suited his purpose. They believed that they had sought him out. In reality, it had not been difficult for him to attract them. He would have preferred to remain in the mountains of his home islands, desiring familiar territory in which to execute his attack. But it was not to be—that meddler from Tokyo had seen to that.

They had asked for his knowledge and he had come, knowing that what they sought was a thing that was easy to bestow. It merely needed devotion, and they had that quality in abundance. He had left one island chain for another, abandoning the peaks and rice fields of his ancestors, spurning the cities that had grown up in sterile imitation of the West. His new pupils understood the decay that the West created. They, too, resented what had been done: legacies spurned and lives rendered pointless. The old teacher spoke to them through translators, but when his eyes looked into theirs, he saw a familiar glint. The anger and resentment needed no translation.

It was not a difficult task to teach them the techniques of his art. To create the warrior's spirit was a deeper challenge. They were willing to fight, but had spent so long hiding that their impulse was always for ambush—a vicious blow to the back of the head, or the strike from a distance—a peaceful morning rent by the blast of a car bomb. It was sometimes effective, the old man knew, but it was a tactic ultimately shaped by fear. It was ironic in some ways. They hated the nations that had made them weak, and yet their very weakness drove them to rely on the technology of the people they hated.

The rushing bloom and fire of explosions entranced them. The old man watched them swell with pride and power as they spoke of it. They ignored the imprecision and gloried only in the fear that it created. The old man thought them foolish. He valued few things in this world, but precision was one of them.

Yet, he persisted in instructing them. They knew of guns and bombs, the things that brought death from afar. He had different, more feral skills to impart.

Deep down, he felt contempt for their tactics. They had chortled in glee at the video footage from New York, seeing in the storm of concrete dust and black smoke a great battle won. The old man did not care one way or the other about the lives snuffed out as the buildings pancaked down into the ground, but he knew that the true warrior faces his enemy. What their brothers had done was not the act of warriors, whatever they called themselves; it was homicidal demolition.

He did not speak to them about the warrior's code. Instead, he made them into weapons themselves. This, at least, was a thing they understood, these young men from the hot, dry places of the world. It was their strength. They knew that the West searched for weapons in the hands, not in the eyes. It was a weakness in their enemy that they appreciated. And the old man helped them cultivate fragments of an ancient wisdom that would give them strength.

After a time, the young men grew to respect him, drawn by the bond between *sensei* and student. But their leaders watched with suspicion, their eyes bright and their hands fluttering as they murmured to each other in the throaty language of their home.

He was still an outsider, and while some of them trained with him, the group elders never fully trusted him. They demanded proof, a test of his effectiveness. It was a tradition from the isolated desert camps where so many had gotten their early training. The old teacher thought them foolish—such tests were wasteful. A good test was a dangerous thing, not to be undertaken lightly. And in an art that dealt with life and death, a flaw in technique would be disastrous. He felt contempt for the leaders—they were like impatient children eager to try new toys. They ran risks for no good reason. For men who sang the glories of an ancient way of life, they seemed to have forgotten patience. He shrugged inwardly, knowing it could not be helped. Their cause was not his. He was using them as surely as they were using him. The test would go forward as they wished, but he would shape it to ultimately serve his purpose, not theirs.

He had smiled grimly at their request. His face was a round one, although lined with age. His teeth were uneven and pointy, and his face was almost comical until you looked in his eyes. The more gifted of his students could feel the invisible energy roiling out of him as his anger flared in a brief eruption.

"You wish to see proof?" he had said, his eyes narrowing. "So. It is easily done." He had selected his best students, pointing them out one by one with the iron-ribbed fan he habitually carried. They were solemn-faced, these young fighters, under the dual gaze of the *sensei* and the senior member of the brotherhood.

"To defeat an enemy," the old man taught, "is not just to shatter his body. You must destroy his pride as well." It was a dictum he had thought long and hard on. So he told them how they would go about the attack to prove themselves to the senior men.

In a crowded city, a kidnapping is strikingly easy to effect. And some of the men he trained had financed themselves in the lean years through just this means. When the targets had appeared, it was relatively simple. Their route was known beforehand. The panel truck pulled up and the targets were snatched away like so much walking laundry. The smothered cries and flurry of arms were swallowed up in the jostling noise of the streets.

But he had not come all this way merely to refine their approach to abduction. The targets—two U.S. servicemen—were delivered to an empty warehouse. A video camera recorded what followed. As their captors cut their bonds, the victims assessed their surroundings, rubbing wrists and eyes. The Americans scanned the ring of expectant faces. Their eyes widened as the fighters approached them—they were soldiers and sensed the approach of battle. The realization that they had been kidnapped for a purpose more sinister than ransom dawned on them and they set themselves for what was to come.

The council of elders reran the video to watch it again. Things of this nature should not take long, and the old *sensei* was glad to see that his students had learned at least that much. The attack against the soldiers had been unleashed with maximum force, like the great winds of his home islands that swept upon the unwary, churning the sea and sky into a maw hungry for destruction.

In the video footage, after the bodies lay broken and still on the ground, the old man saw himself approach. It looked as if he were checking for a pulse. The camera's angle could not detect the paper he had slipped beneath one body. Which was as he planned. The footage ended and he left them to their self-congratulations and returned to his quarters.

The moon shone on him. His eyes captured sparks of light and glittered there in the shadows. He moved silently, drifting across the floor like the fog that gathered in the mountain hollows. He approached the sword rack. His *daito*, the paired long and short swords of the samurai, rested in their stands. The scabbards were dark and highly polished, but they felt warm as he touched them. The blades gave off an energy of their own. He could feel it. His ancestors told tales of weapons so inherently evil that they drove their owners mad. The old man knew of this ancient force, but he believed that it could be bent to a will that was powerful enough. His will.

His muscles were warm with the comforting ache of good use. But he knew his time was short, that the days burned away with finality. He needed to goad his victims into the trap while his strength was still with him. The video killings were the first step. Before he made the long trek to a strange land, the old master had pondered strategy for countless nights. His rage burned like an ember smoldering in the ashes. And, finally, a plan had crystallized, like some occult jewel emerging from a furnace.

The old man bowed before the wooden rack that held his swords. He lifted the *katana*, the long sword, and drew it from its scabbard. The blade was a milky white in the moonlight. The men he now trained had no use for the old techniques, and that was fine. The old man still had much to teach them. He made them into weapons of a different design. But he still held onto the old ways, and the discipline of his ancestors was both a challenge and a comfort in this strange place. He worked the blade through the darkness in exercises that were centuries old. The sword cut through the air again and again as his spirit fed on a new certainty. And, as that insight came, the sword sang a new song in the growing darkness.

With a final swoop, the katana was returned to its scabbard. Night spread like spilt ink and the camp grew quiet. The only noise was the rustle of leaves and the static-like chorus of insects. It had begun. He would test himself one last time. To revenge what had been lost. The old man closed his eyes and, motionless, could feel the silent weaving of his plan as it came together.

6

SMOKE

Yamashita says we're surrounded by subtle vibrations—the energy the Japanese call *ki* that fills the world like an electric charge. If you're adept, you can feel it buzzing in your head and playing along your skin. I've seen my *sensei*, a being alive to an invisible world, stop in mid-technique and let his eyes gaze inward as the surge of *ki* washes over him. And I've felt it, too, but not as intensely. The experience of *ki* is tactile and aural and inexplicable, all at the same time. But it's elusive: for many of us, the sensitivity comes and goes. It's just as well. Everyone needs a break.

I sat in a corner desk in the reading room of the Dharma House, logging in books. The air is still here. Not much aggressive energy. There was the low-level hum of chanting from a distant meditation room. The scent of old incense drifted through the air, soft, diffuse and almost undetectable. For me, the press of *ki* is a thing most often associated with danger. And the Dharma House is a refuge of sorts, so I was off my guard.

A wealthy and eccentric Manhattan socialite had created the place as a center for the study of Tibetan Buddhism. I knew the head *lama*, a remarkable teacher and mystic named Changpa. Not too long ago, we had shared an experience that still troubled him—even holy men have nightmares. He had given me a job when the university let me go, letting me serve as a type of librarian for the center's expanding reading room. It was a good deal for all concerned: Changpa was able to follow the Buddha's admonition to be compassionate. I got to pay my rent.

Those who came to the Dharma House were different from the people I worked with in the *dojo*. Here, they were often fragile and frightened: thin, pale young men with scraggly beards; women with wet, wide eyes and drab, formless clothes. Changpa stretched his arms out in welcome to them and there was an almost chemical reaction when he did so. The tension in their shoulders melted away, their faces grew calm, and their movements less jerky. It was an amazing thing to see: the spectacle of human unfolding under the guidance of a master teacher. It was part of what I enjoyed about working there.

I was a seeker, too, but of a different sort. If Changpa was like a soft breeze, a nurturing wind to his disciples, my teacher Yamashita was like a furnace. He forged the human spirit through hard effort and remorseless training. Changpa turned his pupils' eyes inward, the better to see the world within themselves. Yamashita had us focus instead on the world around us, believing that the experience of the flashing strike of an opponent's sword, a moment white hot with urgency, made you one with everything.

Over the years, I had come to experience some of what Yamashita had promised. It was a revelation that was as breathtaking as it was terrifying. And it held a fascination of its own. By the time you were capable of the insight he sought for you, Yamashita's training had changed you in subtle ways. It wasn't just skill or endurance. It was an appalling realization that you were most alive listening to the whirr of the blade's edge as it razored through the air toward you.

I didn't think I really fit in too well at the Dharma House. It was another place where I was present, but not connected. We were all walking paths toward the same goal, of course. But my path winds through some rough territory and it leaves marks. Perhaps that intimidates people. Some of Changpa's more advanced students knew about me. I could see their troubled facial expressions when they thought I wasn't aware of the scrutiny. They murmured occasionally to each other about me as well. Maybe all that meditation had made them more sensitive to inner states and they sensed my turmoil. More likely, they'd read the stories about me in the papers. Occasionally, I'd catch them looking at my hands, as if there would still be blood on them.

I log the books in and out of the reading room, trying not to let them bug me, enjoying the quiet. I'm grateful for the work. Or maybe it's that I like the fact that the flow of *ki* is slowed here, the air so thick with prayer that little can intrude. Sometimes I need a break from the *dojo*. In the Dharma House's reading room, the work was monotonous, but your hands stayed clean.

The reading room is tucked away toward the back of the first floor, but you can still hear quite a bit of the comings and goings in the building. People are in and out all day to attend classes or prayer sessions and to use the meditation room. At night, there is even the group of archers training in the Japanese art of *kyudo* on the lower level, the beauty of the art enhanced by a woman named Sarah Klein.

The sound of footsteps was clear and sharp on the wood floor of the hallway leading back to the reading room. In the Dharma House, people tend to walk softly in a reverent shuffle. It's the combination of sandals and noodly muscles that does it. But whoever was coming my way was striding, not shuffling, down the hall. I looked up, curious to see who it was.

I thought I was out of place.

He wore what I later learned was the new blue Army service uniform. His black shoes were so highly polished they looked as if they were wet. The left chest of his jacket was crowded with ribbons. They didn't mean much to me, but I did recognize jump wings and a Combat Infantryman's Badge pinned to the top of the display. In his military splendor, he looked as out of place in that room as I felt. Their monks wear colored robes, but other than that American Buddhists are a pretty subdued group when it comes to clothing.

"Hello Dr. Burke," the soldier said to me. He had a pleasant voice, which was a bit of a surprise. I'm a victim of childhood stereotypes created by B movies. I expected him to sound like Aldo Ray.

I stood up from the desk and watched him approach. He wore the silver oak leaves of a lieutenant colonel. His hair was flecked with gray and freshly cut—you could see the white line of skin around the edges of his hairline. His eyes were brown and he had the look of someone who spent a lot of time outside. His cheeks had been scoured by the wind and the skin around his eyes was seamed from squinting into the sun. He smiled as he extended a hand and the lines at the corner of his eyes became creases. "I'm Randall Baker."

"Hello, Colonel," I said, shaking his hand. "Art told me that you might drop by."

He took a step back and looked at me, as if trying to mesh what he'd been told about me with my appearance. Then he glanced around at the reading room. "My understanding is that you're working until three today." He looked at his watch—a stainless steel affair with a black face and luminous dial. When I was a kid, we called them skin diver watches. Every man of action had one. "If you're free, I was wondering whether you'd like to come with me."

"Sure," I shrugged. "Where to?"

"A martial arts demonstration," Baker said.

"Right up my alley," I told him.

Baker had a car waiting on the street. It was a late model Chevy sedan with white government plates. It looked like it had just been washed. My tax dollars at work. A sergeant opened the back door for us without a word and then got in behind the wheel. We took off.

"This is Sergeant Hanrahan," Baker told me.

"Hi," I told the back of Hanrahan's head.

"Pleasure, sir," the driver said. But he didn't turn around. Hanrahan's hair was cut so close as to be almost invisible. He had a neck, thick with muscle, that bunched up where it met the base of his skull. He kept his hat on in the car.

The Saturday afternoon traffic was manageable. Hanrahan took us up the East Side to the 59th Street Bridge and into Queens.

I looked at Baker.

"You've been told a little bit about me, Dr. Burke?" he asked, and then continued before I could answer. "I'm involved with the development of unarmed combat systems for the Army. There's a big martial arts tournament at a local high school today. As part of our recruitment activities, a demo team is going to be participating." He looked out the window at the passing cars, the buildings. You got the impression that he was a man who watched things carefully. Then he turned to look at me. "I thought it would be a nice way for us to meet and for you to see some of what I've been up to."

The expression on his face was pleasant enough, but I felt that he didn't really expect a response. I didn't give one. People like Baker don't do things on a whim. It may have been true that he wanted me to watch his people perform. But I knew that Baker wanted to watch me. This wasn't just an excursion on a Saturday afternoon. We were on our way to a contest, and I was the one being judged.

I sat back in the seat and relaxed. I've spent more than a decade with a teacher who could probably show Baker a thing or two. I'm used to being tested. It happens every time I walk into Yamashita's *dojo*.

The high school was a big box. The brick was an ugly mustard yellow that told me it was built sometime in the early '60s. The windows were covered with metal grilles. The halls were washed in fluorescent light and lined with metal lockers. It smelled like a school—the air had an aroma shaped by equal parts disinfectant, paper, and resentment. And the gym was full of people.

We walked in and made our way to the recruitment table, draped with a black and gold banner that simply proclaimed "A Force of One." There were two sergeants there, wearing the same sort of distinctive blue uniform as Baker.

"I thought the Army wore green," I offered. There hadn't been much in the way of small talk up until now.

"The Army's always had blue dress uniforms," Baker stated, "as well as white and green ones. Class A's were green, but command has decided to simplify things and they're phasing the other out in favor of the blue version."

A steady flow of kids fingered brochures tentatively while the soldiers went into their recruitment pitch. You could see parents hovering in the background, some apprehensive, others encouraging.

"How's the fishing at something like this?" I asked the Colonel.

He smiled. "In the all-volunteer service, recruitment is always a challenge. But we offer young people something that they don't seem to be able to find in civilian life . . . " his voice took on a reflective tone for a moment. Then he snapped back to his usual crisp, efficiency. "We do fine, Dr. Burke."

The two recruiters stiffened to attention when Baker approached. Baker waved them back to their conversations with the kids.

There was a spot at the bottom row center of the gym bleachers reserved for us. The four soldiers sitting there shot to attention when Baker approached. He went through the same wave routine and said, "As you were." He didn't introduce me and they didn't ask who I was. But you could see them take a peek at me out of the corner of their eyes after I sat down.

The soldiers on the bench were young and fit looking, with broad chests and narrow waists. They were wearing the new camouflage trousers known as ARPAT, Army Combat Uniform Pattern, and boots. They had on black T-shirts whose V-neck and sleeves were piped in gold. Their heads were shaved and they looked like a pack of attack dogs. They seemed impassive enough, but I'd have bet inside they were quivering with eagerness.

I was sandwiched in between the Colonel and Hanrahan. I looked at the driver and nodded at the crowd in black shirts. "This the demo team, Sergeant?"

"Yes sir," he replied. He was a very serious young man. He had hands the size of shovels, with big broad fingers. Is that why he was a driver? I looked at his tunic and saw that he had jump wings like Baker, another one with a helicopter in the middle, and a third that looked like a flaming torch. His uniform's left sleeve had small patches at the shoulder. One said "Ranger," another "Special Forces." Hanrahan didn't say much, but he obviously had many skills—sort of an Army renaissance man.

A fuzzy introduction boomed out of the PA system and I turned to watch the demonstration.

It had been organized by a group of Korean martial arts schools in the area. The Koreans have been tremendously successful in propagating their version of karate in the U.S. Part of the success is due to the no-nonsense nature of their arts. Part of it's because they're shrewd businessmen.

The Japanese *sensei* tend to look down on their Korean counterparts, and the feeling is mutual. There's not much love lost between the two peoples. The Imperial Japanese government instituted a brutal colonization of Korea, and Korean resentment still smolders. The Koreans had been influenced by modern Japanese martial arts before the 1940s, but over the years had given them their own distinctive flavor. Part of it was driven by innovation, part by resentful nationalism.

In any event, Korean empty-hand systems were built on a foundation that was at least partially Japanese, although the Koreans work hard at denying it. They have tons of different systems—*tae kwon do, kang duk kwon, mu duk kwon, tang soo do*—but when you watch them in action, it's Korean karate. The stances differ a bit from the Japanese, there are minor stylistic variations, and they tend to use a lot more kicks. But it's karate, one way or the other.

Athletically, it's pretty impressive. All that kicking requires a tremendous amount of energy. The young men and women who performed that day were strong and supple, and possessed tremendous physical ability. Their uniforms were very similar to the traditional Japanese *gi*, although some had black piping along the collars and sleeve ends. Other participants had opted for a more sporty pullover top with similar piping.

They wore a rainbow of belt colors. Some had little stripes on the belt ends as well. The Koreans had learned that Americans loved the whole belt system, with its graphic representation of advancement. As a result, some schools had a seemingly endless series of belts or stripes that could be earned. The black belts tended to be embroidered with name and rank spelled out in gold thread. They wore patches and flags on their sleeves. Some outfits looked more like billboards than uniforms, which, in some ways I suppose, they were.

Yamashita doesn't use belt colors for rank. You need black belts in a few systems just to get in the door of his training hall. The uniforms we wear are all the same: plain, deep blue, and utilitarian. My teacher isn't interested in advertising, or in making you feel important. As far as he's concerned, you earn respect through competence, and that's something revealed through movement, not fashion.

Groups of students demonstrated the *kata*-like routines they called *hyung*. I recognized a few of them as being similar to the Japanese *Heian* series. A less charitable observer would have said they were copied, but I'm a font of tolerance. The movements were crisp and hard, the control at a very good level.

There was a lot of board breaking. The Korean styles are big for this. Twelve-inch squares of pine, an inch thick, were snapped in two in various ways: knife hand technique, back hand, lunge punch, front and side kicks, elbows. The crowd loved it. One of the junior instructors broke two different sets of boards held on both sides of him with a double flying side kick. I got tired just watching it.

There was a brief intermission, then the Army demonstration team was introduced to enthusiastic applause.

Hanrahan strode up to the microphone and gave a brief introduction.

"Good afternoon, ladies and gentlemen, I'm Staff Sergeant Robert Hanrahan, part of the demonstration team for the United States Army's Martial Arts Program. It's a pleasure to be with you today and see so many of these fine athletes." There was more polite applause.

"The Army Martial Arts Program is composed of techniques such as strikes, throws, and holds that are meant to assist the soldier to close with and defeat his enemy. More than that, it's also a system designed to instill every aspect of the warrior spirit in each trooper.

"This close combat program was revamped in 1996 with the input of leading martial artists. It's undergone continuing refinement and today includes combat-tested martial arts skills and close-combat training techniques that are combined with core

Army values and leadership training."

You could hear the crowd growing a bit restless with the explanations. They were an action-oriented group. If Hanrahan's canned commentary got much longer, he'd lose them.

But this was obviously a well-practiced routine. While Hanrahan spoke, the demo squad was setting up floor mats behind him. They finished just as he wrapped up. "It's our pleasure to be able to show you some of the more physical aspects of the art here today, part of the skills we're proud to display as soldiers in the United States Army."

Basically, it was a good, solid demonstration of effective self-defense. There were no frills. They were obviously a fit bunch, and they were pulling their blows, but they went through a series of attack and defense vignettes that showcased their ability to break out of choke holds, immobilize various strikes, and bludgeon an attacker into a helpless heap. They used their boots a lot and I didn't blame them. The basics were a meld of judo and karate-like techniques combined with the more ruthless propensity for target areas typically banned in martial arts schools that worried about the cost of liability insurance.

I watched closely. After Micky and Art had told me about Baker, I took some time to try to find out what I could about what the Army was up to. There were some short video clips on a Web site, as well as text outlining the history of the system, but there's no substitute for watching people who train in a particular style move for an extended period of time.

The soldiers finished their demonstration, put away the mats and then sat back down with us on the bleachers. They weren't even winded.

Then the regular activities resumed and things wound their way down. For a finale, the local Korean headmaster set up a circle of hapless students. Some held boards, others bricks. Their teacher smashed his way through them all, a tough, wiry dynamo. Then, while the debris of shattered wood and brick still littered the floor, the headmaster was blindfolded and a student was placed in front of him with an apple set atop his head. The old teacher crouched down as if winding his muscles up, cocked his head briefly, then launched into the air, executing a spinning back-kick that smashed the apple off his student's head to the wild applause of the crowd.

In the car, Baker asked me what I thought. I reflected for a minute, remembering the sight of the hapless student standing stock still, balancing the apple, and squinting in anticipation as his teacher launched himself into the air. "I think," I told Baker, "that sometimes the measure of a really good teacher is what they can get their students to do for them."

"You sound like you speak from experience, Dr. Burke," he said. "But that wasn't what I meant."

"Yeah, I know," I told him.

"So? Do you have any comments? About the troopers."

I shrugged. "Seemed pretty solid stuff. But I'd probably need to see a greater variety of attack scenarios to really evaluate it."

Baker nodded at that. "We routinely have various experts do that sort of thing for us . . . look for areas we can improve on."

"How's it worked out?" I asked.

Baker made a shaking motion with his hand. "Sometimes it works, sometimes . . . " He looked up at the stolid driver in the seat in front of us. "Remember that last guy, Hanrahan?"

"Permission to speak freely, sir?" Hanrahan asked.

"Sure," the Colonel said.

"What a cluster-fuck," he told me, looking briefly over his shoulder.

"I know that the Special Forces did an experiment with some aikido training a few years back," I said. "It was like two groups of people speaking completely different languages."

"Before my time," Baker said. "But I read the book."

"Me too," I said. "It was good comic relief."

Baker smiled. "I hear positive things about you, Burke, but I want to make sure you 'get' what we're all about . . . "

"Locate, close with, and destroy the enemy," Hanrahan said. It was the kind of thing he didn't say at high school recruiting events. The parents would swoon.

"What did you think of the tae kwon do today?" the colonel prompted.

I shrugged. "They sure can jump."

"That's it? You're not impressed with their skill?" His eyes had an intentness about them that I hadn't seen before. And, ever so faintly, I got the tingling sense of an energy field pushing against me.

I waved a hand. "I don't know. They're impressive athletes, but fighting? It's so much smoke." I thought about the time Yamashita had squared off against a student of *ninjutsu*. The guy could do handsprings across the room. Yamashita had told us ahead of time that such techniques were mostly designed to throw you off balance because they were unexpected. If, however, you weren't flustered . . .

During the match, the *ninja* had tried to leap across the room. Yamashita simply waded in and caught him by the throat in mid-cartwheel.

"But didn't you see that last technique?" Baker pressed. "The blindfold?" He sounded incredulous, but the eyes were still watchful. I noticed the subtle twitch of Hanrahan's neck muscles and knew that he was listening carefully as well.

"Baker," I said wearily, "it's a good stunt. It takes a lot of practice. But in the long run, you know what?" I paused.

"What, Burke?"

"I don't train to fight fruit. And I bet you don't either."

The Colonel sat back in the seat and smiled. "What do you think, Hanrahan?"

"He'll do," the sergeant said.

7

HAMON

He's not talkative even at the best of times. Yamashita has spent a lifetime following the path of an art that prizes efficiency: the slamming precision of a strike or the smooth, pivoting projection as you find and take hold of the fulcrum that's present whenever two bodies meet in attack. So when I told him of Baker's proposition he didn't react. My teacher prizes timing as well as technique: he would comment when it suited him.

I was worried about his reaction. Yamashita seemed preoccupied lately. I was doing much of the instruction and, although he was present like a predator gliding around the edges of the class of straining trainees, he sometimes seemed focused on an interior reality the nature of which I could not fathom.

I didn't know what was going on with him. But I rarely did. Part of the warrior's art was to give away as little of yourself as possible to the world. You remained always watchful, guarded. And even after all this time and all that we had been through, in many ways my teacher was still a mystery to me.

I had waited until the last of the students had left the *dojo* and the lights were turned down low in the cavernous training hall. Yamashita drifted up the stairs to the loft area and beckoned for me to follow. I ascended into the soft lighting and simple décor of his living area. It was a familiar view; there were a few easy chairs and lamps. The walls were white and dotted with framed *sumi-e* paintings—the stark and elegant ink drawings of Japan, and resting on a table in pride of place, his swords.

The *daisho*, the two swords of the old samurai, are emblematic in many ways of the art Yamashita follows. They are a melding of esthetics and functionality, highly refined products of master artisans whose ultimate purpose is savage beyond description. I've seen their use firsthand, and wondered how such danger can be contained—or justified. Once I had asked my teacher this question. His eyes narrowed and the answer was brief. "Discipline," Yamashita told me. "And wisdom."

It's a hard path to walk.

Sensei lifted his swords out of their rack and set them down on a table. He brought out a small wooden box, slid back the lid, and removed sheets of fine, soft paper, a small vial of oil, and a stick with a round fabric ball at the end. Yamashita knelt by the table and, bowing to the blades, began to inspect them.

When handling swords, there is an unyielding etiquette. Any time a sword is unsheathed, the potential for danger is released as well. For this reason, Yamashita held the long sword horizontally in front of him and slowly drew the blade from the scabbard with his left hand, pausing after a few inches of steel was revealed and then slowly continuing. The *katana*, the long sword that people typically think of as a "samurai sword," is usually drawn with the right hand. By using the left, and removing it slowly from the glistening black scabbard, Yamashita was symbolically demonstrating a lack of offensive intent.

Once the sword was fully drawn, he set the sheath down and raised the blade to the vertical. The handle was wrapped in sharkskin and silk cords and the metal fittings were simple and balanced. The blade itself was an arc of deep silver, wrought centuries ago by skilled sword-smiths laboring in an atmosphere made dense by heat and Shinto prayer. A delicate wave of shadow ran in undulating lines along the single, razor-sharp cutting edge. The pattern, known as a *hamon*, was created in the forging process itself. It was a subtle mark of distinction, of personality. For the Japanese, all things have a spiritual essence. And the power and beauty of swords make them a locus of strange energy. Folktales tell of swords that hum to warn their masters of danger, that leap of their own accord to battle. Of swords that can make a warrior great or that can drive the bearer mad.

Yamashita worked quietly, precisely, on his swords. His eyes concentrated as he regarded the blade he held before us. He slowly oiled the surface, wiping the metal gently with soft polishing paper made expressly for the purpose. Then he took up the stick and ball and tapped the fabric end of the implement all along the edge of the sword. It absorbed excess oil that was left from the polishing.

Yamashita stretched the sword between his hands, one hand on the handle, the other cradling the blade in a folded sheet of the paper. A sword should never touch skin except in the instant of attack. He focused on the handle, checking the bamboo pin that held the sword firmly in place within the handle.

"The *mekugi* is sound," he said quietly to me, referring to the pin. "Even the finest blade depends for its utility on the most simple of things . . . " It was a commonplace observation, but his tone implied a deeper meaning.

Sensei slid the sword back in its scabbard with a fluid, gliding, almost magical motion that took my breath away. He did it with the grace of nature. I work every day of my life to try to emulate it.

Yamashita stood and placed the swords back in their rack. "So . . . " he said, "it appears as if you will be traveling, *neh?*" He wandered into the kitchen and I followed him.

"*Sensei,*" I started, but he waved me to silence.

"Your brother has spoken of this to me, Burke," Yamashita said. He let out a small, hiss of breath. "Coffee?" he asked.

"If you're going to have some," I answered.

He made a small grimace. "Tonight, I think not." It wasn't like him: This was the second time he had given up this indulgence. Yamashita has been a coffee connoisseur for as long as I've known him. Before I could say anything he switched gears, asking "What of the new students?"

"That's for you to decide," I told him. "You're the *sensei*."

The lighting in the kitchen was muted, but I thought I detected a twinkle in his eyes. "Ah, but it is you who teach them their lessons, Professor." There was a playful tone in his voice. He was walking back out to the sitting area as he said that, but I could pick up the nuance anyway. *Sensei* sat down and beckoned me to a seat beside him.

"I'll only be gone for a week," I explained. "Ken or one of the other senior people can help you. Then I'll be back."

Yamashita smiled tightly, as if he didn't quite believe me. But he said nothing.

"I need the money," I added lamely.

His smile grew broader. "There is that need, always," he commented, shaking his head in resignation. "But for you, there is more to this . . . "

I started to say something, but he held up a hand. "I know you, Professor. There is within you this need . . . " he searched for a word, " . . . to prove yourself somehow. Over and over again."

I nodded because there was no sense in denying it. I had spent my life pursuing various goals: a doctoral degree in history, black belts in the martial arts. And no matter how much I believed they were real achievements, I had come to realize that much of their value lay in the respect they elicited from others. Yamashita knew this as well. It's a motivator he had used over the years to drive me along the hard path he laid out for his students. And now I use the same technique when I teach newcomers. It's a curious blend of raw emotion and subtle psychology, percolating through the chemical surge that hard exercise creates.

"Your father was a soldier," Yamashita mused. "Your brother and his partner also. These are men you respect. And you wish to have them respect you as well."

"It's not as simple as that," I protested.

My *sensei* waved a hand. "Important things rarely are. This for you is important, *neh*? A chance to assist your countrymen in training. To earn a living, and to prove something about yourself as well as your art." He sounded so very matter-of-fact, and his acceptance of my decision surprised me. Yamashita sighed and looked at his hands, as if the creases of his palms held the words he wished to speak. "You will do well, I am sure, Professor. You will be missed here, but we will be glad to see you return." I looked up at that. It wasn't the kind of thing my teacher said very often.

Yamashita's head came up, too, and he looked at me with the dark and oddly forceful eyes he has. I used to find the look disconcerting. Now, it was a relief to see something of my teacher's old ferocity back in evidence. "Two things to remember," he said.

"What's that, *Sensei*?"

"These are young men you will be training with. They will be resilient in ways that you are not." I started to protest and he smiled as he continued. "You will be almost twenty years older than most of them, Professor. You are more skilled, but your muscles are not as young. You will be sweating and straining. Watch against dehydration. I have found it useful to drink a beer in the evening. It helps you retain fluids."

I smiled at that, even though he was perfectly serious. "I think I can handle that," I told him. "What else?"

Yamashita grew somber. "Consider the virtue of *isshin*—single-heartedness. Can a person who is in so many places ever be fully present anywhere at all?"

"Yamashita's right," Sarah Klein told me. "I think this whole thing is some odd excuse to prove yourself to the men in your life."

Sarah has a real knack for being blunt, but is also adept at taking much of the sting out of her comments when she wants to. She's utterly direct, but charming. She's got a heart-shaped face and very expressive brown eyes that shine with a type of tolerant amusement at most things in life. Tonight her face was stern as she spoke, and the warm wood and subdued lighting of the Japanese restaurant where we were eating created an atmosphere of calm that couldn't subdue the urgency of her words.

Sarah studies *kyudo*, Japanese archery, and Yamashita has taken her under his wing. He likes her intensity, he confided to me once. My teacher thinks she has the makings of a good warrior. For me, the attraction is at once both more complex and subtle than that.

I tried talking with Micky about it. I'm not terribly articulate about these things. It's the combined impact of growing up Irish American and then spending my adult years with the Japanese. Many things are intensely felt; few are discussed. I tried any number of analogies when I talked with Micky about Sarah. I tried magnetism. Chemistry. Kismet. Micky heard me out patiently, letting me squirm with what for him was good-natured patience. When I was done, my brother squinted at me and smirked.

"You're in love, you dope," my older brother explained.

And maybe I was. I sometimes slip down into the lower level of the Dharma House, the place where the archers train, just to watch Sarah. She's unaware of my presence most times, and moves through the motions of her art with a focus and grace that make me smile in contentment. Sometimes, when I close my eyes, I can see her in another place, wet and muddy, eyes wide with the curious mix of fear and determination that I've come to think of as bravery, as she fires arrow after arrow into a fight none of us really expected to survive.

I know Sarah remembers that event, too. And while we're drawn to each other in many ways, her memory of that time also makes her fight the attraction. In battle's heat, we sometimes learn things about people—ourselves and others—that we would prefer not to think about.

There's a dark side to what I do. And it worries her. I sensed that tension, even in the calming atmosphere of our favorite restaurant. "Hey," I said defensively, pushing a crab dumpling known as *shumai* around my plate, "this is a really good opportunity for me to do some consulting work. It's not like my career is taking off anywhere else . . . " That, at least, was hard to argue. I'm an academic without a home, an expert on an obscure aspect of Asian history, over-educated and under-employed.

Sarah sipped thoughtfully at her cocktail and squinted at me. "Consulting, huh?"

"Sure," I responded brightly. "I get to review the training system the Army has set up down in Fort Bragg, watch them work out, make some suggestions." I shrugged. "It'll only take a week, and then I'm back, with a nice fat check from Uncle Sam."

In reality, the check was not really going to be that fat, but the Burke universe is not one awash in money. Everything is relative.

"It's not the mechanics of it that bother me, Burke," she told me. In the rare tender moments we've had, she whispers my name, Connor, in a way that makes my stomach flip. But mostly, and especially when she's annoyed, I'm Burke. The waitress brought our entrees and Sarah paused while the plates were set down and arranged. The waitress topped off my glass with more beer. I smiled gratefully. I had the feeling I was going to need it.

"I'm sure that it's something you *can* do," Sarah continued. "I just wonder whether it's something you *should* do." She looked at me significantly. "For a man who can be so focused, you're all over the place sometimes."

We've had these sorts of discussions before. Sarah has watched me struggle to find out where I fit in, and she has her own very clear idea about that. But there was more to her uneasiness than that. The martial disciplines are a disconcerting blend of idealism and brutality. When Yamashita wields a sword in the flowing movements of the solo performance called *kata*, it's a thing of beauty. Each performance ends with a tight swoop of the sword before it's sheathed. To the uninitiated, it's a dramatic flourish, an artistic embellishment. In reality, it is something called *chuburi*. The action is designed to shake blood and human tissue off the sword blade. It's a reminder of what it is to know the way of the sword.

Sarah, on the other hand, is an archer. For students of *kyudo*, the esthetic of action is all-important. They stand at a distance from their targets. It makes it easier to imagine yourself as simply an artist, a performer. In Yamashita's world and mine, you can feel your opponents' body heat, smell their breath. It's harder to maintain the illusion of calm and serenity.

The struggle in the martial arts between beauty and brutality, power and transcendence, is one that bothers Sarah. And she hates it when my actions remind her of it.

I shrugged at her statement. "Seems to me the government needs all the help it can get." She made a face at that. "You know what I mean . . . " I protested.

"I'd feel better if I could be sure that was all there was to this, Burke," she told me. She wasn't letting go. I sighed inwardly. A nice night out. Some salad with ginger dressing, *shumai* and *yaki-tori*. Perhaps some warm *sake*. The primitive romantic cunning of the Burke clan linked fine dining with romance. I looked at Sarah

Klein with longing. She was pretty and self-assured, her dark hair shining in the subdued lighting of the restaurant. She sat there across from me, supple and sparkly, alive to so much of life—and tonight, totally impervious to my charm.

She looked searchingly at me for a minute, then turned her attention to sliding one of the pieces of chicken off a bamboo skewer. She ate. I followed her lead, glad to be doing something non-controversial.

"Come on," I finally urged her. "It's a little thing. After the Trade Center, it's the least I can do . . . help out in some way." I could see that this statement registered with her. She'd been in the City that morning and had seen the boiling wall of gray ash come racing up the streets. Some things you can't forget, no matter how much you wish you could.

"Look," she replied in defeat, "you're going to go. And on some level, I accept it. I know you want to help and that's okay." She looked at me earnestly and I was surprised to see that her eyes looked shiny. Sarah reached across the table and touched my hand. Lightly, her fingers slowly resting on the skin where the small white scars showed. "I just don't want you getting . . . " she let out a tight jet of air through her lips as she struggled for a word, "sucked in, okay?"

I smiled at her. "Don't worry about me, doll." It was my patented Humphrey Bogart imitation. Perhaps I should have worn my trench coat for the full effect. But it's crumpled at the bottom of my closet—the various buttons keep popping off and I lost one of the epaulets.

Sarah smiled sadly. "I'm serious. You're a good man, Connor Burke. But remember what Changpa said." I nodded. Chanpga Rinpoche, the Tibetan holy man who runs the Dharma House, had once described the martial path as a razor's edge. One slip could result in your destruction. And he wasn't talking about simple physical danger. Changpa felt that we harnessed force to a good purpose, but that power is seductive. This path required discipline and care and commitment. To slip, he felt, would destroy you spiritually.

"I know, I know," I nodded. Yamashita has this awareness, too. He scrutinizes his pupils for years, trying to sense the quality of their character. I had thought for a long time that those narrowed eyes only focused on technique; now I understood that he watched for the indications that revealed something of the inner self, like the *hamon* of a sword blade.

"You know," she chided me, "but you keep finding yourself in these . . . situations. Don't you?"

"Hey," I smiled at her reassuringly, "don't worry about me. I'm all grown up." Sarah looked at me skeptically. And I couldn't blame her. I spend large chunks of my day working with wooden swords, practicing an art that was archaic a century ago. And I've seen more bloodshed than I care to think about. I tried a different tack.

"You know why they use young guys for soldiers, Sarah?" She shook her head, no. "Mostly because they don't know any better. They haven't seen enough of life to be really scared. And they haven't built much of a life that they can worry about losing."

"And you?"

"Me? I've been scared plenty." But I waived that away. "The real issue is that I've got too much to lose." I gave her hand a squeeze. "And I know it. So. I'm gonna go to Fort Bragg and review some manuals. Get some exercise with the grunts. Help them fine-tune some technique. Nothing more."

"Promise?" she asked.

"Absolutely," I replied.

She looked skeptical for a time, but slowly relaxed. Maybe it was what I had said. Probably it was more the good meal and nice surroundings. Whatever it was, the night began to get better. We smiled more. And after a while, the waitress brought *sake*. The small white ceramic cups were warm with the promise within. We lifted the cups up in a silent toast. I smiled. I don't know whether I'm a good man, but I am an incurable and persistent romantic.

8

WATCHER

Even in the mountains of the tropics, it was cool in the mornings. Hatsue could hear the coughing of the villagers as the morning fires in their huts smoldered into life. Chickens cackled and scratched. The light was burning through the night mist and washing the slopes and the small mountain village in a pearl-like haze. She rolled off her camp cot, her clothes damp with humidity. She shivered into a fleece jacket and rubbed her hands through her spiky hair, cut short for her sojourn into the field.

The field. The floor of the hut was packed dirt. You could smell the earth everywhere in these hills. It was damp and rich and aromatic. She lit her small kerosene stove to heat the day's tea water. Hatsue had set gauze sheeting over the window and doorway to keep the bugs at bay—and to provide some privacy. She peered out through the screening into the village that had been her world for the last ten months, and the cloth created an impressionist image: a blurred universe of moist greens and dark wood tones. Dirt and wood. The screen netting was a filter that softened the reality somewhat—but not enough.

The Japanese were nature lovers. But their nature was carefully managed: pruned and manicured and manipulated for esthetic effect. Hatsue's childhood had been a world of razor-neat gardens, postage stamp-sized plots tended with ferocious zeal. Bonsai trees twisted and bent to human intentions. But here, nature was a wild thing, unpredictable and overpowering. Like the smell of earth, it seeped everywhere, a riot of growth and decay.

She sat at the rickety table she used for a field desk. She stared at her hands. They were small and she worked hard to keep them clean, but the line of dirt under her nails was always there. It wasn't that she did not struggle against it; it was simply that the mountain jungle was too strong.

She felt warmth in her eyes and made a grimace of disgust. *Idiot*, she thought. *Don't start feeling sorry for yourself again.* She busied herself making her breakfast, the small, sure movements a reassertion of some sort of control. *It will be so good to be back in Boston.* Hatsue moved some notebooks aside and opened her calendar journal. She carefully inked another day off. *Two more months. You've done it this long; you can hold out 'til then.*

When she had won the research grant to come to Mindanao to complete her doctoral research in anthropology, she had been excited. Her professors smiled quietly and congratulated her, but they looked at each other with strange, private expressions—something in their eyes that had made her uncomfortable. It wasn't until she had actually entered the field that she realized what they were thinking.

Fieldwork was the last hurdle for an aspiring anthropologist. The academic discipline prided itself on a tradition of sending its young researchers to experience firsthand the peoples and tribes they studied. Hatsue, the product of a tightly controlled and cosmopolitan upbringing in Japan, had been caught up by the romance of studying exotic cultures. There was something so uncontrolled and free about it. She had plunged into graduate studies at Harvard with a determination to excel. She read unceasingly. Debated obscure theory with her equally engaged classmates. Researched and wrote endless papers. It was a world of books and ideas, supercharged intellects and fragile egos. Graduate study had sharpened her mind and her pen. It had made her an able debater. But, despite all her enthusiasm, it hadn't prepared her for the immersion into a world of primitive hill farmers, of complex personalities and emotions. Sickness. The unceasing sweat of the mountain farmer. The dirt.

Fieldwork was the last cruel trick her professors had played on her.

But she was from a proud family. She had been groomed for success; first at the best preparatory schools Japan had to offer, then at Harvard. She would not destroy her career because of emotion. She would not let her family down. She would persevere.

You occasionally heard stories of graduate students who washed out in the field. Their trips were cut short and they came back, strangely quiet about what had happened "out there." They lingered at school for a course or two, but if you looked hard at them you could see the essence of an academic career evaporating. Eventually, they simply disappeared as well.

Hatsue knew this would not be her fate. She opened the water-proof locker and looked at the notes she had taken, careful records of observations and conversations, hastily set down at the time, then more neatly organized and analyzed later. Pages of ink—you used pens here because the humidity made the graphite of pencils smudge and fade. She fanned through page after page of data. It was a frequent ritual, a reminder of progress and purpose. And as the notebooks filled and were carefully placed in the locker along with small packets of desiccant, they, too, told her that soon she would be gone from this place.

She set herself to her breakfast and another day.

Villagers were stirring. Someone was hawking up phlegm in the next hut. Children were calling like small birds. An old woman was scolding someone in the rapid syllables of the language of the Higuanon tribe. The thud of a metal blade sinking into a piece of wood set a rhythm to the morning as fuel was chopped to feed the fires.

Morning with the Higuanon, a Philippine hill tribe, she thought, creating a mental caption for the sights and sounds around her. She wondered how the process of writing up her notes would leach the immediacy of experience from her description. The smell of morning fires, the cool air of the hills on your skin as you set out with the women to the small clearings known as *kaingin*. It was here that the Higuanon hacked out a spot on the hillside to grow their crops: corn, dry rice, water grass, sayote, and white beans.

They were a small people, much like the Japanese, light-footed on the narrow mountain trails. But, despite all her preparatory studies, she had not really been prepared for the plunge into their world. They were a people who had fled to the mountains generations ago to carve a primitive living out of the hillsides, steep and covered with vegetation that sprang from the rich dark soil of old volcanoes. On an island of increasingly militant Muslims and evangelizing Christians, they held to the old beliefs of animism. To the Higuanon, the world was alive with spirits, powers for good or evil. The inexplicable, even the inevitable arrival of sickness and death, were the work of unseen forces.

Hatsue had talked of these things with the villagers, curious and yet skeptical. She wasn't supposed to judge these people, but she couldn't hide her disbelief. They, in turn, had laughed at her. She came from the world of cars and radios and other wonders. How could she be so ignorant of the basic things in life? The world was filled with spirits. Of this there was no doubt. When she had looked at them in disbelief as they told her tales in the night, the patient *datu*, the headman of the village, had gently taken her by the hand and led her out of the hut into the absolute darkness of a mountain night.

The villagers rarely left their huts after nightfall. It was pitch dark, and her eyes were still dazzled by the firelight in the hut. Hatsue could feel the hard, dry skin of the old man's hand as he led her into the village center. The *datu* grasped her by her shoulders and turned her to face off across the valley. In the distance, cherry red embers glowed on a remote elevation. It was Mount Kamatayan, the center of the Higuanon universe. There, the old man explained in the bubbly language of his tribe, the dead traveled to be judged at the end of their lives. By night, their campfires were visible. Even during the day, the smoke of their fires vented from the mountainside.

The mountain was called Balatukan on her official maps. She knew that the fires and smoke were from the venting of volcanic action. But here, in the close darkness, with the jungle breathing on her, the surety of science and cartography seemed distant and unpersuasive. The world was alive, the old one told her.

Hatsue nodded. Later, she noted the conversation in her journal. But she did not write a word about the feeling of unease the conversation had created. In the darkness, the jungle pressed in on her, speaking in the visceral language of the hills.

After breakfast, she joined the women and children as they wound their way along the grassy trail that led to the fields. *Tiger grass*, she noted almost automatically, vaguely pleased at her growing knowledge. That morning the villagers were gay as birds, the turbaned women balancing rattan baskets on their heads, the children darting along the trail, alive to the slightest diversion. On their flanks, off among the trees, there were benevolent shadows. The *alimaong*, the tribal guards, were with them.

The Higuanon held to the high ground in the hopes of peace. It was in many ways a tranquil life; one measured by the pace of dry seasons and wet ones, of the growth cycle of crops. But the jungle slopes were not always quiet. More than just spirits haunted the deep woods. The Muslim tribes, the old Moros, still struggled for independence. The central government fought back. Truces were made and then broken. There were times when the faint ripping of automatic weapon fire could be heard, even on the high slopes of the Higuanon farms. Hatsue had shrugged off the danger: there were very few places left in the world to study tribal peoples. Most of them were curious blends of shamans and Kalashnikovs, of Stone Age farming and geopolitical struggle. It came with the territory. Literally.

That day passed like most others. Hatsue had long ago paced off the dimensions of the hill fields and inventoried the crops grown. She had reduced what she could of Higuanon life to facts and numbers, but that effort was soon completed and paled in comparison with the challenge of really understanding these people. She watched the daily pace of their lives and hoped for insight through the experience of the mundane.

Hatsue resigned herself to another sleepy day on the mountain slopes, to the buzz of insects and the distant calls of birds, and the desultory conversations with the women. Only the children offered some relief. They hovered around her, fascinated by the spectacle of a grown person who, even now, knew so little about their world. They offered to take her into the forest to show her a troop of monkeys or a tree as old as the world. They brought her curious insects, cupping them in the cage of their small hands and smiling at her feigned surprise. The sun made the fields steam with heat and they moved into the shade of the trees for relief. The weeding done, the adults, Hatsue included, culled the fields for the evening's meal and collected wood for the fires. She straightened up for what seemed like the millionth time and rubbed the small of her back. An old woman saw her and grinned. The old one's face was creased and leathery, her few teeth discolored from chewing betel nut. Her ageless brown eyes glittered with silent understanding: she too rubbed her back. Then bent again to pick up another piece of firewood.

Late in the day, a runner toiled up from the river valley, his face streaked with sweat and his secondhand sneakers covered in mud. He spoke quietly with one of the guards, who nodded him along the trail toward the village. Then the *alimaong* checked the action on his old M-1 carbine and ushered the women and children out of the fields.

There were strangers on the slopes.

Hatsue had been through these types of alerts before. The Higuanon prized their isolation and any outsider was viewed with deep suspicion. Sometimes it was nothing to fear. The blonde-haired evangelist from a Chicago mission society would sometimes make the long trek by horseback up to see them. He was greeted politely and was respected for the rudimentary medical care he could give people. The *datu* listened to the missionary's stories of Jesus with pleasant tolerance. There was also a team of scientists stumbling around down in the valley, occasionally lugging boxes of instruments upslope to measure volcanic action in some of the older craters.

But this time the runner spoke of men with guns.

The women shouldered their loads and slipped down the trail quickly and efficiently. They cast an occasional glance back along the trail where the sentry stood watch, but their feet moved quickly toward the village. The children, whose energy level seemed to spike shortly before the evening meal, hooted in excitement. The elders hushed them with a severity that was unusual and squatted in a circle to debate a proper response to the mysterious intruders. Hatsue edged closer to learn what she could.

The sky was still bright, although when you lowered your eyes to the ground it was amazing how dim the forest looked. The yellow of small cooking fires seemed more vivid and the tips of cheroots glowed red in the glowing gloom. The men of the village smoked and squatted, speaking softly and quickly to one another. It made it difficult to hear. The women busied themselves with cooking and distracting the children, but Hatsue was drawn to the circle of men. She drifted closer and they stopped suddenly, all eyes rising to look at her. The wise brown eyes of the *datu* were cold and remote. A woman came and gently tugged Hatsue away from the council.

The air began to blue with the approach of evening. Fires were stoked into life and the evening rice prepared. Young men continued to filter in and out of the village, conferring with the headman. From their expressions, it was obvious that the search for intruders had yielded nothing. What was more disturbing, Hatsue wondered, the idea that a stranger was present, or that he could not be found?

She did not ask the question, knowing that in the quiet time after the evening meal, there would be more talk. And the women would tell her what they had learned. Part of Hatsue bridled at this. She was a product of a different place, and had been encouraged to find things out for herself. It was one of the freedoms that she treasured about her life at Harvard, and one of the things she feared losing on her return to Japan. So she slipped out of her hut and into the forest, drifting quietly through the brush, alive to the possibility that she could succeed where the men could not.

Hatsue had learned to move along the wooded slopes, having been taught with eager glee by the children. She could recognize the worn pathways of wild pigs and avoid them for safer trails. She no longer froze in fear as a snake coiled its way down a nearby tree. She could weave through the trees, the noise of her passing nothing but a part of the general rustling and snapping of the forest.

At first, the mountain forest had been a disorienting place. But it offered a type of privacy she never had in the paper wall culture of Japan and she found that she liked the isolation. The pressure of constantly being on display, of being observed by the villagers was wearing. It never occurred to her that they might feel the same way. But over time, Hatsue had made it a habit to walk alone in the forest as the sunlight waned and the space under the leafy canopy grew darker and the air grew cool. It was her time alone, and something she came to treasure. It was one more odd habit that marked her as different from the people she studied. For them, the coming night awoke the malevolent spirits of the forest. They clung to the safe circle of firelight with a deep and feral appreciation of nature's peril. Hatsue, whose world was both more sophisticated and less perceptive, was immune to that wisdom.

Now, she moved quietly, eyes roaming across the foliage, listening for the telltale noise of an intruder. She inched slowly toward a spot where a rockfall had carved a scar in the mountainside: it would provide an excellent vantage point.

The small hand grabbed at her and the surprised rush of Hatsue's breath was smothered in the humid air. One of the village children squatted under a bush, face taut with tension. The boy pulled Hatsue down next to him. She sank to his level and looked at him questioningly. The boy held up a hand in warning.

"Moros," he whispered, and turned his head to face up the rock slope.

High above, their faces streaked with camouflage paint, small wiry men with automatic weapons were quietly watching the trail that led to the village. Hatsue could feel her heart thudding in her throat as she crouched down in the brush. The child next to her unconsciously moved closer, seeking comfort. With a nightmare inevitability, the men with guns began to pick their way downslope toward the trail to the village. She felt a jet of alarm. Most contact with outsiders like this was accidental. Chance collisions as groups of armed men traversed Higuanon territory. But these men were heading toward the village. She could not imagine what they wanted, but she feared these men and what they would do to her village. *Her village.* Hatsue would have smiled at the thought in any other situation, but now she realized in alarm that the line of armed men was heading toward her hiding place. Her hands were cold as she gripped the child and whispered urgently in his ear.

"Run," she told him. "Warn the datu."

The child slipped off into the darkness under the trees. Hatsue held her breath as the child disappeared into the forest. Then she slowly began to move in the opposite direction, hoping to shield herself from view in the underbrush. But she was not as skilled as she imagined. With a shout, the men spotted her. Hatsue sprang up and raced downslope, mouth open in fear.

Her flight had no rational direction. She ran downhill, pulled by gravity. Her ears burned and her shoulder muscles were tense with fear. Would they shoot? Hatsue slapped her way through an obstacle course of branches. Roots and creepers snatched at her feet. She stumbled, but continued on, willing herself not to look back.

It was just as well. The watchers poured after her, cascading downward with the darkness like animals seeking prey.

9

BEAST

The urge for order is strong; it fights for dominance in the most unlikely places. You see it in *reigi*, the etiquette of the *dojo*, where precisely scripted courtesies exist side by side with barely restrained fury. So Fort Bragg was both familiar and strange at the same time. It was neat and orderly. All that marching and uniforms and saluting. But underneath, something dangerous lurked. I got the feeling of a tremendous psychic tension, the faint creaking of chains stressed to the breaking point with the effort of keeping something elemental under control.

A uniformed driver had picked me up at the Fayetteville airport late in the afternoon of the evening before. The corporal from the 82nd Airborne was lean. His uniform was creased. He had large ears that stuck out from his shaved head like radar dishes. He looked like a twelve year old—an extremely lethal twelve year old with a familiarity with automatic weapons.

The corporal was polite and efficient, but not a very gifted conversationalist. He had a checklist on a gunmetal clipboard with extremely precise instructions about me and it seemed to occupy the greater part of his attention. We pulled in off Rte. 24, had our IDs checked at the base gate, and were logged in. I was ushered into a building identified as the Soldier Support Center and taken upstairs. A succession of bored looking clerks, beefy non-commissioned officers, eyed me skeptically. My escort gave them a sheet of paper, and then the fun began.

This was obviously not your run-of-the mill processing job. They read the corporal's instructions. The senior man present, a master sergeant with jowls, took the sheet and left to make a phone call. The others conferred and talked about a variety of forms, many of them with cryptic titles comprised of letters and numbers strung together. Critical thinking in today's armed forces.

The master sergeant came back scowling, but he had an idea what to do, and that seemed to make everyone feel better. Computer keyboards were tapped. Files accessed. Laser printers whirred. I was given a pen with black ink and ordered to sign and initial a flurry of pages by the dour non-com. They raced through the process with a smooth yet self-conscious efficiency, trying to make up for their earlier confusion by now getting me in and out as quickly as possible. I entered a civilian and left a temporary employee of the Department of the Army. I was photographed with a digital camera and issued a shiny new identity card on a lanyard. It was, my escort informed me solemnly, to be worn at all times. The card was still warm from the laminator as I slipped it on.

The boy corporal handed me off to a sergeant who stuck me in a room in the Transient Bachelor Officers Quarters. The corporal gave me some material on the base, instructions from Baker, and my schedule for the coming days (I had to sign for them). He straightened up and almost looked like he was going to salute. Then he got hold of himself, spun around on his polished shoes, and left with barely suppressed relief. I dumped my bag onto the bed and listened to the springs squeak.

There was a beat-up desk facing a window and a stack of binders waiting for me. Homework. The three-ring binders looked like something from high school, but the contents were like nothing I could ever have imagined then. Laid out with the mind-numbing organization and precision I was beginning to associate with military paperwork, was the curriculum for unarmed training in the Special Operations Command.

I shuffled through it in the course of a boring evening, letting my eye scan over the pages but not really registering much. Or so I thought. I slept fitfully and woke while it was still dark. My eyes shot open and, for a moment I couldn't be sure whether a sound had roused me or whether it was just something in my head. Then I heard the beast.

It was dark out, with that damp coolness you get just before the night begins to slip away. Somewhere out there, I could hear the throaty sound, faint yet fierce, of large numbers of people shouting in unison. I looked at my watch and sighed. Morning with the XVIII Airborne Corps.

I have my own routine. At dawn, my old injuries prod me into remembrance. The muscles are tight and bones moan faintly. Yamashita says it's a function of approaching middle age: he's a font of good news. I rolled off the bed and began the sequence of stretches he'd taught me. There's a sequence to them that he insists on, including an almost yogic series of work with the back and stomach muscles. Afterward, I run.

I shambled outside and, off to the east, the horizon was clearly visible. I had looked at a map of the base and mentally laid out a route for running last night. I got to it.

I don't enjoy running. But I don't not enjoy it anymore, either. Yamashita insists on the need for endurance and strength training from his students. And his demands have only increased over the years. "As skill grows," he admonishes me, "effort diminishes."

"This is a bad thing?" I ask. But I grin to let him know I'm kidding. He looks at me with that flat expression, but he pulls his chin down so his jowls appear. I don't know whether he gets my humor completely, but at least I get this reaction from him. It's taken years.

So that morning I ran, taking the spectacle in. A military base at dawn is bustling with activity. Bodies in large clumps move at varying speeds, tied together with invisible thread and controlled by sung cadence. They wind along the roads, serious-looking blocks of identically dressed young people with shaven heads, moving in unison like a machine. Sergeants confer at doorways, creased and impeccable and looking deeply annoyed. Cars and trucks cruise by, a mobile sampler of camouflage styles ranging from woodland green to desert brown.

I trotted along, untethered and unnoticed. Or so I thought. I was on the last leg of my four miles when a sedan with flashing lights shot past me and pulled across my path. Two very serious young men with sidearms got out.

"Good morning, sir, may I see some identification, please?" one said. Or that's what I eventually figured out. In the military, everyone seems to speak quickly, with little or no pauses. The usual verbal cues like inflection are missing. So it really sounded more like, "guhmornsuhmayseeIsuhidenticationplease." He held his hand out and his partner watched me warily, gunhand free.

Their uniforms were different from the civilian world, but I've been rousted enough times by the authorities to recognize the general drift of things. I had wisely slipped my ID card over my neck before setting out. Didn't want to disappoint the corporal with the big ears. For all I knew, he could have dropped a dime on me this morning just to make sure. The two security men eyed the card, then radioed in for directions. Eventually, they bundled me into the back of the car and delivered me to my quarters.

A captain was waiting there for me. He watched the car approach with his hands on his hips and a lopsided grin on his face. He was wearing the new-style camo fatigues that are made up of tiny pixel-like squares of color. He seemed friendly enough.

"Dr. Burke?" he asked, hand extended to shake mine. "I'm

Dave Ashby. Training cadre asked me to escort you down to the training site this morning." Ashby had a big face and a thick neck that made his fatigue hat look small sitting up there on the top of his head. His eyes glittered and he seemed quietly amused.

The security people had eyes that were considerably less sparkly. They were not happy, even though they got to pawn me off onto Ashby. Their parting shot was the curt directive that in the future I was to clear any unaccompanied movements around the base with security before setting out.

"Man," Ashby said. "You've been here . . . what? . . . twelve hours? And already you've gone off the reservation."

"It's a gift," I admitted.

Ashby grunted. "Hnhh. You had breakfast yet?" I shook my head, no. "OK," he said, glancing at his watch. "Get changed and we'll grab something quick." I headed up the steps to my room feeling that this was the most friendly contact I'd had on the base so far, and that things were looking up. Ashby called out after me. "Hey! You like grits?"

Then again, maybe I was being overly optimistic.

"Colonel Baker says he brought you in to do some analysis on our hand-to-hand," Ashby said.

"That's right," I replied. "He wants to bring someone with a different background in to analyze your system. Says he's done it before."

Ashby's glance was evasive. "Well . . . you know the Colonel . . . he's always up to something. And he's got some major juice with Special Operations Command. I never knew that training was one of his areas, though . . . "

"I got the impression that he uses consultants of one type or another on a regular basis," I told him.

Ashby waved a hand. "Side effect of the downsizing of the military. We got a lot more civilians picking up peripheral support functions. Combat stuff tends to be kept in-house, though."

"Things change, I guess."

"Maybe," Ashby replied, but he didn't sound sure. He thought for a minute. "Colonel Baker's typically not someone focused on training and analysis. He's more of a 'problem solver' kind of guy. More action-oriented, if you know what I mean."

"Sure," I said. Somewhere off in the distance, I could hear the report of small-arms fire. "He must fit right in here."

"He's got an outstanding reputation," Ashby said in all seriousness. "He's one squared-away trooper."

I just nodded. We had arrived at the training site—a nondescript warehouse with some humvees parked out front. Ashby paused before entering. He looked at me. "These soldiers in here are pretty squared away, too, Dr. Burke."

"I'm sure they are."

Ashby shook his head as if I wasn't hearing him. "No. I mean these are all very well-trained people. They know their business. Between them, they've done nearly every program the Special Operations Forces have. I'd tread lightly with them. The only reason they're gonna give you the time of day is because Baker's asked them to." His eyes had developed a hard edge. Ashby was an interesting guy.

"Understood." I looked back at him to let him know I got the point. "Are you going to let me in, or are you just hoping all this Green Beret stuff is going to scare me off?"

Ashby smiled, but it wasn't a warm one. "I just wanted you to be clear on things before you go in there."

"I appreciate it," I told him. He was probably worried that the civilian consultant was going to be mauled. But I had gone into scarier rooms.

I stood in the middle of a circle of soldiers and I could smell the antagonism in the air. They eyed me stonily. I sighed. Teaching people is difficult enough. Teaching them when they don't want to learn from you is even harder.

They were all sergeants of one type or another. Fit and hard. I knew from the briefing material I had gone over last night that they had all been through a prototype advanced unarmed combat course. They'd done Airborne and Ranger and Special Forces training. Some were just back from a tour in Iraq. Their body language clearly indicated that they didn't think I had anything to tell them.

Ashby introduced me as Dr. Burke and started to give a quick synopsis of my expertise. It was standard stuff, the Ph.D. and books, the blackbelts I had earned. It was a miracle no one snickered out loud. I waved Ashby off and stood in the circle.

"I'm Connor Burke, " I said to them. I looked around the circle, taking in their faces, reading their stances and the different body shapes. "I think you've all done things I haven't and have that knowledge I don't." You could see they liked that. We all want respect. "But," I continued, "that cuts both ways. You guys work with a range of weapons. I work with blades and sticks and bare hands. For you, close combat is anything under three hundred meters. In all my fights, you can smell the opponent's spit. So I can probably teach you some things as well." But their eyes told me that they were still skeptical.

I thought about my brother Micky and the discussions we'd had over the years. Micky is a pragmatist. He's suspicious of the exotic. It's only in the last few years that he's grudgingly admitted that Yamashita's training isn't an exercise in delusion. And I had to have the same sort of conversation with these people around me now, only it all had to be compressed into a few days.

"Look," I continued, "I don't break boards or claim I can levitate. I work in an old tradition that has much the same goal as yours."

"What's that?" a compact, swarthy soldier asked.

I smiled. "To locate, close with, and destroy the enemy."

The soldier made a grimace that I think was a smile. "Fuckin' A," he said, and heads nodded. But they were still wary.

"The bottom line is that you're professionals," I continued. "It's your responsibility to learn every possible thing that can help you in getting the job done and maybe help you stay alive. I'm here to see what I can contribute to your mission readiness." The reading last night *had* come in handy. "Okay?" A few heads nodded. "Let's see what you've got," I told them, and the workout began.

I spent two whole days watching them move. All systems tend to emphasize a finite range of actions and techniques. It's what creates stylistic patterns. Individual capacity and talent introduces minor quirks and variations as well. So I observed the training to see what areas were emphasized and what additional things they could benefit from.

No style is complete—the range of possible attack/response scenarios is infinite. And this sort of training was only part of what these soldiers were expected to do. They had focused on a general range of techniques and emphasized specific skills in hand to hand work. It made sense, in a way. Yamashita would have said that they were neglecting "basics," but he's also someone who believes it takes three years to teach students the correct way to grip the floor with their toes.

Every night I had to produce a written report for submission to Baker, the combination of my analysis of the written syllabus and its application in training. It made for a full day. Every dawn I ran with the training cadre. Then I watched and participated in the drills. Ashby took me to and from the mess hall, picked me up in the morning, and tucked me in at night.

By the end of the week, I was tired of it. The soldiers I watched were still not particularly interested in learning anything from me.

It reminded me of the situation I had just had in Yamashita's *dojo* with the new trainees.

Besides, the Army had a basically sound system. They worked on drills to get the technique right and then did the applications in full gear, to get a sense of what it would be like in a real fight. It was an important point. Just going through the motions with a helmet on was important. All that weight on your head tended to change your balance and the way you moved.

In fact, if there was one thing I thought they needed, it was more drill in full gear. A soldier in the field would probably be wearing body armor that weighed about twenty-five pounds. Plus a field pack and other equipment that could mean he'd be carrying sixty pounds. Throw in gloves and goggles, elbow and knee pads, and what you got was someone who had to move in completely different ways. Balance would be a problem. Nobody was going to do much kicking—it's hard enough to carry that weight on two legs, never mind one.

I was reminded of one of the more obscure *kata* in judo—*kojiki no kata*. The moves are odd and stilted, very different from the other forms that *judoka* practice. But that's because that particular *kata* rehearses movements that would be made in full armor. It's a holdover from the days when the samurai in armor still stalked the battlefields, and a recognition that the mechanics of fighting can change technique considerably.

During a break, I mentioned that idea to a few of the senior instructors, and for once they nodded. "What else you got?" one asked.

I shrugged. "You're basically on track with this stuff. Short, hard strikes. If anything, make them shorter. Nothing fancy. Get close in. You can use the weight you're carrying as a weapon. You do it right, you could probably break someone up just by falling on them."

They liked that, but had a funny way of showing it. "Man, Burke," one asked, "they pay you for stuff like that?"

Some of the faces seemed a bit more friendly after a week. Maybe I was just getting used to the atmosphere. Testosterone and aggression make for distinctive social dynamics. But there were still a few faces that were decidedly unfriendly.

One of them spoke up. "You ever fall down and hurt anyone, Burke? Or just yourself?" It was not a rhetorical question. There were some snickers from the group.

I looked at the printed name on the chest of his uniform—Fields—then up into his eyes. They were small and blue and watched me like I was prey. Was it D.H. Lawrence who wrote about the blue-eyed killer? The man with the gun? Here he was.

"What do you wanna know, Fields?" I asked him. My voice was as unfriendly as his. The place was rubbing off on me.

He gestured at me with his chin. "Mr. Expert. What do you know about any of this? You ever been in a firefight? You ever killed anyone?" He snorted in disgust.

"What the fuck kind of question is that?" I snapped out. Like I said, it must be something in the air. I got up real close to Fields, projecting energy as hard as I could. You could see him stiffen. "Grow up, Fields. *You* don't know what you're talking about." I looked around at the group. "The question is not whether I've ever killed anyone. I know drunk drivers who've managed to pull that off. The question is whether I've been in places that scared me shitless and stayed anyway and did what needed to be done." I knew the answer to that. I was calm and ready when I finished by saying, "That's the real question."

I don't know what would have happened next. Fields was big and dense and did not look particularly happy with my response. His nostrils flared spasmodically as he waited for me to throw the first punch. But I didn't, even though I would have liked to. The discipline I follow teaches you to do what you should, not what you'd like.

"Stand down!" a voice barked, and punched through the tension. Ashby stood there, glowering. "Fields," he said dismissively, "as you were." His voice had a compelling quality to it—what the military calls "command voice." They say some Zen masters can use a shout to impel trainees into enlightenment, pushing them there by the blending of psychic and aural force. It's a very similar sort of thing. Yamashita, of course, can paralyze students with his commands. Ashby was nowhere near as good, but he was still pretty impressive.

"Burke," he ordered, "come with me." He spun on his heels and I followed him out of the building.

"Am I in trouble, Ashby?" I asked sarcastically as he steamed toward a parked car. He went around to the driver's side and looked at me across the hood.

"Hunh?" He looked puzzled for a minute. "Oh. No." Then he smiled slightly. "I told you they were a hard crew, Burke. They push you a little bit?"

"No problem. I pushed back," I told him.

"Shame I had to stop it. It would have been interesting to see what would have gone down. Fields can be a pain in the ass."

"So why did you stop it?"

"Colonel Baker sent for you. Your clearance came through."

"Clearance?"

Ashby grinned at me knowingly, and his eyes had a hard and wild look to them. "Fun is fun. But now your real work begins, Burke."

10

BLOOD MONEY

The video image had been enhanced and considerably cleaned up. As a result, it made the little details easier to see. Not that you wanted to see the details. We've all watched so much Hollywood mayhem that when we see the real thing, it seems almost flat and without drama. But it's horrible nonetheless: the gasps and muffled thud of meat and bone, the sawing of desperate breathing. The faint spasm and drumming of heels as a man dies and the body comes to a final, terrible stillness that looks different from anything else that I know.

Ashby had brought me onto a different part of the base, an area of well-kept brick buildings and brisk efficiency. Officer country. I got whisked down a hall to a meeting room, where three men in suits were clustered at the end of a long wooden conference table. They all had little ID cards pinned to their jackets. Baker was there, in a uniform shirt with creases that looked like they could hurt if you touched them.

"That's all, Ashby," Baker said in dismissal. My escort shot back out the door. "Burke," he said, and gestured me to a chair.

"Hello, Colonel." I eyed the others, but Baker didn't seem inclined to introduce them. The men around the table seemed like they were all cast from the same mold—dark suits and short haircuts—but I figured the silver-haired guy at the head of the table was in charge. They all watched me like I was some sort of lab specimen.

"I'd like you to review a video clip for us, Burke," the Colonel said. He patted a file folder. "I've been reading your nightly reports and reviewing your file in general. I'm hoping you can help us out with something."

"Us?" I prompted. I looked at the guys in suits. They hadn't fidgeted or said a word since I came in the door. Finally, the man with silver hair spoke. He had a Midwestern accent of some sort and a very quiet voice.

"Let's say, we're your friends from Virginia." He smiled at me without warmth and his companions did the same. Jokesters from Langley, no doubt.

"We've come across a video . . . it's got some hand-to-hand fighting on it and we'd like some help in analyzing the techniques," Baker started to explain.

"Who'd you get it from?" I asked. "What did they tell you?"

Baker looked at his companions. The soft-voiced man said, "The previous owner is no longer able to comment on its provenance."

Ah. "But you've got some idea," I pressed.

The spook shrugged his shoulders in reply.

The Colonel took up the thread. "There are some distinctive . . . " he paused for a minute to select the right word, then found it, "elements on the video and we want the benefit of your analysis, Burke. That's it. You can leave the other stuff to us."

Baker's expression was flat and final. So I sat down and let them show me the thing. It wasn't what I expected. When the clip stopped, I swallowed and said to them, "You know what this is?"

My friend from the CIA said, "Why don't you tell us what it is?" He had a knack for sitting very still. But you could sense the intensity that he kept tied down and see a hint of it way back behind his eyes.

I thought about what I had just seen. "Where'd it come from,

Malaysia?" Some of the people in the clip were clearly from some-place in southern Asia.

"The operational area is not your concern, Dr. Burke," another of the quiet suits told me. "What can you tell us about the techniques used?"

"Why?" I pressed them. I was getting a little tired of dealing with these guys.

Baker reached across the table and ran the clip again. I didn't particularly want to see it another time, but the doomed figures on the screen drew my attention.

It was filmed in a warehouse of some sort, a big space, where high, dingy windows let in enough light to make filming possible. The floor looked like concrete. It was stained, and by the time the film was done, there were new smears darkening the surface. Vague shapes of furniture or equipment loomed in the background, but the central area of focus was empty except for the fighters.

Although I probably shouldn't call what happened a fight. It was more of a ritual execution. And it was pretty obvious that the victims never really had a chance. They were simply there to pro-vide fodder for the men who worked on them. And, when it was over, the two bodies were pulled into the center of the floor and the camera panned on their faces.

"These two men were Marines," Baker said in explanation, his voice a raspy growl. "Embassy guards."

"The Jarheads usually take care of their own," the man from Langley explained, "but they're looking for some help on this one."

"Special Operations Command has some local assets that could be significant for this," another suit added tersely. It sounded like a rationale that had been presented before.

Baker's jaw tightened and he grunted in dismissal. "I don't give a damn about interservice rivalry. We all follow the same flag. And I'm going to figure out who did this, track them down, and nail them to the wall." He glared at me and I had the fleeting thought that I would not like to be someone who Baker was going to track down.

"Okay," I breathed. "Run it again."

I screened that video any number of times, trying to let the flow of physical action imprint itself on my brain. Watching for movement patterns, habits of particular training styles, gaps in technique. I broke the hideous sequence of events down into more manageable discrete chunks that could be analyzed. It made it easier, but not much. I watched. And watched again. Made notes on a pad.

"Can you slow it down?" I asked. They could. "Can you make it louder?"

"Why?"

"I need to hear their breathing patterns."

They waited in silence, running and rerunning the video for me until I told them to stop. They had dimmed the lights, and when they turned them back up, I rubbed my eyes.

"All right. What have we got here, Burke?" Baker turned a small tape recorder on.

"Before we go any further," the quiet man said, "I just want to confirm that this is confidential and, as a government contract employee, you're bound by your agreement not to divulge the contents of what you've learned to anyone on pain of prosecution." It was quite a mouthful. And he wasn't even looking at me when he said it. The question was really aimed at Baker.

The Colonel nodded. "He's been fully processed and the forms are signed." I didn't remember anything like this, but then again, I had signed about ten different things when I arrived on the base. I felt vaguely foolish, but everyone in the room seemed very serious.

The man from the CIA pressed me. "We clear on this?"

I nodded. "Continue, Dr. Burke," the Colonel said.

I looked down at my notes. If I closed my eyes, I could see flashes of the video imagery. I took a breath and began.

"I'll probably repeat the obvious, but since you're not telling me anything, you'll have to bear with me. Start the clip, but run it slowly." The lights went down and the screen lit up. "The victims were young and fit. The way they rubbed their wrists and moved their limbs about suggests that they had been bound for some time. I imagine it impeded their ability to defend themselves." I looked around the table for someone who might offer me a clue, but got nothing.

"It wouldn't have made much of a difference," I continued. "The attackers are wearing hoods, so I can't really be sure, but they look a little bit bigger than some of the Asian figures you glimpse around the periphery. Slightly different builds. Even so, you'd think the Marines would have given them a run for their money. But the attackers were professionally trained in just this sort of thing."

"Stop," Baker commented, and the video imagery froze. "How do you know about the training?"

"Watch the way they approach the Marines. Your guys had some training, I can see that. But it's a very aggressive, lineal approach. The attackers move differently. Start it up." The images moved.

"It doesn't take your guys long to realize what's up. They move in to meet the fight. They knew there wasn't much of a chance, but you have to give 'em credit. They go down fighting." It was probably not going to be much of a comfort to their families. I heard Baker draw in a breath to make a comment, but I continued. "The way they move in is characteristic of people trained with weapons, Baker. They bring the fight to their opponent. I've been watching the soldiers here move all week. They're tough and hard and aggressive. They train with guns and bayonets. The guys in the hoods, however . . . Stop!" Once again, the figures on the screen were frozen in mid-action.

"The attackers are using classic combat stances . . . "

One of the CIA men spoke up. "We had some of our people look at this. It's not judo or aikido or karate based."

I shook my head. "It's older. Those styles are modern forms. They're practiced in controlled environments: flat, regular floors." I nodded at the figures on the screen. "These guys are using stances much more like what you would see in old-style martial arts, the *ko-ryu*. Techniques were designed for actual battlefield use, so stances were different. Start." The video began again.

"The strikes could be a variant of karate," another of the spooks offered.

"There are only so many different ways to hit someone," I countered. "What's really significant are the hips, shoulders, and heels."

"Heels?" Baker sounded incredulous.

I didn't answer him right away. "The movement patterns here are typical of Japanese as opposed to Chinese styles of unarmed fighting—the Japanese think of the torso as a cylinder that should be kept upright when fighting. The Chinese are a bit more flexible." I watched a strike unfold on the screen. "The rotation of the hip into the strike makes me think of Japanese styles as well, although it could be Korean."

"So you're not sure?" The man with the Midwestern accent seemed vaguely annoyed.

I shrugged. "I wasn't, until I saw this. Stop." The resolution on the video was very enhanced: an arc of spittle froze in space.

"The attackers are well trained, but they still show some flaws. Notice the placement of the heel here as he strikes. It's slightly raised. Not much, but the extension of the strike and the rotation of the hip pull at the leg. Even though he's flattening out that back foot, the heel rises up a bit. It's not uncommon. Many Korean styles have compensated by raising the heel up so the back foot rests on the ball of the foot. But this guy is struggling against that. So, again, I'd say it's derived from a Japanese style. Start."

They didn't have much more to add, so I finished with my analysis. I tried to look more at my notes than at the images that flickered on the screen. The end was not pretty.

"Here, where the one attacker breaks the Marine's arm, you see a pretty basic technique. Lots of systems use it. But the flow of the attacker, the way he uses his hands and focuses on the arm make me think it's not a system that works with weapons held in each hand. So various systems from Malaysia and the Philippines seem to be out." I noticed that the CIA people reacted to my mention of the Philippines. They shot Baker a look, but he didn't react.

"Japanese training?" the Colonel asked.

I nodded. "At a very high level. Someone very skilled at combat from the old schools of Japan."

"Any names you care to share with us, Dr. Burke?" One of the CIA men was poised with a pen.

On screen, the attackers finished the two young men off with a tight, concentrated jerk. You could hear the faint snap of the spinal cord. It made me feel faintly sick.

"I don't know anyone with this kind of skill who would train people to do something like that, who would ever countenance this kind of . . . application. The *ko-ryu* are very selective. The masters are not people who share their knowledge with just anyone."

"They share their knowledge with you, Dr. Burke." The soft Midwestern voice was mild, but the implication hung in the air.

I looked once at Baker. His eyes were hard and told me nothing. I stood up and glared across the table. "Do you have a question you want to ask me?" It was an unconscious move, but I could feel my stomach tighten. It was the same feeling I get before combat. There's also some energy projection that goes with it, and I think the man from Langley picked up on it, because he waved his hand

and just smiled tightly.

"You want a written summary of this, Baker?" My voice was raspy with annoyance.

He shook his head. "Ashby will debrief you on tape." The man from the CIA moved his chin slightly as if pointing something out to Baker. "Your notes will remain with me," the soldier added.

"Fine," I agreed. "If there's nothing else, I'll be getting back to the training cadre . . . "

"The debriefing takes priority and will be your final assignment here, Dr. Burke." The soft-spoken man from Central Intelligence stood up and his attendants began disconnecting the computer and shutting things down. "Thanks for coming by." He said it without sincerity and watched me without expression, arms motionless at his side.

It was hot in that room and I was glad to get out. Ashby was waiting for me. He looked slightly uncomfortable. "Do you know what I was watching?" I asked him.

"Yes." He nodded solemnly and gestured for me to follow him down the hall. We entered a small room with a desk and two chairs. A small tape machine and microphone were waiting. On the otherwise bare walls there was a Special Operations Command plaque, a black oval with a gold spear thrusting upward, searching for a target.

"I don't get it, Ashby," I told him. "Why wait so long to show me?"

He tested the tape machine and looked at me. "We were waiting for some security clearances on you."

"Clearances?"

Ashby shrugged. "Sure. Standard operating procedure for consultants. They do some basic checks on you. The Colonel wasn't about to show you anything until he was reasonably sure about you . . . "

"And?"

"And we were waiting to see—who you were. We didn't want someone who, you know—who trained to fight fruit."

He'd been talking with Baker. But I let the thought go. "I don't get the feeling that the civilians were happy about me seeing the video."

Ashby grimaced and waved them away. "The spooks? They've been having a bad few years. I wouldn't take it personally. They're cranky about everything. Important thing is that, one way or the other, you passed muster with Colonel Baker. That's what counts."

Then he got down to business and slowly walked me through my analysis of the video. He was calm and unhurried. He would ask a question, note my response, and go on to something else. After a few more inquiries, he'd ask the first question in a slightly different way, probing, seeking new details I may have omitted. It was a different side of the man. He had spent most of the week being a sort of good-natured escort and nursemaid, watching me with a slight smile on his face. But now the smile was gone.

"You've done this before, I think," I told him. We had finished the interview and Ashby ejected the tape, labeled it carefully and slipped it into a manila envelope, concentrating precisely on his actions. Only when he was done did he look up at me.

"Sure," he nodded. "It's what I do."

"You're not with the training cadre, are you, Ashby?" But I said it without inflection. It wasn't really a question.

"I've been through it," he said. "But I specialize in other areas . . ."

He got up and we left the building. Ashby had a car parked and waiting. There was no driver for a change. I slid in the passenger side and he started it up. It was a Chevy of some sort, a nondescript four-door sedan perfect for government work. The motor ticked smoothly. Heartbeat of America.

"Now what?" I asked him.

He picked up a clipboard from the backseat. An envelope was stuck on it. It had my name typed on the outside. "This is the consultant fee for the week as agreed upon in your contract," he said. He handed me the clipboard. "Open it, make sure that it's correct, then sign the receipt for me, please."

"Pretty formal, Ashby." But I did as I was told and signed.

He took the clipboard back. "Thank you, Dr. Burke. I've got you booked on a ten p.m. flight to New York tonight. It should give you time to get back to quarters, clean up and the like. A driver will pick you up," he looked at his watch, "about seventeen thirty, okay?"

"You don't want the final report on the training?" I thought I knew the answer, but wanted to be sure.

He waved his hand, "You can mail it in to us." He reached over to put the car into gear and I stopped him.

"You were never really interested in my help with your training, were you, Ashby? You were just hanging on to me until you did your final checks."

He turned his head to look right at me, his eyes flat and noncommittal. "I told you, Baker wanted to check you out himself."

"I don't like being jerked around like that."

Ashby grinned tightly. "Welcome to my world, Burke. Yours too, now."

"What do you mean?"

"You ever hear of the king's shilling, Burke?" I shook my head. "Old English military recruiter's trick. You send a soldier in to a bar to talk with a bunch of guys; he tries to sell them on the glory of a soldier's life. But they think they're too smart. So the soldier keeps talking and then offers to buy them a drink. Well by now, they're all feeling pretty smug, so they say sure. And after they finish the soldier calls in the rest of his guards and drags them away."

Ashby leaned slightly toward me and with a twinkle in his eye, he continued. "When they accepted the drink, they were really taking the king's money and were now legally obligated to serve. Same thing with you, Burke."

I felt a jet of alarm. "Whattaya mean?"

He laughed then, and slipped the car into gear. "Relax. You're only a consultant." His tone was condescending and I quelled a surge of resentment. "Guys like Baker have made the big commitment. They dedicate their lives to the greater quest. They don't get tricked into taking the king's shilling, they go in search of it. You got tricked, Burke, and the king calls the tune. But the nice thing for you is that you can take the money, go home, and forget about what you saw. "

I swallowed my guilty relief.

11

VOID

The jerking was subtle, but ominous, because I knew what it meant—the heaviness in my limbs, the blackness, the roaring in my ears. Whoever he was, he was working the hold in tighter, trying to cut off the blood flow to the brain. Once the minute jerking adjustments start, you know you're in trouble. It means that the chokehold is almost in. You've got maybe five seconds to break it before you lose consciousness. But while you struggle, the hold is tightening and the flow of blood is starting to slow. If you struggle too much, you use up the last of the oxygen and you black out. But if you don't get free, they'll crimp the carotid arteries and you slip away, spinning down to a place you may never come back from.

And I thought that I had left it too long. I couldn't move. The roaring in my head grew stronger. I tried to break free, but couldn't.

Then the chime sounded and Art reached across the aisle and nudged me until I opened my eyes.

"Wha'?" I asked thickly and brought the seat back up.

"We're making our approach. Should be landing in ten minutes or so."

I was still groggy, half in the dream world where someone was choking me to death. Life slowly came into focus: the sound of jet engines, a slight pressure in the ears, the stewardess slowly walking down the aisle, gently trailing a manicured hand over seat backs as she made sure her first class passengers were strapped in and ready. Her nails were painted the color of blood.

The plane bounced a bit as we came down through the thermal layers—it must have been what I felt in the dream. The stewardess was all smiles. My heart was pounding—in some ways I was still back in that dark place where someone was trying to kill me. Micky came down the aisle and squeezed past me to his seat. I looked from Art to my brother, and took a few deep breaths. I rubbed my face, remembering where I was. And why.

It didn't make me feel any better.

The Army had said goodbye without much fanfare. Ashby had met me at the car before I left Fort Bragg and handed me another envelope. Inside was a black laminated ID card. It had my name, picture, and the logo of the Special Operations Command on it. The back of the card had a paragraph identifying me as a consultant and listed two different phone numbers and an e-mail address, indicating that the bearer was entitled to use these numbers to make contact with the training cadre, USASOC. Any and all government employees were, upon receipt of the card, to provide communication assistance to the bearer.

"So what's this, Ashby?" I had asked. "A get out of jail free card?"

He smiled. "Colonel Baker thought that you might have some additional insights on that video. You come up with anything —a hunch, a guess, anything—he wants to know. Anytime. Anywhere."

"Yeah. But why this?" I asked, and held up the little card.

"Colonel Baker moves around, Burke," Ashby told me. "The numbers there will route you to a comm center that will know where he is and can get you in contact with him within a few hours."

"My tax dollars at work," I said. I slipped it in my pocket, but didn't figure I'd ever use it. I was glad to be getting away from these people and didn't think I wanted to talk to Baker again.

The commuter flight back north to New York was so brief that they barely had time to give out the tiny bags of snacks they use to distract you from the tedium of flying. I opted for the cute little blue potato chips. So good, and so good for you. But I figured Yamashita would sweat it out of me within a day or so. Any time you miss practice for a while, he tends to ratchet things up a notch. Just his way of saying welcome back.

I was eager to talk with him about the video. About the techniques and body movements. Part of me wondered why Baker didn't just ask my *sensei* to look at the video in the first place. But I thought of the men from CIA. They weren't crazy about me seeing the thing, and that was after they had a run a security check. Imagine how they would have felt with a Japanese national in the room.

I had scarfed down the chips and was trying to brush the tiny crumbs and salt off my shirt when one of the attendants came by. His nametag read "Geoff." Perhaps he was named after Chaucer, but I had my doubts. In the neighborhood where I grew up, I had known a few people named Jeff. Anyone spelling it G-E-O-F-F would have been in for a severe pummeling.

He had a manifest in his hand and glanced up at the seat number to make sure. "Dr. Burke?" he asked.

"That's me. What can I do for you?"

Geoff wouldn't make eye contact. "Oh nothing, sir. Merely double-checking the flight manifest."

I nodded. "It's a post-9/11 world, isn't it?"

He nodded back but moved on and checked a few more seats. He seemed a little nervous. Then again, I imagine the airline people don't like you mentioning major air disasters while in flight.

Geoff eventually got back to his station just behind the cockpit. He picked up a phone and spoke into it. I didn't look directly at him, but I could see him glance at me as he talked. Something was going on.

I sat there and felt the steward's energy pulse down the aisle toward me. There's a type of vibration people give off when they're focusing on you. And it doesn't matter whether they're actually looking at you or not. It feels like you're a target. At least that's how I interpret it. The martial arts training hall is a place where the psychic flow of energy related to aggression and fear makes the air pulse. You have to be pretty thick not to notice it eventually. But once you start registering feelings like that, you eventually start to pick up on other, more subtle variations. My teacher Yamashita encourages it, believing that a warrior needs as much sensory input as possible to stay alive.

But what I was picking up on this flight was still a mystery to me. Was it anxiety? Fear? Certainly not aggression. Geoff did not strike me as a major threat. They still tend to recruit smaller people for jobs as flight attendants, and he was no exception. He was young enough to tussle, I suppose, but his neat hairdo and the immaculate light blue windowpane uniform shirt did not project the image of someone eager to mix it up. I didn't imagine that lifting little serving baskets filled with potato chips did much for muscle tone, either. But he was clearly watching me.

I tried to figure out what I had done. The government had paid for the plane ticket, and those checks don't typically bounce. I hadn't tempered with the smoke detector in the bathroom. I kept my seat belt on during the whole flight and had refrained from using unauthorized electronic devices. I felt the vindication of the truly innocent.

But it wasn't much of a surprise when we landed and two of the beefier types from the Transportation Security Administration came on board and escorted me off the plane and down the boarding ramp. They didn't say much, just asked me my name and requested I accompany them. Nobody slapped the cuffs on me right away, so I figured things would work out. We squeezed by Geoff on the way out the door. He looked like he was going to faint.

Then I saw who was waiting for me at the gate and my stomach gave one quick, tight lurch.

"Is it Mom?" I asked my brother Micky. Since my dad died, she has developed into an increasingly fragile thing. Feisty, but brittle. Someday, time will snap her in two.

"No," Micky said tightly. He looked around at the flow of people. Announcements bounced off the poured concrete walls of the round terminal. It was a no-frills carrier and the departure area looked like the inside of a cement silo. You could see Micky's mind working and deciding that this was no place to have a conversation. "Come on," he told me, and headed out without looking to see whether I was following or not.

My brother has been a cop for almost sixteen years and it shows. He was always an intense kid, and the life he's chosen has proven to be a good fit. He has the hard look some cops get: eyes that see everything, even the things you don't want seen. As a result, people tend to shy away from him in crowds. He steamed through the terminal at JFK like an icebreaker and nobody got in his way.

There was a black Lincoln town car idling in the pick-up zone. A uniformed Transit Authority cop was standing by as well. The TSA guys brought my luggage and the trunk lid popped up, seemingly by magic, and they tossed my bags in, looking vaguely pleased at a mission accomplished. It was probably the most excitement they had all day and beat sifting through people's unmentionables.

The car gleamed. I looked at Micky. "Nice ride, Mick," I said. "Not really your usual style, though."

He squinted at me. "Yeah, well, it's not. Get in the back." He opened the passenger door next to the driver, gave the TSA cop a nod of thanks, and got in.

I opened my door and caught a glimpse of a pair of pinstriped-clad legs in the back. They belonged to a youngish Japanese man whose dress shirt was so white it almost glowed in the subdued lighting of the town car.

"Dr. Burke," he said as I got in, "allow me to introduce myself. I am Kenjiro Inouye, second undersecretary for intergovernmental relations at the Japanese Embassy here in Manhattan." His English was faultless. I don't think that I could say intergovernmental without doing a far poorer job. Inouye extended his *meishi*, his business card, to me with both hands. I bowed and took it as etiquette required.

"*Hajimemashitte*," I said automatically. Then I looked at my brother, sitting stolidly up front next to the uniformed chauffeur. "Where's Art?"

"He's home. With his family."

"Oh." I could tell Micky was annoyed.

"Yeah," my brother said. "You may recall, before I was diverted into a new career running a car service for you, that I had one, too." Micky gave Inouye a look of pure malevolence.

"Your assistance is very much appreciated by my government, Officer Burke," the Japanese man said smoothly. Micky's glares tend to unsettle most people. Inouye seemed totally at ease. "We may go," he told the driver, and the Lincoln rolled out into traffic, smooth as melting butter.

"What's going on here, Mick?" I asked. My brother didn't say anything, just jerked with his chin toward Inouye and waited.

I sat back and looked at the second undersecretary. He reached down to the floor and withdrew a file folder from a leather briefcase. He set it on his lap and began talking.

"Nine days ago," he began, "a young graduate student doing research was kidnapped . . . "

"Research?" I asked. I had a hard time equating research with danger. Most libraries are only dangerous if the shelves fall on you.

"She was working on her dissertation research in anthropology," Inouye explained, "studying the hill tribes on the island of Mindanao." I nodded and he went on. "Hatsue Abe," he slid an 8½ x 11 picture across the seat, "is the daughter of one of our leading industrialists." Inouye looked at me. "She is a child of privilege, Dr. Burke, reared in luxury, educated at the best schools in Tokyo. Graduate work at Harvard . . . "

I looked at the picture. It was professionally done, a posed shot. Hatsue had delicate features and an expensive haircut. She had the look of someone who was very self-confident, someone who was accustomed to a world where the systems worked very smoothly, a meshing of gears that would propel her along life in comfort. I tried to imagine what the expression on her face would have looked like when she was kidnapped.

I looked from Inouye to my brother. "I'm very sorry Inouye-san, but I don't see . . . "

"Just let him talk," Micky said.

Inouye slipped the photo back into his folder and consulted some notes. "A ransom note was received, along with a photograph of Ms. Abe holding up a newspaper . . . "

"Newspaper?" I asked.

"Proof of life," Micky said. "The newspaper is there to confirm the date the photo was taken. Shows that the victim is still alive at that point." He said it very matter of factly. I glanced at Inouye, but he didn't seem bothered by the discussion.

"Her family was obviously eager to do all in their power to get her back," the diplomat said. "Given their wealth and connections with the government, they were able to make arrangements rather quickly and collect the funds needed for the ransom payment."

"Did the cops get involved?"

"The Philippine authorities were working the case, but under the circumstances, I am sure that you can understand that the family's first priority was obtaining the release of Ms. Abe."

"Sure," I said. I could imagine what it must be like, having someone you love taken. The ransom was everything. Justice probably seemed a luxury, an abstraction that was burned into irrelevance by the white-hot urgency to get your kid back.

Inouye continued. "The financial resources were at hand and only awaited certain other arrangements . . . " he paused here. Traffic was light and we moved smoothly toward the Midtown Tunnel. The whirring of the tires was magnified as we entered the curving tube that would take us under the East River.

Inouye sighed slightly. "It was hoped that the ransom process would take place without complication. The police were involved, of course. And at the same time, elements from our government were monitoring the exchange . . . "

Micky was shaking his head. "Must have been crowded at the drop point, Inouye. Way too many actors for my taste. It was bound to spook somebody."

"Indeed. So I have been told. It was unfortunate . . . " Inouye said nothing for a while.

"What happened?" I eventually asked. The car climbed out of the tunnel and headed up town.

"I do not have all the details, Dr. Burke. Suffice it to say that events did not go as planned." In the front seat, Micky snorted at the diplomatic understatement. We rolled on for a few blocks and then headed west. I wasn't really surprised—the Japanese Embassy was on Park Avenue between 49th and 50th Streets. Inouye seemed to be gathering his thoughts.

"From what I understand, the situation was . . . messy," Inouye said. He frowned a bit at the untidiness. Diplomats prefer their world to mirror their language—smooth and without unforeseen complications. Inouye and Hatsue probably had much in common. "The Philippine government is not pleased with my government,

Dr. Burke. The Abe family is most distressed that their daughter has not been recovered, not to mention the loss of several million dollars in ransom money. And now, of course, we fear that the goodwill of the kidnappers has been lost."

Goodwill. It seemed an odd quality to attribute to felons, but I got his point.

"I am very sorry to hear all of this, Inouye-san," I told him. The car floated to a halt. "But I am not sure how I am involved or even how I could begin to help." I looked at Micky. The disgusted expression on his face suggested that he knew more than he was letting on. "Perhaps the FBI . . . "

Inouye held up a hand. "Please, Dr. Burke. We seek you out not because of your professional background." This was not a surprise, since Ph.D.s in history are not on anyone's list of first responders.

The second undersecretary continued. "There is, however, a personal link here which, combined with your skills, suggests to some in my government that you could be of help to the Abe family."

Then he and Micky told me the details, and the bottom fell out of my world.

They gave me a fuller briefing at the embassy. I met a more senior functionary—I nodded at his name and then forgot it, still stunned. He was pretty smooth, despite the obvious tension that buzzed in the room. He discussed the Abe family's willingness to assist me if I would assist them, fanned out a series of papers with travel details and vouchers, and for all his smoothness I could see the urgency in his eyes.

My brother had sat there with me, his face a mask equal to that of any diplomat. He didn't watch the people from the embassy. He watched me. I turned to him.

"What are the odds?"

He shrugged and for a minute the play of subdued lighting

in that hushed and elegant room made him looked tired beyond words. "Hard to say. Kidnapping is an industry in most of the third world countries. They do it for the money. Now that they have the money, who knows what they'll do. Whatever's easiest would be my guess."

It wasn't what I wanted to hear. "How're the cops?"

Micky shrugged. "They're like cops everywhere, I suppose. The good ones are only as good as their resources—as good as they're allowed to be. The rest . . . " he trailed off for a minute, then looked up at me. "She disappeared somewhere in the hills, Connor," he said in reference to Hatsue. "Indian country. They play by different rules in places like that. The cops, too." My brother shook his head. "It's a deep dark hole you're thinking of going down."

As if I really had a choice. That certainty covered me like a cold, inescapable net. Every step in my life had led me to this juncture, and every stratagem I had ever devised to repress fear and avoid the final plunging step into the unknown was shattered. I wasn't sure that I could do this alone. I wasn't even sure I could do this at all. So I swallowed and asked the question we both knew was coming.

"Will you go with me?"

My brother grunted, and asked for a phone.

Departmental wheels were greased. Formal diplomatic requests made and honored. And two NYPD detectives were assigned to take a trip in an effort to promote intergovernmental cooperation between law enforcement agencies. That's what the men with the smooth words cooked up.

I saw the worry in Deirdre's face when she dropped Micky off at the airport. She turned her head to face me, her expression flat and angry, her eyes glistening with emotion. "You bring him back, Connor," she told me, hissing with urgency. "Bring him *back*."

I heard it in Sarah Klein's voice when I called to tell her where

I was going.

"I've got to go," I told her simply.

"I know," she answered, discipline fighting with sadness in the timbre of her voice.

The ransom drop had gone wrong. Someone—maybe one of the Filipino cops, maybe one of the Japanese security guys shadowing the man carrying the ransom to the rendezvous—had somehow been spotted by the kidnappers, and a gunfight had erupted. It didn't matter. The man carrying the ransom had been snatched as well, and the kidnappers took him and the money, melting away into the busy city streets.

"Who was the poor guy?" I had asked.

The man from the embassy cleared his throat. "I'm sorry, Dr. Burke," he said, "I thought you knew."

I shook my head. The man looked at my brother as if asking for help.

"Connor," Micky said, "It was Yamashita."

12

CAGE

The rain fell and muffled her weeping. Hatsue yearned for the coming of darkness, when her captors would leave her alone in the night. It was the tail end of the rainy season, and she knew that soon the winds would shift to the northwest, blowing the scent of salt water up to the mountain heights where they had their camp. In the past, the smell of the sea had brought comfort—memories of childhood and home. In this place, it seemed another element in a cruel season. Late afternoons often brought rain, making the men in the camp seek shelter. For that, she welcomed the odd, dim green light of the storms as a kind of refuge.

They had run her down easily enough and brought her away from the Higuanon territory. Hatsue flailed through the underbrush, panic robbing her of any agility. She heard the pounding of their feet and the slap of their bodies whipping through the underbrush as they rushed downslope. She drove herself forward at the same time that the muscles in her back and the skin on the rear of her head strained to sense what was approaching. Terrified, it was almost a relief for her when they ran her to ground: the shock of impact, the jet of adrenalin that made her heart leap, and then the collapse. Dry-throated and winded, she hadn't made a sound as they started to drag her off. When she recovered her voice and started to scream, one of her abductors jerked her around by her hair and slammed the butt of his rifle into her midsection. The force of it almost made her faint. In some ways, the shock that someone would physically attack her was almost more disturbing than the sensation of the blow itself. Her face spasmed in a mix of confusion and pain. The man watched her dispassionately—a swarthy figure in a drab and dirty T-shirt, an olive green bandana wrapped around his sweaty head. He was young and unremarkable except for the rifle he held and the look in his eye.

The man with the bandana watched Hatsue gasp for air. She retched and spit, then straightened up and started to protest.

He slammed the rifle into her again, but with more force. The others watched impassively. She fell to the ground and the man straddled her. Hatsue looked up at him, a dark form looming over her. He was a hulking shape silhouetted by a distant sky that was slowly surrendering its light to darker things.

"Shut up," the man said in fairly good English, glaring down at her. "You make a problem, I hit you. You make a noise, I hit you. Okay?" He jerked the rifle to emphasize his point. Hatsue flinched defensively at the movement, hating herself for the reaction. But she nodded her understanding.

The young man said something to one of his companions in a dialect Hatsue did not know. They bound her hands behind her back. She tried to be as cooperative as possible, but it did not seem to mollify her captors. They jerked her bonds so tightly that her hands began to tingle almost at once. When they were done, the man with the bandana slapped the side of her head with a casual brutality. His hand was hard and horny with calluses. It seemed an old thing for one so young. The impact made her head ring. He gestured that she should follow the fast-moving line of men, already disappearing into the forest. Hatsue's head buzzed with pain, her ear on fire, but she stumbled after them in silence.

They traveled along mountain trails, slowly working their way north and west in the growing darkness. Dropping down to a dirt road, they trundled her into the back of a rusted white pickup truck. Men piled in after her, and in the crowded confines of the truck bed, their bodies rubbed against her. She tried to pull away. One of them noticed her motion and said something to the others. They laughed, but it wasn't a happy sound. For a while, the vehicle bounced along the slick ruts of a backcountry track. Eventually, it led to a highway. At this point, the men wrapped Hatsue's head with cloth to blindfold her and shoved her under a muddy tarp. She could smell the moist earth on the fabric, a scent grown familiar through her months with the Higuanon. But the smell held no comfort for her now.

Hatsue tried to make sense of the abduction. It wasn't random —these men had come looking specifically for her. The fact that they spoke English to her indicated they knew something of their victim. The question was why she was chosen. These men were not locals, and while there was no shortage of armed groups in the region, she saw no political point in taking her hostage. During her fieldwork, she had stayed clear of any action that could be construed as political in any way. Besides, the guerilla factions tended to seek fights on their own terms. Kidnapping a foreign scholar seemed a good way to bring far too much government attention to a group. So perhaps it was simply an act designed to generate ransom. Her family was a wealthy and influential one. She was sure they could negotiate a deal.

The thought offered some solace. Hatsue tried to stay attentive to whatever details she could note about their journey—the patterns of turns, the engine sound that suggested rates of speed. It might help later on. She had never known such fear, a fear so intense it warped her senses. She compartmentalized her terror into a little box and tried to stay alert for a way out. Her ancestors would have approved.

They drove in shifts through the night. Hatsue eventually

dozed, a sleep with no real rest in it. The truck ground through gears. Its tires whined along the highway. She could smell the faint scent of tobacco from the cigarettes that the men smoked.

At dawn, they stopped for a meal. The men dragged her out of the truck bed like a sack of rice and dumped her in the weedy grass by the roadside. Birds called in the heavy, wet morning air. She could hear the men moving about, talking quietly, laughing occasionally. Still blindfolded, she waited in the dark world of the prisoner, tense with expectation and stupid with the dullness brought on by emotional strain.

After a time, someone jerked her to her feet, untied her hands, and led her off into some bushes so she could relieve herself.

They rebound her hands when she was done and led her deeper into the underbrush.

Then they raped her.

It was a thing made more horrible by the bonds, by the darkness of the blindfold. She was battered and stripped and entered, crushed by unseen bodies. She raged and struggled, but was ultimately forced into a world dominated by fear, pain, and the body odor of her rapists. They left her collapsed and gasping on the ground, alone with the smell of crushed plants, oozing their green essence into the earth.

When they hauled her out of the truck a few hours later, Hatsue thought they were going to rape her again. She trembled, her shivering making her teeth chatter uncontrollably, and fleeting sparks danced in the blackness behind her eyelids. She tried to sense what would happen, to reach out somehow beyond the blindfold and divine what was next. Her imagination conjured up the approaching forms of new attackers. Her body ached, but it was a distant sensation, a muffled experience. It was as if the rape had severed some connection. She was alive only to the threat of the outside world. She jerked tensely as she heard new voices. Then the noise of the truck as it whined into reverse. Rock and dirt sputtered under the wheels. She felt the impact of them as they struck her legs. Then the vehicle faded away. For a moment, hope flared—perhaps she had been abandoned.

But her hopes were quickly extinguished. Other hands took her by the arms and prodded her forward. An involuntary sob escaped before she could catch it. Then suddenly, she was yanked to a stop. There was the sudden, cool hardness of a knife blade next to her skin. It made her flinch, but strong hands grabbed her head and held it still. There was no care for her welfare in the action, just a hard efficiency. The blindfold was sliced away and Hatsue opened her eyes to the muted greens of the forest. As her eyes adjusted, the muted tones differentiated themselves into a half dozen men dressed to blend with the trees. Each man was armed with AK-47s, and they watched her expectantly. On a silent signal, they set off with Hatsue in tow, moving up the narrow path into the hills.

Despite similarities in appearance, this group seemed different from the men in the pickup truck. She had been trained to observe human action and note the subtle nuance of things like body language as clues to the mystery of human behavior. And, battered as she was, it was a comfort to resort to the familiar mind-set of the observer.

These men spoke less frequently but Hatsue quickly discerned the hierarchy among them. The two taller men, clearly not Filipinos, spoke to the others quietly, but they were obeyed. There was no small talk. No smoking. And, as she watched the men around her out of the corners of her eyes, Hatsue did not see the surreptitious glances at her or have to endure the casual bumping and rubbing she had experienced in the truck. It was a relief, but a small one. For the efficiency with which they moved farther into the bush and higher into the hills, sweeping her away from any succor, had a colder, more profoundly dangerous feel.

They were dressed in jungle camouflage and each wore a web harness with various pouches hanging off it. All the men had black headbands and moved with a quick efficiency that struck Hatsue as vaguely military. They moved in formation, with a scout out ahead and someone lagging behind for security. Their weapons were clean and well oiled.

She staggered along the trails, propelled by the harsh urgency of the men. At a stop, they sat her down and one of them let her drink from a canteen. Her lips were puffy from being struck and it hurt to drink, but the lukewarm water was welcome. She looked at the man holding the container. One of the foreigners. She watched his face for any sign of compassion, of a willingness to connect with his captive. His eyes were brown and he looked at her with clinical dispassion. They rested for a few minutes, then he called to the others and they began again.

Eventually, they reached a camp high up in the mountain forest. They were greeted by sentries who emerged, wraithlike, from among the trees. A hillside clearing, perhaps thirty meters square, was bounded by huts and tents of various types. They brought her across the open ground and into the shade. She was shoved into a chair and made to hold a newspaper in front of her chest. A man took her picture, muttered unintelligibly when the flash failed to go off, then took two more for good measure. He said nothing to her and left as soon as he was done.

Once again she was dragged across the camp. They led her to a well-constructed hut that, unlike the other tents and lean-tos she saw, was raised off the ground. Also, unlike the other shelters, this hut had a sentry who stood at the bottom step. When she was brought to him, the sentry went up the two steps to the veranda and called respectfully into the hut. Hatsue noticed all the men standing straighter, and looking toward the door with expectant tension. Captive and captors alike waited on whatever was inside.

He emerged and she blinked wildly in confusion. He was so unlike what she had expected, another assault on her sense of reality, that she was struck with a desire to shut out the chaos of the world around her.

He was a short Japanese dressed in a dark gray kimono, and he held a large old-fashioned fan like the ones Hatsue had seen in formal posed photographs from her grandparents' day. She tried to remember what they were called, but couldn't. His feet were encased in spotlessly white *tabi*, the split-toed socks of old Japan. He glanced at them cursorily, then looked down to slip his feet into straw sandals before stepping out onto the veranda.

One of the non-Filipinos who had brought her to the camp approached the Japanese man. He bowed to him—Hatsue would have smiled in amusement in another life—and spoke quietly and deferentially. She couldn't hear what was said. The old man nodded and approached the edge of the steps. He looked down at her. His face was round and his high cheeks were flushed and ruddy. A long, bent nose ran down to a small mouth. When he spoke, she could glimpse his teeth, small and jagged like those of an animal. The old man looked at her, but said nothing. His glance made her conscious of her filth, the thin material of her T-shirt sweaty and clinging to her chest.

"Who are you?" she finally whispered. She said it in English.

He cackled at that, and answered in Japanese. "So. You have set even the language of your ancestors behind you? Like an animal . . . I wonder if you even understand me."

"Wakarimasu," Hatsue replied. I understand. The old man smiled at that, his pointy teeth showing.

"I doubt that you do . . . " he said. "But you will. In time."

"Please . . . " she began.

The old man waved his fan to silence her. "Who I am is not important for now." His eyes narrowed and he folded the fan and pointed it in her direction, his movements imperious, like the gestures of samurai commanders from the old days. "What is important is who you are."

"You know me?" she asked.

He nodded. "I know of you. It is enough."

"But why? What have I done?" she pleaded.

He cocked his head as if hearing a distant sound. "Done? Why nothing. It is enough, Abe Hatsue, that you are who you are."

She looked at him, speechless with confusion, waiting for an answer. He watched her clinically for a moment then smiled. It was a gesture that held no comfort.

"You are," he said, " . . . a means to an end."

He gestured with the fan and they dragged her away to her cage.

13

SIMPLE THINGS

The jet settled to earth with a rumbling squeal of tires and we staggered down the covered connector into the terminal. We knew that someone would be waiting for us. I had expected a contact from the Japanese Embassy. What we got were the cops.

It was all polite enough—the elliptical courtesy of Asia couched in careful language—but you needed a machete to cut through the wall of resentment. Micky and Art had pulled some serious strings with the NYPD and had a friend at headquarters fax a personal request for professional consideration to the Manila police. The Japanese had told us that they could set things up, but wanted to stay in the background. I thought even at that time that that was odd. On the other hand, the Filipinos are working closely with the U.S. on anti-terror issues, so Micky figured they might be cooperative. But first impressions made me think that the locals were not real crazy about our presence.

Chief Inspector Tomas Reyes—"call me Tommy"—ushered us down through the Customs concourse after introductions. The airport was a busy place, with wiry Asian travelers churning in all directions, shoving themselves along personal pathways invisible to the casual observer. Fuzzy loudspeaker announcements in multiple languages added to the intensity. I picked up a young, fit, well-dressed Asian man, trailing along behind us, just out of the periphery of vision. Yamashita had taught me that little trick of staying in a target's blind spot and I knew enough to scan any area for just this sort of thing. I didn't say anything to the local cops about the man I spotted.

My mind had been churning since we boarded the plane in New York. I was left with two insights: The attempt to save my *sensei* was, at best, a long shot and if I was going to succeed, I needed everything I had ever learned from my teacher. Primary among his many lessons was the need to contain emotion, to focus, and not to give too much away to your opponent. I would wait and watch to see where—and with whom—danger lay.

The processed air of the terminal was barely cool. You looked out the plate glass windows, beyond cement landing strips striped with rubber from countless landings, to where a flat gray sky met the distant trees, and got the sense of moisture and heat barely kept at bay. Reyes looked like he was feeling it. He was wearing one of those tropical shirts that spilled out over his pant waist. It didn't flatter his hips. And when he reached a plate glass door set off from the concourse and opened it to invite us in, you could see dark half-moons of sweat staining the underarms of his shirt.

He was a prosperous-looking guy. Fiftyish, with jet black hair swept back into place and given luster by heroic amounts of hair cream. The Inspector had multiple chins; it looked like the fat from his thick neck was trying to push up into his jawline and finding it a tough go. The effect was completed with an aftershave that smelled like lime. But he was a cop. He had the look.

We filed past him into the room. As he brushed by me, Art said very quietly, "Book 'em, Dan-o."

The conference room was hushed and the air whooshed around in a cooling flow. Inspector Reyes sat down gratefully. He had two other guys with him, but they got to wait outside. The room was in one of those swank club areas they have in airports for rich people who travel a lot—the Ambassador Club, or the Captain of Industry

Club, something like that. It was not Burke clan territory—we fly infrequently on low budget carriers that herd you like cattle. For the Irish, all travel is a form of pilgrimage, and so should entail some degree of suffering. But I had to admit, the Club lounge was nice. The lighting was soft and the chairs were comfortable. The table was highly polished dark wood. There were soft drinks arranged on a tray, cans pearled with moisture, some glasses, and an ice bucket waiting for us.

"May I offer you something to drink, gentlemen?" Reyes asked. We shook our heads, no. He shrugged and grabbed a can of Coke. He held it to his forehead, his eyes closing briefly in relief at its coolness. Then he sat up straight in his chair, popped the top, and poured himself a drink. You could see the effervescence dance in the air above the glass and hear the hiss of the gas as it dissipated.

Reyes observed the fizzing for a while, regarding the drink with calm dispassion. That's how you knew he was a cop. He knew how to wait and watch. Then he carefully placed some ice in the glass, took a cautious sip, and set the drink back down on the tabletop, looking content. There was a folder that he had placed flat on the table. He ignored it, even though he knew we wondered what it held. Reyes gave every appearance of being fascinated by the unique fizzing qualities of a glass of Coke, a large man engaged in the small and simple things of life.

We all waited. I was surprised that Micky went along with the whole thing. Then I looked from my brother to Art and then to Reyes. All three sat there, impassive. Alert but calm. Watching each other. And, in an unexpected way, for all their differences, they seemed very much alike

There is a time before the fight is joined in the *dojo* when the world cools down to a very still place, where only you and your opponent exist, waiting and watching each other. In India, wrestlers sometimes say that "the body becomes all eyes." The Japanese call the experience *haragei*—a subtle process of intuitive knowledge or non-verbal communication. I've trained with Japanese masters who possessed the impressive abilities of *haragei* and as I watched the three policemen surrounding me, I got the sense that I was witnessing three such masters at work.

The Inspector took another sip of his Coke and sighed appreciatively. He held the glass and, looking at the faint ring of moisture it left on the table, set the glass down slowly, exactly in the same spot, covering the ring. His hands were swollen looking, but they handled the movements with great delicacy. Then he looked up at us and smiled.

"The communication from New York expressed interest in a case we are pursuing here. May I ask what is your interest?"

My brother sat forward. "We received notification that a U.S. resident had been kidnapped."

"Indeed. In fact, two have been kidnapped. But I had thought they were Japanese. You say a resident?" the Filipino cop commented. "Not a citizen?"

"We're talking about Mr. Yamashita. A resident alien, but a long-time resident of New York," Art explained.

The Inspector held his two hands out, palms up. "How generous of your police department to show such concern . . . "

"Yamashita is very well connected in New York," my brother said. It was a great lie in that is was partly true and totally misleading at the same time. My teacher is well known and respected by the small community of elite martial arts *sensei* in Manhattan and elsewhere. He runs a school that isn't listed in the Yellow Pages. It's difficult to get him to even let you apply for admission. He looms large in my imagination, but to the rest of the world, Yamashita's almost invisible.

"He must be quite the celebrity," Reyes said. "To merit the attention of two detectives." He swiveled in his chair to face me more directly. "And what is your role in this little trip?"

"He's my *sensei*," I said.

"*Sensei?*" the Inspector asked.

"My teacher," I explained.

Reyes' eyes narrowed. "I am familiar with the term. In years past, my country had quite an exposure to Japanese culture."

The tone in his voice was bitterly ironic. I had worried about this. The memories of Japanese Imperialism, the savage excesses of the Emperor's armies, were things still vivid in many parts of Asia. How a people like the Japanese could be responsible for so much that is beautiful and refined, and yet have been the authors of so much brutality, is a continuing sadness to me. Unfortunately, it's not a mystery. Westerners tend to idealize the exotic East, but all cultures are similar in this: They're attempts at keeping the beast at bay, and more often than not they fail. The miracle is that we continue to try at all.

I had thought about this on the flight over. The men from the Japanese Embassy were correct; the plight of a kidnapped Japanese expatriate was not going to generate much sympathy from the Filipinos. I looked at the Inspector. He was a professional and would certainly do what was required. But I knew from working with my brother that on any given day a cop has about a million things demanding his attention. When push came to shove, would Inspector Reyes pay more attention to a case involving a Filipino or a Japanese visitor? It wasn't hard to figure. But maybe they'd cooperate with a few Americans.

"Inspector," I said, taking a breath, "I know that there are lots of things demanding your time and we appreciate your meeting us. We're really here to find out what we can about my teacher's disappearance and perhaps to help in any way we can . . . "

He bridled at that. "Do you think we're incapable of dealing with this, Mr. Burke?"

"Inspector," my brother chimed in, and I could hear the acid creeping into his tone, "let me get this straight. Some Japanese woman got kidnapped on one of your islands here . . . "

"Mindanao," the Inspector supplied.

Micky waved a hand. "Yeah, whatever." He glanced at Art, who just nodded at his partner in encouragement. "Then you get a photo and a ransom demand, and somehow, Yamashita gets roped into the delivery of the ransom . . . "

"We were informed that he was a trusted friend of the family," the Filipino cop said. The tone of his voice clearly indicated that he hadn't been happy about it. "We were also informed that they would be content only with his involvement in the delivery of the ransom."

My brother snorted as if the whole idea was ridiculous. "Sure. The drop goes down and . . . ?" Micky left the question hanging in the air.

"The family had assurances that once the ransom was paid, the girl would be returned unharmed." The Inspector took a drink, sucking a few ice cubes into his mouth. He crunched at them as he spoke, grinding down unpleasant facts. "Pressure was exerted at the highest levels to keep the police at arms length."

"And you went along?" Micky demanded, his voice incredulous. He looked at Art and rolled his eyes.

The Inspector set his glass down with a crack. He leaned in toward us. You got a sense of the powerful frame that lay hidden under the extra weight. He was not someone to underestimate. "I did not. The Japanese had their own men—armed men in *my city*—who they claimed would take care of things. I advised against it. And we shadowed them to the drop point for the ransom delivery."

"The drop went bad," Art said quietly.

"It was the Japanese," the Inspector hissed. "They are so arrogant . . . they underestimated the kidnappers. Your Mr. Yamashita delivered the money as arranged . . . "

"Drop location specified ahead of time?" Micky asked, and his technical question served to reign in some of Reyes' emotion.

"No. They kept him moving around, giving directions on a cell phone."

"Trace?" Art asked.

"They used different phones for each communication."

"Pros," Art concluded.

"What happened?" Micky prodded.

Reyes sucked a few more ice cubes into his mouth and the crunching began anew. "Someone must have been spotted. At the moment your Mr. Yamashita was approaching with the money . . . "

"The girl wasn't present at the meet?" Art interrupted.

Reyes shook his head, his top chin swiveling, but the rest staying in place. "She was to be released in a public place within ten minutes of the delivery of the ransom."

"And your negotiators bought that?" my brother demanded.

The Inspector looked at him and spoke through a clenched jaw. "By this time, private elements associated with the Japanese had taken control of the process. My force was to serve only as a liaison and support group."

Micky and Art shook their heads, in equal parts commiseration and exasperation.

Reyes opened the folder and pushed out some photographs, sliding them out like a dealer at a casino. "Our surveillance cameras recorded the drop. Here is your Mr. Yamashita lugging the ransom."

Micky looked at the shot. "Public park?" he asked. Reyes nodded.

"Lots of access routes," Art commented. "Various people coming and going. Green space so vehicles are kept at a distance. Good choice." His voice said you didn't have to like who did this, but you could admire their professionalism.

The pictures had the flat, two-dimensional look of shots taken with a telephoto lens and then blown up. It was jarring to see Yamashita there, a stocky Japanese man in a short-sleeved shirt with a black duffel bag slung from his shoulder. At first glance, he was unremarkable. But the photos were good enough that you could see some of the intensity in his eyes if you looked closely.

The pictures were shot in series, and with a little imagination you could string together the sequence of events. My teacher approaches the rendezvous. He is met by two Filipino men in sunglasses. They inspect the bag. Two more men approach, flanking Yamashita. One looks up in alarm and spots something in the distance. One of the flankers points a pistol at Yamashita and the other yanks away the ransom bag. Two of the men cover the guy carrying the duffel and you can see the set in Yamashita's hips as he prepares to follow the ransom. In the next shot, both blockers are down on the ground and Yamashita is moving toward the man with the duffel. The pistol is aimed at Yamashita, and in the next photo he is being dragged away.

I felt a surge of adrenalin as I looked at the last picture, an electric jolt right through to my core. "They shot him?" I protested in alarm. No one had told us this.

Reyes nodded and passed us another picture. "With this." I looked at what he showed me, but my expression must have betrayed my confusion. "It is a tranquilizer dart, Mr. Burke. Of the type used in zoos to quell dangerous animals."

"So he's not . . . dead?"

Reyes looked at me and shrugged. "I assume if they wanted him dead that there are simpler ways of doing it." It was one of those cop observations—technically accurate but not very comforting.

I looked at Micky and Art for help. They didn't seem to respond to my alarm at all. If anything, my brother appeared calmer than at any time since we started the trip.

"Ransom was for how much?" Micky asked Reyes.

"Two million U.S. The usual details: small bills, non-sequential."

"Is that big money for a snatch in this part of the world?" Art asked the inspector.

"It is a considerable sum, but not unheard of. My understanding is that the family is wealthy."

"So it would take a little time to put this together? Get the funds and everything?"

"A few days," Reyes shrugged.

"Smart," Micky pointed out. "A hefty ransom, but not too hefty." He looked at Art. "These guys knew what they were doing; the cell phones, the drop location. And they got the cops sidetracked by the family."

"Pros," Art commented again.

I looked from one to the other. "Is this good or bad?"

"Dealing with pros is always better," Micky said. "Fewer surprises."

"And it can help in the investigation. Pros have records." Art looked at Reyes and pointed to the pictures. "Any luck ID'ing any of these people?"

"We are currently looking for some suspects," Reyes admitted.

"And?" Art prompted.

"They are, as you say, professionals, men for hire. They hide well."

"But I don't get it," I said. "Why take Yamashita if they already had the ransom money? Why not just take the money and release the girl?"

Reyes looked at Micky and Art expectantly, as if they could explain something. After a pause, Art merely asked Reyes whether they could keep the pictures.

The inspector nodded and gestured toward the file. "Background material is here as well. I will keep you informed of the progress of our investigation as a . . . professional courtesy." He took out a business card and slid it across the smooth surface of the table. "Let me know where you are staying." Reyes got up, nodded, and headed toward the door. I started to say something, but Micky laid a hand on my arm.

"What is going on?" I hissed when Reyes was gone.

Micky looked at Art, who said. "Oh boy."

"What!" I demanded.

"Connor," Art said, "this is going to get dicey."

Micky snorted. "Like it isn't already."

I took some deep breaths and waited. Finally, my brother explained. "This is way more complicated than I thought, buddy boy. And I don't think our pals from the Embassy gave us the entire picture, either."

"There's a shocker," Art added. I just looked at him, so he went on. "The New York Embassy tells you Yamashita got caught up in something trying to deliver a ransom for some friend. Bad. But this is worse. The kidnapping was genuine enough, I guess . . . " He looked at his partner, who was paging through the contents of the file Reyes had left for us.

Micky nodded in agreement. "Yeah. The snatch looks real enough. And so was the ransom demand."

"But they went through with it. The family came up with the money . . . " I started.

"Sure. And the local cops think the drop went bad and the kidnappers grabbed Yamashita 'cause they were pissed. But I don't buy it. How about you, Art?"

"Not me." He looked at me, held up his hand, and ticked some points off on his fingers. "One: They ask for a ransom and who gets to deliver it?"

"Yamashita," I said, "but that's because he was a friend of the family . . . "

"Connor," Micky said, "her family's loaded and influential. They want their kid back. You think the only person they can get to do this thing is some guy from halfway around the world?"

I didn't know what to say to that.

Art continued. "So they arrange the drop. But, of course, the girl will not be present. You like that arrangement, Mick?"

My brother snorted. "I'm handing over two million bucks in small bills to a complete stranger, I'd want to make sure he had what I was buying."

Art nodded. "And when the hand-off occurs, what happens?"

"Something spooked them," I said. "There was a scuffle and they grabbed Yamashita and the money and took off."

"Yes, they did," Art agreed. "And these guys are professionals. They do this for money. Did they have possession of the money?"

"Sure," I said.

"And were they suddenly alerted to the fact that someone was watching them?"

"Yes. It's what spooked them."

"Connor," Micky told me, "anyone who does this knows that the chances are good they're going to be watched. Being watched is not going to freak them out."

"Getting caught freaks them out," Art told me. "Losing the money freaks them out."

"These guys like to get away," my brother said. "It's what makes them pros."

"So what's your point?" I responded.

Art continued. "These guys need to get away, and what do they do?"

"They grab Yamashita,'" I said.

"Yeah. They grab Yamashita. And if you want to run away, do

you drop everything except the money and run, or do you grab more luggage?"

I could see were he was going.

"And think of this," Micky added. "They don't just grab Yamashita. They shoot him with a tranquilizer gun." He looked at Art. "Is this standard issue for most kidnappers?"

Art pressed his lips together in thought, then said to himself, "Hmm, rope, tape, paper for a ransom note, maybe a gun . . . " He looked up. "No. Tranquilizers are typically not part of the standard kidnapper's kit."

And I thought of what Reyes had said about the dart: like something used in zoos to subdue dangerous animals. Micky saw the light go on in my eyes.

"Are you getting it, Connor?" His voice was quiet. "The kidnapping wasn't arranged just to get the ransom. It was arranged to capture your teacher. They knew from the beginning that they were going to take him. And they knew he would be a handful, which is why they had the tranquilizer with them."

"But why?" I asked.

Art shrugged. "Hard to say. But chances are they'll communicate their demands soon. Kidnappers usually want something." He looked ominously at Micky. "It's just simpler when all they want is money."

Micky snorted. "And since when is life simple?"

His partner looked at us both. "Since I've met you two? Hardly ever."

14

LOCAL KNOWLEDGE

The fit-looking Asian guy was waiting for us when we came out of the Club lounge. He spoke briefly into a small silver cell phone, but his eyes never left us. They were dark eyes, set back above high cheekbones. They had that flitter you see in a hunter when the underbrush comes alive.

"Dr. Burke?" he asked, presenting a *meishi*. The Japanese business card is an essential tool for commerce in Asia. It's designed to tell you about the person you're meeting: his identity and status, his position in the world. The quality of the card, its texture and esthetics, send subtler but more important messages.

"I am Ueda Koji, from the Embassy," he continued. I looked at the *meishi*. It gave his name, and the address and contact numbers of the embassy, but nothing more. That was unusual. The Japanese are highly status conscious and their language is full of various ways of speaking that are contingent on knowing the status of who you're talking to. Part of the whole rationale for exchanging business cards is to establish issues of relative rank between strangers. Yet, here was Ueda with no status established at all.

"And what is it you do at the embassy, Ueda-san?" I asked him. It was a shockingly direct question in terms of Japanese etiquette, but it had been a long flight and with the information Reyes had passed on to us still filling my head, I didn't much care.

Ueda smiled at me. "I am a . . . cultural attaché for our government, Dr. Burke." His eyebrows lifted slightly as if I were to join in on a private joke.

"He's a spook, Connor," Micky broke in. "Thank God. We're gonna need all the help we can get.

"I'm here to offer what help I can," Ueda said in reply. I registered a slight hesitation in his voice.

I introduced Micky and Art to give me a moment to size him up. Ueda shook hands firmly, with none of the awkwardness and half bowing you sometimes get with Japanese. It told me that he'd been around. He eyed the duffels my brother and Art were carrying and the scuffed backpack I had. "Luggage, gentlemen?" he inquired. We shook our heads.

"Only thing I wanted to bring I couldn't," Micky had grumbled. He meant his gun.

"All those bullets just upset the stewardesses, Mick," Art answered.

Ueda ushered us through the terminal. He didn't say much and the message was clear that this wasn't the place to talk. So we followed him. He moved well, his muscles working smoothly, his hips driving him forward in a type of glide. It's a characteristic of people well schooled in the martial arts. I glanced at his hands and saw a faint enlargement and discoloration of his knuckles. You get it from whacking things repeatedly.

"What *ryu*?" I asked him.

Ueda turned his head to talk but didn't slow down. "Kyokush-inkai," he told me. I grunted. The karate trainees of Kyokushin-kai were notorious for their breaking techniques—boards, bricks, bottles—they hacked through them all. Some even practiced breaking baseball bats with their shins. You had to admire their persistence. Me, I prefer breaking baseball bats on someone else. I wondered if that kind of skill came in handy in the cultural attaché business.

We emerged through the rotating glass doors of the terminal into the dense, warm air. Taxis formed a jagged line that stretched along the curb, engines idling and filling the air with exhaust. Past a center island, limousines and shuttle buses waited, their tinted windows making it hard to guess who was inside. Motorcycles and scooters wove in and out of the passing traffic. It was a typical airport scene, and only the distant vista and the faint aroma of humid green hinted that you were in a foreign land. That and the presence of the brightly colored jeepneys—the distinct jeep/bus hybrid of the Philippines.

Ueda stood and slowly scanned the scene. He may have been looking for his car, but I suspected that he was looking for other things as well. He may not have been expecting anything specific, but I'd bet that the cultural attachés who lived to retire developed this habit pretty early in their careers.

He grunted faintly in satisfaction and looked toward a black limo. "There," he told us.

As we approached the car, the trunk lid popped open and we threw our bags inside. We could have fit in there as well. A uniformed driver got out of the front and opened the rear door. You felt the cool of air-conditioning rush pass you in a little cloud when he cracked the door open. We climbed into the gloom of the backseat. Ueda stood for another minute and then got in the front.

It was dim in the limo after the brightness of the day, but I could see him clearly enough, and I could see from my brother's face that he also recognized the man sitting there—Mori.

The last time we had both seen him, he was driving off from a crime scene, protected by his diplomatic status. Events had culminated to his satisfaction. He had been hunting a rogue killer from his organization who had made it to the U.S. It was a convoluted story, but it ended simply enough, in a late night sword fight in Manhattan. Micky and I both had to do an awful lot of explaining, and I got to take my first serious ride in an ambulance. We hadn't been crazy about him before that night. Neither of us was very happy to see him now.

Mori's face was square and flat and expressionless at the best of times. He watched us settle ourselves and react to his presence. Then he spoke. His voice sounded raspier than I remembered, like a man who prefers silence.

"Dr. Burke. Detective." He nodded at each of us. "And you must be the partner," he said to Art, "Pedersen. I was glad to hear that you had recovered from your wounds . . . "

Mori was impeccably dressed as usual, his white shirt glowing faintly in the dim recesses of the limo. His dark suit jacket fit perfectly. His feet, flat on the floor, were encased in gleaming black leather. His posture was perfect but there was something in the set of his shoulders that exposed his exhaustion. Despite that, it seemed to me that he was going to persist in the pattern of polite small talk that is the hallmark of Asian conversation. Still, he couldn't keep himself from glancing at his watch with a grimace.

"I am sorry, Mori-san," Ueda told him. "The policeman met them and I thought it best to remain unnoticed."

"I understand," the older man grunted. He took a breath and turned towards me, as if summoning up energy for an unpleasant task.

"I . . . " he paused and swallowed " . . . regret extremely the situation that brings you here, Dr. Burke." His head came down and his torso jerked forward in a small bow. Even in the confines of the limo, it was an obvious act of humility.

"*Shigata ga nai*," I told him. It can't be helped. I wasn't interested in hearing apologies from Mori; I wanted what information and help he could provide to get Yamashita back.

"You know what I want to know?" Micky broke in. "I want to know what brought Yamashita here in the first place."

"What do you mean?" Mori answered. "Surely the embassy officials in New York explained the situation to you, Detective."

"Don't blow smoke at me, Mori," Micky told him. "I know how you work. We get told exactly what you want us to know, and nothing more." He sat forward on his seat and gave Mori a hard stare.

Art put a hand on Micky's arm, reminding him of the need for restraint. "Mr. Mori," he began calmly, "this is an extremely complicated and dangerous situation."

"I would agree," Mori said gruffly.

Art nodded encouragingly. "So you can understand our need to get as much information as we can. If we're going to help find Yamashita *Sensei*, we need you to tell us what you know."

Mori looked at us and nodded. "I am prepared to do that. Ueda-san has been fully briefed on the situation and will provide you access to the support I have arranged."

"We wanna hear it from you, Mori," Micky pressed.

The older man looked again at his watch. He smiled tightly. "I regret that I will only be able to remain here a little while longer, detective. It seems that my . . . activities to date have not been well received by the Philippine government. As a result, I have been asked to leave the country. I am boarding a flight shortly. So perhaps it is best to ask me the most pressing questions now and Ueda-san will fill in what gaps remain?" His voice was reasonable, but his eyes darted from one to the other of us, wary of what we would ask.

"Why was Yamashita *Sensei* used to deliver the ransom, Mori-san?" I pressed him. "Why? What's the link between him and the kidnapped woman?"

Mori closed his eyes. "The reasons are multiple," he said finally. "The woman kidnapped, Abe Hatsue, is the child of my only sister. I care deeply for my niece, Dr. Burke, and sought a trusted friend to help me, someone capable of dealing with a difficult and dangerous situation. Was I so wrong in reaching out to your master?"

I looked at Mori. He and Yamashita had a long history together, serving in an elite section of the Imperial Household Agency tasked with training guards for the Imperial family. That had been years ago, but the bonds of loyalty and obligation are strong ones in Japan. And the links formed in the elite ranks of that organization named Kunaicho were even stronger. If that were not enough justification, there was also the fact that Yamashita was one of the most capable and dangerous men either of us knew.

But there was something wrong here. I could see it in the way Mori set his face and the slight jerking of his eyes.

"Yamashita *Sensei* is a skilled *bugeisha*," I admitted to him. I thought of Micky and Art's earlier discussion as I continued. "But he is an older man now and was half a world away at the time." I gestured at Ueda. "I am sure that there were many skilled and capable men available for this duty who could have been summoned in half the time, Mori-san. So I'll ask again, why Yamashita?"

Mori fidgeted slightly. "Over the years, I have seen your teacher in many situations. Ones you have no knowledge of. He was . . . is . . . without peer." But Mori was still evading me, and I pressed him on it.

"No, Mori-san," I said, shaking my head in emphasis. "It doesn't wash. Kidnappers work to keep the families of their victims off-balance. They make outrageous demands and insist that things happen quickly. They force you to play their game. The delay in getting Yamashita from New York would have set off alarms. If you cared that much about your niece, I don't think you'd take the chance . . . "

"Unless there's something else you're not telling us," Micky said.

"Wouldn't that be unusual?" Art added snidely.

Ueda was watching Mori carefully from the front seat. "Mori-san," he prompted quietly.

Mori's head shot around in anger and he glared at the younger man. "Silence!" he commanded.

"*Ie*, Mori-san," Ueda responded. "If you will not tell them, I will."

Micky sat back in the seat with an anticipatory sigh. "I told you there was something hinky here," he muttered to Art.

You could see Mori struggling. He was a proud man and accustomed to being in control. I don't imagine he admitted to failure, much. And the situation he had on his hands was a debacle. His niece hadn't been ransomed. His family was out a few million dollars. And the colleague he had brought in to help had been abducted. Now, to add further humiliation, he was being pressed by *gaijin*, foreigners, to reveal something he did not wish to. I almost felt sorry for him. Almost.

I was sitting on the limo's jump seat, directly across from Mori. I leaned forward. "Listen to me," I hissed. "Stop wasting my time. I'm here to get my teacher back. It seems that you are the cause of all of this and I want to know why! And I don't care about your sense of shame or your dignity. You have an obligation to your friend, and a duty to help me find him. If I have to beat it out of you," I saw Ueda tense and I held up a hand to calm him, "and your driver and anyone else you throw at me, I will. I'm here to get Yamashita back." By this time, my face was maybe an inch from his and I was looking right into the black of his pupils. His lids had narrowed in defense. I spaced my next words out and jabbed his chest with a hard index finger to emphasize each one. "Do—You—Understand—Me?"

Mori's lids closed slowly and his body sagged wearily. Then he straightened up with a great deal of internal effort. "The kidnappers specified that only Yamashita would be acceptable to deliver the ransom," he said quietly.

"Shit!" Micky exploded.

"You idiot," Art added. "It was a set-up."

I looked at the two cops and the certainty in their eyes. It made my stomach sink.

"Did he know?" I asked wearily.

"What?" Mori said.

"Did *Sensei* know they had asked for him to deliver the money?"

"No," Mori admitted. "He only knew that I asked his help."

Micky shook his head. "You are some piece of work, Mori. How many friends do you have, anyway? I mean ones that are still alive?"

The air conditioning was working hard in that car, but we were all beginning to sweat a bit. Ueda broke in.

"Dr. Burke, I agree with you. Whatever the circumstances that have led us to the place we are in now, our first priority needs to be finding the two kidnap victims." Ueda was working hard to bleed some of the tension off things. "Mori-san's continued presence in this country has been strongly objected to by the Philippine government . . . "

"They're not alone," my brother mumbled.

Ueda didn't miss a beat. " . . . and I am here to represent the Abe family's continuing interest and to provide you with the resources you may need to assist in the search for your teacher."

"Big deal," Micky said. "You guys created this mess. The least you can do is help clean it up."

That was too much for Mori. "I was operating in the best interest of all concerned," he began to protest. Ueda read the expressions on our faces and broke in with some comment about the time and Mori's need to clear security before take-off. It provided the older man with an excuse to leave. It was thin, but Mori took it with alacrity.

He looked at me one final time. His face was somber and pale. His chin was pulled in and he looked old and fleshy. Again, he bowed toward me in silent apology, but couldn't bring himself to say anything.

Mori left the car. The chauffeur and Ueda got out to accompany him to the entrance of the terminal.

"What a turd," Art commented.

Micky snorted in agreement. Then he looked at me. "You, on the other hand. Whattaya been eating, raw meat?"

"The whole finger-jabbing thing was very impressive," Art agreed.

"Not like you at all, Connor," my brother concluded. "I like it."

I watched the three Japanese men conferring on the sidewalk. "Let's get our ducks in a row," I said, ignoring the comments. "What do we need right away?"

"We need a continuing line to the PD in this town and whatever info they're collecting," Art started. "Probably have to be unofficial, since Reyes is not going to be on fire to help the Japanese."

"Okay," I nodded.

"We need weapons," Micky said, "and whatever associated gear necessary, as well as transportation."

"Mostly," Art told me, "we need a guy with connections and knowledge of the local scene. Cop or ex-cop. Someone who knows the players and how to grease the skids to get things done."

"You think Ueda's the guy?" I asked them. The cultural attaché had bowed and Mori and his driver headed toward the terminal doors.

"No," my brother answered. "He can help. Probably mostly in terms of a bankroll. But we need a Filipino."

Ueda reached the car and, as the door opened, the sounds of traffic grew in volume. There were any number of noises—car horns faintly blaring in the distance, the hiss of tires along the road, doors and trunks slamming, and, growing with the insistent buzz of an approaching insect, a high-revving motorcycle.

Ueda got back in the car and the noise was muffled, but I could see the thing as it came into view. It was a bright yellow racing bike, the helmeted driver bent low over the machine as he wound his way through the traffic, leaning and swaying through narrow gaps with an urgency out of sync with the rhythm of drop-offs and pick-ups.

I looked from Mori to the approaching biker to Ueda and had a mental flash—a geometric diagram unfolding with a terrible inevitability.

"Ueda!" I said, and reached for the door. He looked at me, then glanced out the window. The attaché had good reflexes. We jumped out of the car almost simultaneously.

There was perhaps thirty feet separating us from Mori. It may as well have been a mile. Ueda called out a warning, but it was blurred in the ambient noise of airport traffic. The motorcycle shot up to the terminal entrance with a squeal of tires. Mori looked up in surprise. The biker's helmet encased his head and wrapped around the lower jaw. The dark visor was in its down position so that the rider's face was totally hidden.

The motion was so smooth and so fast that Mori really didn't have time to react. The biker's arm came up and he shot Mori in the head. I saw an eye blossom red and Mori collapsed. The rider tracked him down with the pistol and put two quick, accurate shots into Mori's chest. From where we were, the shots made popping noises, but it must have been louder by the doors. People screamed and tripped over their luggage in clumsy attempts to get away.

The chauffeur cringed near Mori, certain he was next. But the biker simply dropped the gun to the pavement, revved his bike, and bolted away into traffic. In seconds, the angry whine of the motorcycle was fading.

Ueda reached Mori and knelt down. He looked up at me and shook his head. Micky and Art were right behind me.

"You get a make on the bike?" my brother asked Art.

"Nah," his partner grunted. "Never really got a clear look at the tags."

"He's dead," I told them. Blood oozed from Mori's wounds and had begun to snake across the pavement. The white of his shirt was quickly soaking into a dark crimson. The suddenness of the shooting was disorienting and numbing. I didn't care much for Mori, but nobody deserves to go that way. I felt the same way I always felt at the spectacle of violent death—shaky and humbled and guiltily glad to be alive.

"He was dead before he hit the ground," Micky said. Sirens were approaching from the distance. He looked at Ueda. "Now what?"

Ueda spoke quickly to the driver, giving him instructions. Then he got on his cell phone and gave someone else more instructions. As he spoke, he ushered us back toward the car. He was quick, but not flustered.

"I prefer not to have you gentlemen involved with the police at this time," Ueda explained. "We need to leave."

Micky shrugged. "We can sort things out later. But, leaving a crime scene . . . "

"We've been in this country, what? Two hours?" Art asked rhetorically.

"And already we're in trouble with the authorities," Micky added.

"Gotta be a record. Even for us," Art finished.

I said nothing. Ueda got behind the wheel and slid the limo out into traffic while behind us flashing lights converged on Mori, faceup on the pavement, his once clever eyes robbed forever of all knowledge.

15

ESKRIMADOR

The three of us sat in the cool dim corner of the hotel bar, waiting for Ueda. The man behind the bar kept his eye on us. He moved quietly along the terraced rows of bottles, their labels providing subdued flashes of color in the artificial twilight. It was late afternoon and the pre-dinner crowd hadn't come down. We, on the other hand, were getting an early jump on things. The bartender polished the counter and worked on his set-up for the evening, cutting lemon peels and arranging cocktail napkins. He didn't say much to us, but when the beer got low, he was right there with some replacements. We were all conscious that we needed to keep our wits about us, but no one had the heart to discourage him. It's always a pleasure to see a professional at work. Even if it wasn't the first time that day.

"A hit like that," Micky said, shaking his head. "Pretty smooth."

"Someone knew what they were doing," Art agreed.

"So we're dealing with pros again?" I asked. "That's good in some ways, right?"

"Sure," my brother said. "Whoever capped Mori does this for a living . . . "

"Which means Reyes will have a good idea of who it might be, but will probably have a hard time pinning it on them," Art finished. He didn't seem particularly upset. He saw the look on my face, though. "Don't worry, Connor. There's a beauty to being—whattaya wanna call it, Mick—unofficial operators?"

My brother sipped at his beer bottle, swallowed and nodded with a smile of wicked satisfaction. "Sure. Irregulars. With any luck, we get to operate under the legal radar."

"Which means?" I asked.

"It means that we tear through this town until we find Yamashita and hopefully the girl and then boogie outta here before Reyes catches up with us."

Art brightened up. "I like this plan. Simple. Direct. With the possibility of creating untold trouble."

"It's the Burke way," I reminded him.

"Tell me something I don't know," Art said. "We just gotta hope that Ueda can get us someone with some good inside info."

Marangan was maybe in his mid-fifties with close-cropped hair and deep grooves running from the sides of his nose to the corners of his mouth. He didn't look like a happy camper. The second floor office Ueda led us to was poorly lit and the walls were decorated with old posters for sporting events. The words in Tagalog were made even harder to read by the fact that the humidity was curling the posters right off the wall. An oscillating fan pushed at the air sporadically in useless fits. Marangan sat and looked at us balefully. We looked back. No one was impressed on either side.

"I believe that the *batikan* Marangan can help us. *Batikan* is much like our term *sensei*," Ueda explained in an aside as he led us up the stairs. "It is the title used here for a master of *eskrima*."

"It's a Philippine martial art," I told Micky before he could open his mouth.

"Here we go again," Art mumbled.

Now we sat in the stuffy office and waited to learn why Ueda was so optimistic.

"The *batikan* served for a number of years on the Manila police force," Ueda began. "He was later seconded to an intelligence unit dealing with the southern provinces. He has family on Mindanao, and the variety of his contacts can be extremely useful to us."

Marangan sat there like a reptile, never blinking, barely even breathing. He didn't seem particularly interested in talking.

"How come you're off the force now?" Micky asked. Between Marangan and my brother, I suspected we had located two of the world's worst conversationalists.

Marangan sat forward. "They wanted a clerk. I am a *mandirigma*."

"A warrior," Ueda translated, then continued. "There was some conflict, gentlemen between the *batikan* and his superiors . . . issues of means and ends, really." He said it like we were all men of the world and could forgive a little excess zeal here and there.

Micky's eyes narrowed as he weighed the Filipino. Marangan looked back. If they were dogs, the hair on their necks would have been bristling.

"Okay," my brother finally said. He didn't sound happy, just resigned.

Marangan pulled open a drawer and fished out something to write on. "The usual pay arrangements?" he asked Ueda. It was one of the few times I saw any spark of interest in his face. The Japanese nodded. Marangan sat forward. "Then we begin."

Ueda briefed him on the events to date—the kidnapping in Mindanao, the disastrous ransom attempt, Yamashita's kidnapping, and now Mori's murder. After a while, Marangan stopped Ueda's narration and pulled an old rotary dial phone across the desk. He made perhaps five phone calls, talking in a low clipped voice.

When he finished, Marangan looked at Ueda. "I wish you had come to me earlier. In matters of this type, it is important that the trail not grow cold." Ueda said nothing, just sat there, and finally the Filipino shrugged. "We will see what we will see." Then he looked at me.

"You are friends of the kidnapped?" Marangan's voice was dry and didn't contain much inflection.

I nodded in response. To describe Yamashita as my friend doesn't begin to characterize our relationship, but I wasn't interested in long explanations. "And you two . . . " he continued, looking at Micky and Art.

"We're cops," Micky said. "Partners. From New York." Marangan opened his mouth to ask another question, but Micky forestalled it. "He's my brother," he told Marangan. It was part explanation and part excuse.

The Filipino nodded. "Ah."

"When Yamashita *Sensei* was kidnapped, they agreed to help me out," I added.

The word *sensei* triggered a response in Marangan. He looked quickly at Ueda. "*Sensei*? Of what, Ueda?"

"Yamashita *Sensei* is a master of the sword and other arts," he began. But Marangan jumped in. If he were a cobra, his hood would have swelled out in excitement.

"And you are his student," he told me with a slight air of satisfaction. "Come to rescue your master." He smiled then, and you saw that his teeth were crooked and stained and long like his face. "I honor you for the effort." Marangan stood up. It was a smooth motion, like a spring uncoiling. "Perhaps you would be interested in my art as well."

"We gotta waste time with this?" Micky hissed in my ear as we followed Marangan.

"Yeah," I told him. "Shuddup." I *knew* Marangan. I've spent most of my adult life with people like him. When he had described himself as a *mandirigma*—a warrior—it sounded a bit over the top. But people like him lose themselves in a world of their own making. It doesn't matter whether the art deals with fists or feet or sticks or blades. The pursuit of the art takes hold of you if you do it long enough. It becomes in many ways a reality bigger than reality itself. Everything is judged in terms of it. Including people. Marangan would need to know how I fit in his world. It would tell him how far he could push me and how far I would push him back.

We were in a strange place where the rules were unknown to us, clues were few and far between, and the need for haste was almost paralyzing in its insistence. For me, it was going to be a comfort and a release to have to deal with something as elemental and familiar as fighting. Besides, I rationalized to myself, I needed to show Marangan that I was *not* going to be pushed.

I flexed my hands gently, stretching muscles in anticipation. Art looked at me with a worried expression.

Marangan led us out of the office and down the hall. Double doors were propped open to reveal a large, high-ceilinged place. There was a faded sign over the entrance that announced the Kapatiran Marangan Kali. I didn't understand Tagalog, but I knew a training hall when I saw one.

These places are all different and all the same. Spaces empty of embellishment or ornamentation stripped down and filled with the smell of sweat and the lingering psychic charge of effort and adrenalin. A Japanese training hall may be matted or have a hardwood floor. There may be some weapon racks hugging a wall and a small Shinto shrine tucked into a corner. But those are the sorts of details only a novice focuses on. The real essence of these places is something more subtle.

Marangan's training hall had a dingy floor and smudged gray walls. Wiry young men in black T-shirts and sneakers worked alone or together, some with rattan sticks, others using their hands and feet. The wooden floor thudded with their movements and the sticks filled the hall with clatter. If you listened, you could pick up the grunt of effort, the hiss of breath, the emotional give and take of attack and defense. It didn't have the understated geometric precision of a Japanese *dojo*. But I knew this place.

We filed in along a wall, out of the fray. When Marangan entered, the students stopped and came to attention. Their master waved them back into activity.

"We train for both armed and unarmed fighting here," Marangan explained. "Your karate is good, Ueda," he told the attaché, "but an armed attacker is far more lethal."

"The art is called *kali*?" I asked.

"It is a broad term," the Filipino explained. "We combine the various forms of *arnis* and *eskrima* here." He saw me looking at the different types of weapons arrayed along a wall. "Sticks and blades, Mr. Burke. Perhaps it is the same with your *sensei*?"

I had seen *eskrima* before. *Eskrimadors* usually used two rattan sticks about two feet in length to fight. Sometimes one of the sticks was replaced with a knife. I saw swords on the wall and gestured at them. "Do you train with long blades as well?"

Marangan gave his jagged-tooth smile. "Advanced students sometimes use them. Our islands have a variety of sword traditions." He led us over to the wall and as he identified them, he touched the swords affectionately.

"The *barong*," he ran a finger along a heavy, leaf-shaped sword about two feet long. "Quite common in Mindanao. The various Moro tribes use them." He moved to a thin, wavy blade whose guard crossed the top of the handle at an angle. "The *kris*. Found all over Southeast Asia." He stopped at the longest of the weapons. It must have been almost four feet long. "The *kampilan*," he announced with satisfaction. It was nasty looking. The blade started out narrow and flared gradually to a jagged, angled point. The pommel was forked and the entire thing looked like something engineered to do frightful damage. "Sea Dayaks used them. Headhunters. These blades are widespread in the southern islands here." He touched the handle. "The pommel is said to represent the jaws of a crocodile." Marangan turned to us. "The Japanese are not the only people with martial arts." There was a defiant gleam in his eye as if he looked forward to debating the point with Ueda. But no one said a word.

"Perhaps you would enjoy seeing our *eskrimadors* at work," Marangan suggested, "or experiencing our arts firsthand?" I felt the familiar inward shift, half anticipation and half dread, and nodded in agreement. This was the whole point of him bringing us here. His little natural history exhibit of the swords of the Philippines was beside the point. This was when Marangan got to push me and see if I could push back.

He led me to a rack and showed me a range of *baston*, the sticks they used. There was a long one there—almost four feet in length. It was pretty close to the *jo* staff I use in training with Yamashita— a white oak shaft maybe an inch in diameter and about fifty-four inches long. Marangan told me that the one I picked out was called a *bangkaw*. It wasn't an exact match to the *jo*, but it was close. I like to stay with what I know.

Marangan called out to his students. They flocked around him and he singled one out. Marangan draped a hand over the younger man's shoulders and gave him some instructions. The student wore track pants and a black T-shirt with a red insignia on the chest. They told me later it was a fighting cock, a pretty popular martial image in the Philippines.

I sized him up. He was about my size, which was good. In combat, the length of an opponent's arms and legs can be critical. Unfortunately, he was probably ten or fifteen years younger than I was. You hate to admit it, but over thirty your body doesn't work as well as you'd like and is more subject to injury. In purely physical terms, he was probably my match. So I'd have to use some finesse. Cunning was a technique not well appreciated by the young.

My opponent was whipcord thin with angry eyes, a younger

version of his master. It's funny how we all tend to become copies of our teachers. I know guys in New York who have developed Japanese accents. I'm not sure how I've come to resemble my own *sensei*. I'm taller and thinner and stamped with the genetic markers of County Mayo. But sometimes in the mirror, I catch a glimpse of the same flat mask Yamashita wears—the expression that seems so neutral but hides the fact that you're watching everything, analyzing angles and distances, and, in fact, seeing the universe as a series of fluid scenarios of attack and defense.

I wonder, sometimes, what it is I have become.

But too much thought is a danger. The masters say that it makes the mind "stick"; it creates gaps in your defense. There is a time for thought and reflection, and the practiced feel of a wooden weapon in my hand let me know that this was not the time or the place.

After a brief ritual salutation, Marangan's student came at me. He was using two sticks, wielding them in a series of complex patterns that made it difficult to judge potential angles of attack. I engaged my opponent cautiously, then backed out of range again and again as I assessed his skills.

Most times in the Japanese arts, you're going up against a single weapon. They have a preference in Japan for the commitment this engenders. But, of course, it also tends to create a flaw in your training. After all, the old samurai carried a long and a short sword. What if an opponent used them both?

There are varieties of double-handed weapon systems in the Japanese arts. Miyamoto Musashi was famous for his *nito* style, using long and short blades simultaneously. And you occasionally run up against people in a *kendo dojo* who use it today. As a matter of fact, Yamashita would sometimes insist that I watch these people and train with them. Not to adopt their style—"the road to perfection is steep enough carrying one weapon, I think, Professor"—but to learn how to combat it.

And what had I learned? Basically that if you've got one weapon and the other person has two, you're in for a rough ride. And the only way to beat them is to use an attack that is so precise, well timed, and focused that it cuts through the cloud of uncertainty that the opponent has created. And that's not even it. You have to feel the opponent's pattern in your gut and then when it happens—if it happens—your response snaps out like an electric spark, almost independent of your control.

You just have to hope you don't get pounded to death while you're waiting for the spark.

The rattan sticks came at me, one baton threatening a head strike and begging for response, while the other baton waited, cocked, to exploit the opening. He launched himself in a flurry of attacks, and I couldn't just parry them—if you committed to one defense, then the other side would whir in at you. I had to parry and move and dodge, whirling my staff around and threatening him with its longer reach, jabbing for the throat with all the venom I could generate.

Within maybe thirty seconds, he had clipped me more than a few times on the wrists and shoulders. It stung, but I wasn't going to let anyone see that. When the batons connected, you could see the lights go on in his eyes. He liked to hit. And he thought he was winning.

So what I tried to do was frustrate him a little. I kept moving and thrusting, keeping him a little farther away than he liked. It was hot in that room, and it was getting hotter. Our weapons clattered, our sneakers squeaked on the floor, and I could hear the blood rushing in my ears.

He was younger than I was, but I thought I could outlast him. It's a trick you use on the young. They are dangerous because of their energy, but you can slowly bleed them of it while you wait for an opening. And in this case, the *esksrimador* had been selected by his teacher to fight me. It was an honor, and the young man in the sweaty black T-shirt wanted to show that his master had made the right choice. My opponent didn't want to wear me down. He wanted to *prove* something. It would make him feel the need to attack even when he shouldn't.

He tried to close the gap and the batons whirred at me. I parried frantically and turned slightly, as if wary of being hit. As he came in range, I snapped a vicious roundhouse kick out, taking him on the side of the left thigh. He faltered slightly, but I backed off.

You could see that I had tagged him pretty good, but it didn't slow him down much. He came at me again. I feinted with the same technique, and he jerked out of the way. Fast learner. I could see why Marangan had chosen him.

Unfortunately, when he jerked, his torso turned slightly toward me and his right arm came up a bit. My staff whirled around and I cracked him hard on the right side. It's hard to tell with fit people, since the extra muscle muffles sound, but I'd be surprised if I hadn't cracked a rib.

I used the staff to trap his right arm and leverage him over. He tried to swing out at me with his other hand, but I continued moving and led him around in a circle. He was good and managed to race his feet along so he could force himself up to fight the momentum I was generating. It's an almost instinctual response: the need to reassert control. I could feel the muscle tension in his trapped arm. There was some real strength in him, which was good.

As he forced his torso upright, I switched direction and swept up and back. His feet kept going forward and his body went up and out. At one point, for a split second, he was almost horizontal. His feet lifted off the ground; I stretched him out, pushing with the staff against his throat and upper chest. It was one of those moments when all the elements click and you can feel the technique come together in a type of wild beauty.

Then I slammed him down as hard as I could. Small dust motes puffed out from the floorboards and his head made a nasty thudding sound as it hit. I grabbed the sticks from his hands while his eyes were still faintly crossed, and tossed them across the room toward Marangan.

The room came into focus for me then. The Filipino students were standing in a ring around the walls, staring openmouthed. Ueda gave me a slight bow. Art whispered something in Micky's ear and my brother smirked with satisfaction.

Breath was pumping in and out of me like a bellows. I was sheeted in sweat and I could feel it rolling down the muscles along my spine. I tried to figure out what kind of shape I was in. Nothing was broken. I could taste some blood in my mouth, but that's not unusual. My arms were going to look like the victims of a bad tattooing in the morning. But, all in all, not too bad. While it's never fun, I've come to accept it. That's the sort of business I'm in.

Hollywood's got it all wrong, of course. You don't engage in a fight with bad guys and emerge unscathed. You feel it for days. And it takes a while to get reconnected to the world around you. You don't look up, wipe some sweat off your manly brow, and kiss the well-endowed heroine. In the real world, you tend to just stagger over to the nearest wall and try not to retch.

After a minute or so I looked up at Marangan. My breathing had slowed down enough to talk. "Nice," I said. "Can we talk, now?"

16

CHAIN

There was a lot of noise—motorcycles revving up outside, stools hitting the floor, shouts and the noise of glass breaking. Micky was yelling, "Get outta the way! Get outta the way!" but Ueda and I were too busy to notice.

I heard the *whoosh* of the pool cue as it swung by my nose. In one of those strange moments of irrelevant clarity, I noticed that some chewing gum was stuck on the rubber tip of the cue's base: a weapon and a breath freshener. But the man waving it was not really any good. I let the cue groan by, then I swarmed in and gave the guy a smashing elbow-strike that dislocated his jaw. He sat down hard, looking vaguely surprised. I grabbed the pool cue and spun around, but there were no other comers.

Ueda was fighting a man who wielded a wicked looking knife. He swiped and jabbed at Ueda, who stood, arms outstretched, like he welcomed the opportunity to try his luck. The Filipino with the blade wanted Ueda to jump back and lose his balance, but he only moved a fraction in response to the jerks, just out of the reach of the knife. A jab, and Ueda arched to avoid it, but kept his footing. A swipe—his eyes followed the pathway of the knife, his face totally expressionless, flat with the calm that comes from experience. Finally, the Filipino lunged hard and Ueda used a crescent kick to deflect it, slamming the outside of his attacker's forearm so hard that the knife flew across the room. Ueda's foot came back crisply into the cocked position, resting lightly against the knee of his supporting leg for a split second. Then he drove it out in a classic side thrust kick that drilled into his opponent's middle, lifted him off his feet, and threw him across a table. The table, body and all, tipped over. Ueda followed as if he were attached by a wire. His fist drove down twice like something on a piston and that about did it.

Marangan had taken off after someone down a hallway that led to the alley. I heard the door bang open and then bang again almost immediately as Marangan rocketed after his prey. By this time, Micky and Art had waded through the toppled furniture and stood, brandishing the .38 snub-nosed revolvers with the faded bluing that Marangan had given them.

"The next time, will you get out of the fuckin' way so I can get a clean shot!" my brother demanded.

The master of *eskrima* hadn't taken long to get a tip. It made you wonder about the police and what they were up to. Our main focus was the kidnappings, but Marangan told us to start with the hit on Mori, explaining that there weren't too many people in Manila who could pull something like that off, and that the homicide had to be connected in some way to the abductions. You followed the chain of association to lead you to your target.

"Sure," Art had agreed. "The local cops don't seem to have a clue. The only guy still poking hard at things was Mori."

"Makes sense that the kidnappers would take him out," Micky agreed.

Marangan led us down avenues not contained in the Manila guidebooks. Ueda had a late model SUV. Marangan followed us in a pea-green Dodge Satellite wagon with shot springs. He had two taciturn assistants with him. Our little caravan wound through increasingly run-down streets to a bar where parked motorcycles crowded the front like ticks on a host. There was a flickering streetlight on a tottering pole to one side of the building. The pavement was cracked and poorly maintained, and the bar had the look of a hastily converted warehouse. It had a large window that faced the street, but it was covered in wire mesh with no glass. The door was a thick battered metal slab propped open by a broken cinderblock.

The motorcycles, on the other hand, gleamed with care and polish. Most of them were sleek street bikes, small, powerful vehicles that had aerodynamic fiberglass coverings, like the shells of brightly colored insects. The metal and chrome gleamed, even in the poor light.

"These crotch rockets look familiar?" Art asked.

"A lot like the one Mori's killer was riding," Micky answered.

"They are fast and maneuverable," Ueda told us. "Very popular with the street gangs in city traffic."

Loud music was playing inside and, even though the bar was filled, the bass thudded right through the packed bodies in the building and into the street. People moved in and out of the bar, clusters of men laughing and talking. They were mostly intent on drinking beer and admiring particular bikes.

We got noticed anyway. You could see some patrons eyeing us nervously as we entered, and it was clear that they knew Marangan. A few men pushed away from the bar to stand and face us.

It didn't take long for things to happen. Marangan asked a few questions, moving slowly from person to person. Some answered him; others just shook their heads and looked away, feeling an urgent need to gaze into their drinks. As he made his way methodically around the bar, you could feel the tension ratchet up. Finally, one man bolted across the crowded room, threading his way between two pool tables, headed for a rear hallway. Marangan was after him almost immediately, as if he expected the move all along. That was when Ueda and I tried to follow and things got a little complex.

When we finally managed to follow him out to the alley, Marangan was busy with a man who was cowering by a row of oil drums stuffed with trash. The *eskrimador's* assistants stood at the opening by the front of the alley, discouraging the curious. The alley was unpaved and smelled of moist earth and stale urine. The night had cooled somewhat, but it was still warm and humid and my skin felt greasy. It was hard to see at first, but the unmistakable sound of flesh hitting flesh helped us locate Marangan, that and the ghostly flash of white from his victim's teeth when the pain hit.

I sensed the movement more than saw it—a faint blur in the grayness—and Marangan snapped another finger bone. The man he had chased out there gasped. Then there was a rapid-fire exchange in Tagalog. Marangan was clearly unpleased and, as we got closer, he grabbed his victim's hand again.

I lurched forward to stop it, but Art grabbed me by the arm.

"Easy, Connor," he advised.

I looked from Art to Micky to Ueda, but they said nothing. Nor did they make a move to intervene. It was hard to read the expressions on their faces. Behind me, Marangan's voice demanded answers and his victim's squeal ramped up to something a little more desperate. I glanced over. The *eskrimador* was grinding the bones of the broken finger together.

"Jesus!" I protested.

Marangan looked up at me. "Your *sensei* is with the Moros, Burke. Do you know that they see a world split into two houses? The *Dar al-Islam* and the *Dar al-Harb*?" The *eskrimador* looked at our blank faces. "It means the House of Surrender and the House of War. To them, we are infidels to be conquered or killed. There is no room for holding back."

We all looked flatly at him and he turned his attention to his captive. Marangan ground and snapped and probed in that dark place, intent on getting what he wanted.

"Let him work," Micky said. "It's his turf."

Eventually, Marangan pronounced himself satisfied. I was sweating profusely and feeling slightly sick as we made our way back to the SUV that Ueda was driving. Marangan got in front and sat next to him.

"You okay?" Micky asked me quietly before we got in the car. Even in the dim light, I was probably green.

I swallowed and took a breath. Nodded. "Sorry."

"Don't be," Art told me. "That kinda thing's hard to see. Just remember—you're in a whole other world here. They play by different rules. And we don't have much time." We kept our voices low while we talked.

"I'm starting to get a better picture of what Ueda meant by 'issues with means and ends,'" my brother said.

Marangan's window whined down and he looked at us balefully. "Hurry. I have the name of the shooter." When we got in, Ueda had handed Marangan his cell phone and the rapid-fire series of calls began anew.

Marangan's two assistants trundled the man in the alley over to the Dodge.

"What's going to happen to him?' I asked to no one in particular.

"Eleventh Avenue," Micky said.

"Huh?"

Art's voice was matter of fact. "We can't let him go, Connor. Chances are that as soon as he gets a chance, he'll call whoever Marangan's after."

"So let's take him with us," I suggested.

Art grimaced. "Too much trouble. The secret to doing this sort of thing is to move fast and light. We don't want to have to babysit this guy."

"So. . . . " I persisted.

Micky looked hard at me in exasperation. "Think about what I just told you."

Maybe it was all the flying, or the foreign city. Maybe things were just happening too fast and it was after one o'clock in the morning. But I thought about my brother's cryptic statement for a minute and then it hit me.

When Micky was a young rookie on foot patrol on Eighth Avenue in Midtown, he'd been partnered with an old beat cop. On a midnight shift, they got a call from the night manager of a local hotel, and when they arrived, found the man nursing a huge bruise across the side of his head. His security people had a street bum in custody, but the guy seemed totally incoherent. Micky got the story from the shaken manager: the bum had wandered in a few times during the night and they had rousted him back onto the street every time. Finally, about three a.m., the bum came back. When the exasperated manager had come out into the lobby for one last time, the bum yanked a phone out of the wall by the concierge's desk and beat the manager to the floor with it.

Micky got the report down, and then looked at his partner. The older cop hadn't said much, just watched the bum, who by this time was kneeling in front of a potted plant and babbling at it. Everyone in the room knew that the bum was more crazy than he was violent. Finally, Micky's partner explained things to the manager: They could take the bum over to Bellevue Hospital for observation; they'd hold him for an hour there, then turn him back onto the street. There weren't enough hospital beds in New York for all the walking wounded. Chances are that the bum would be back before dawn. The night manager looked upset, so the old street cop made a suggestion: they could take the bum to Bellevue or they could take him to Eleventh Avenue.

It was Land's End. Beyond the West Side Highway in the concrete no-man's land where Manhattan petered out into the Hudson River. Indian country. The old cop knew that you could load a problem like the bum into the back of a squad car and dump him anywhere on Eleventh Avenue. He might return and he might not: it depended what was prowling on the avenue that night. It was a street solution to a street problem. My brother Micky learned over the years that you sometimes did what was expedient. It might not have been right in a strict sense, but you learned to drive away without looking back.

Every city has an Eleventh Avenue, and Manila was no exception. I watched the Dodge drive away and tried not to dwell on its destination.

Marangan's network of informants was good. Even at that hour, he pulled scraps of information that led us to a motel on the edge of the red light district. It was the kind of place where you paid cash when you checked in and few questions were asked. They turned the rooms over two or three times a night. It was getting close to three a.m., but the streets were still lit with passing cars. Music from bars pulsed in the night air. As we pulled to a stop down the street from the motel, three drunken Americans lurched by. One bent over and gushed a stream of beer into the gutter. Ueda watched impassively from the driver's seat. The rest of us waited for Marangan to say something.

"Shooter in there?" my brother asked, jerking his head at the motel. It was a two story building with an open air hallway that ran across the second floor. There was a light on in the small office on the ground floor and a parking lot in the back. It's a universal tradition in motels: patrons park out of sight.

Marangan rocked his head from side to side. "Possibly so. There is word of a member of one of the motorcycle gangs who has recently come into some big money. Did you notice the color of the motorcycle used in the killing?" he asked.

"Yellow," Art told him.

Marangan nodded. He held up a piece of paper. "I asked an old friend to check for vehicles registered to this man. He owns a Kawasaki motorcycle. It, too, is yellow."

"It's a start," Micky acknowledged.

Marangan slipped out of the car. "I'll speak to the night clerk." He moved off with the muscular, contained glide typical of fighters. Micky let him enter the motel office, then slipped out of the car himself. Art was right behind. They disappeared around the back of the building and returned almost immediately.

"Yellow street bike parked in back," Art told us. "Engine's cool, so it's been there a while."

Micky was examining the cylinder of his pistol, moving it back and forth and spinning it. "This is a piece of shit," he commented. "It's a throw down piece." He looked up at Ueda. "First thing tomorrow, we've got to get some decent firepower." The attaché nodded, but said nothing. He nodded toward the windshield. Marangan was coming back.

"Room twenty-one," the Filipino told us. "Second floor, third door from the far end. He has been in there most of the night."

"Alone?" Micky asked.

"Some girls went up earlier," Marangan said, "but the clerk isn't sure if they left or not."

"That's it, though?" Art pressed him. "One guy?" Marangan nodded.

"Let's go," I said.

Marangan had a key and we moved slowly along the second floor hallway and placed ourselves on either side of the door. My brother grabbed my arm as if to hold me back. I looked at him.

"Let us work this one, Connor," Micky told me. He and Art had their small snub-nosed revolvers out and, for the first time since we had landed, looked comfortable. Art winked at me.

Marangan slipped the key into the door and looked from side to side as if to check to see if everyone was ready. He turned the key and pushed the door slowly in. It gapped open and then caught on a chain.

"Lemme," Art grunted. He backed up and rammed his shoulder against the point where it looked like the security chain was tethered. The door flew open and Art flew in with it, Micky and Marangan right behind him.

The man on the bed was slight and young and clearly stoned out of his mind. He had a wispy little mustache and longish hair. He didn't look particularly deadly, but the naked rarely do. He was tangled up in sheets with two girls. They were skinny and small-breasted, and their black hair was long and dirty looking and snaked across their shoulders. They could have been fourteen or fifteen, but their eyes were much older. They sat up in bed and caught the drift of things much quicker than their companion.

Marangan was on them in a flash. The girls jumped up and Ueda herded them into a corner. Then the *eskrimador* seized the man on the bed, yanked him face down. and bound his hands behind his back with a plastic tie. It was all very slick.

Marangan turned to the girls and snarled something to them. He looked at Ueda. "Get them their clothes. Give them some money and get rid of them." The two prostitutes kept impassive faces. They got dressed, gathered their things, and tried not to look at anyone. They left quickly, spurred on by instinct. Street life dulls many senses, but these two could smell trouble coming easily enough.

The room was a shambles, with empty food containers and liquor bottles littering the floor. You could smell stale perfume and sex, old cigarettes and spilled beer. Ueda went through the place professionally, coming up with a black gym bag stuffed with money. Then he took out a small pocket device and shined it on a few of the bills. He looked at Marangan and nodded.

"You marked the ransom, Ueda?" Micky said. It was a question, but he knew the answer.

Ueda nodded. "Indeed. This is ransom money. At least a part of it."

Art looked at the trussed man on the bed. "Okay. They used part of the payoff to finance the hit. It fits." He turned to Ueda. "We can call the cops now and get them to squeeze him. Probably easy enough to do a test on him for gunpowder residue. We got enough circumstantial stuff to hold him."

Marangan chortled. "And how will you get the information you need, Detective? It will take a day to book him. Then the interrogation will start. In the meantime, the trail grows colder and colder." He gestured at the man with contempt. "He was hired because he is expendable. Chances are good that he would not survive long, even in police custody."

"So what good is he to us?" Micky asked. He was looking from Marangan to the man on the bed to Ueda. My brother had one eye closed and squinted at them, the way he does when he's thinking hard.

Marangan looked at Ueda significantly, then tossed a small bag on the bed and began removing its contents: tape, pliers, a scalpel. I looked at Micky in alarm.

"In our experience," Ueda told us, "people often know far more than they think. It merely takes persuasion . . . " His eyes were hard and for the first time I saw something of Mori in him.

My brother and Art exchanged looks.

"We're out of this, Ueda," Micky said. He and Art moved toward the door together and I followed. Micky grabbed a pillowcase from the bed.

"You touch anything, Connor?" Art asked quietly.

"The doorjamb," I stammered. Micky wiped it down. He tossed

the cloth to Art, who did the same to a few more surfaces. Then we went out. Ueda followed us onto the second floor hallway.

There was no real energy in Micky's voice. He kept it low and matter-of-fact. And he kept moving. "We're not gonna be a part of this, Ueda."

The attaché nodded. "I understand. You are policemen. This . . . is something different."

"Uh, yeah," Art told him, "you could say that."

The Japanese don't typically respond to our sarcasm. Ueda plowed on. "But you will utilize whatever . . . information I am able to coax from him?"

Micky swallowed and nodded.

"So," Ueda concluded. He handed Micky some keys. "Wait in the car. This should not take long."

"How do you know?" I asked, and my voice was raspy.

"I have seen Marangan work before," Ueda replied, and turned back to number twenty-one. The door closed quietly.

We ran the motor for the air conditioning. It dried the sweat but it didn't make you feel clean.

"How's this any different from the guy in back of the bar?" I asked.

Micky rolled the car window down to listen for something. He was watching the hotel intently as well. He didn't turn his head when he spoke. "This is different. Trust me."

"How?" I persisted.

Art put a large hand on my arm. "Connor. This is different. Trust us." Art is big and broad where my brother is narrow and whipcord thin. If Micky is all spiky energy, Art usually exudes more calm. And his voice was quiet as he spoke to me. But it wasn't a comfort.

"I don't get it," I told my brother. "You won't be part of torturing a suspect but you'll use the information Ueda gets? How's that make sense?"

My brother turned to look at me and his eyes were hot. "Hey. Dickwad. You wanna find Yamashita? We gotta use what we can."

"It's a shitty situation," Art explained as if this were a telling debate point.

"I don't control the whole fucking world," Micky continued, and the tone in his voice told me just how angry he was. "Best I can do is control *me*. I don't always like it, but that's the way it is. There's nothing that says ya gotta like it. So grow up a little, huh?" He turned back to watch and wait.

In a while, we heard a muted *pop* from the motel's second floor and Ueda and Marangan crept quietly out of room twenty-one. They didn't bother closing the door. Micky and Art exchanged glances.

Ueda and Marangan got silently into the front of the SUV. The attaché handed Marangan the black gym bag with the money in it. "Thank you, *batikan*," he said to the Filipino. Marangan gave a small, cruel smile, and took the bag.

"What's the deal?" I asked.

Marangan turned to look at me. "Let us term it . . . a finder's fee."

Somewhere out to the east, I knew the sun was racing up to cross the rim of the world. In the back of the car, my eyes gritty with night, it seemed a distant promise. The SUV rolled out into streets still locked tightly in darkness.

17

TESSEN

Hatsue occupied her mind by observing the camp, noting its patterns of behavior, trying to read the ebb and flow of activity, searching for a clue to her fate. After the first interview, she had never again spoken to the hideous old Japanese man. She shuddered at the memory of the way he made her feel.

She knew from what the old man had told her that there was a purpose to her captivity, an end game. She couldn't yet determine what that end game would be. For the first few days, she had driven herself to a terrified exhaustion simply by generating imaginary scenarios. All were equally horrific, and so she stopped, blocking out any thoughts of the future.

During the day, she watched the old man as he drilled the others in martial arts exercises in the clearing beside his hut. Westerners tended to think that all Japanese studied martial arts. In reality, the idea that most Japanese were black belts was as laughable as the idea that most Americans were cowboys. What was more, martial arts training was often associated with more conservative elements in Japan. For many younger Japanese, the arts carried with them the noxious whiff of old Japan, a discredited remnant of imperial embarrassment. To find such a person here, training these men, only heightened her anxiety.

Eventually, the days took on a sameness—her captors permitted her out of her prison twice daily to use a latrine; food and water came in battered old tin pails. No one spoke with her other than to give curt orders. Her guards were Filipinos but she noted the others, the men who surrounded the old man, watching her carefully. Their glances were not curious, nor were they cruel. They looked at her the way a hunter scans a dog working a distant field: a means to an end that would flush prey into motion.

She had decided that these people were from the Middle East, perhaps Arabs judging by their appearance and what talk she had been able to overhear. She tried to use her daily trips out of the cell to collect information. *Sort of a mini-fieldwork*, she told herself bitterly. In a world that had rapidly spun out of her control, the effort of analysis offered the comfort of familiar effort and the illusion of self-determination. Twice a day she moved slowly around the clearing with her guards, stumbling occasionally and acting as if she did not immediately understand their directions. It gave her more time to observe and learn.

The day they brought in the new captive the camp was literally buzzing with the foreign clatter of Arab and Filipino languages. Even if she couldn't understand them, she could tell that this new captive was someone special.

Her cell was on the end of the camp farthest from the main entrance, and it made close observation difficult. Hatsue peered through her small window, craning her neck toward the camp entrance. She could see a group of men, including the Arabs, crowding around the trailhead.

When the crowd parted and they dragged the captive into the clearing, Hatsue felt mildly deflated. He was a short, stocky man, clearly unsteady on his feet. He moved like he was old.

Hatsue had a hard time relating their excitement to the small, defeated figure they dragged across the clearing to the steps of the old man's hut. The Arabs looked up expectantly and the buzz of the crowd died down.

He emerged, that horrible old man, wearing the same traditional and incongruous garb in which he had greeted her and holding the same old-fashioned ceremonial *tessen* fan. Hatsue watched as the old man slowly and menacingly descended the steps from his hut, and she shuddered as the ring of young armed men closed around the new prisoner. After a time, the old one strode back up the veranda steps and gestured imperiously with his fan. They dragged the captive off to a space between two posts, newly installed the day before.

The man was strung up between the posts, his extended arms and legs creating an X. The crowd watched the old man expectantly. He stood there, seemingly oblivious to their inquiring looks. Then with a slow sweep, he gestured.

In her cell, Hatsue jerked back involuntarily as the tessen pointed in her direction. She slunk down into a corner, madly hoping that she was wrong. But the guards came for her.

They dragged her over the rough ground of the camp to stand before the captive. He was an older man, compact, with a shaved head beginning to show stubble. He was Asian. He watched her approach, and, while his eyes seemed clear enough, there was a rim of white around his mouth and a slackness to his face. *He's been drugged*, she thought. Part of her remembered her trip to the camp and she wished faintly that they had done the same to her.

The old man with the fan appeared by her side as if he had glided down the steps of his hut. He cackled at her and she could smell his stale breath.

"Allow me to introduce your rescuer," he told Hatsue. "Yamashita Rinsuke."

She looked at the prisoner suspended between the poles. The man there looked at her and nodded his head ever so slightly in acknowledgment of the introduction. The name meant nothing to her. The slight flutter of hope at the thought that someone was

trying to save her was almost immediately smothered by the reality
of the situation. In her fantasies, she expected armed men to storm
the camp and free her, all dark uniforms, gunmetal, and efficiency.
The prisoner before her looked dirty and unsteady. A man, alone
and unarmed and powerless. *He's no different than me*, she thought.
But she tried to disguise her feelings. When the old man with the
fan saw the lack of response on Hatsue's part, he prompted her.

"This is the man your family pinned its hopes on for a rescue."
He gestured contemptuously at the prisoner and smiled bitterly.
"This!" Hatsue could see that there were emotions roiling the old
man as he struggled to find words. Instead, he moved in and the
folded fan shot out in a blur. The tip drove into the solar plexus of
the captive and his body jerked against the bonds, spasming. Hatsue could see the prisoner struggling against the temporary paraly-
sis of the nerve endings as he fought for breath.

The hideous old man watched impassively for a moment.
When the prisoner finally sucked in a lungful of air, the old mon-
ster drove in again. The ropes jerked, the body contracted, and the
struggle began anew. The men around Hatsue watched, their eyes
bright and expectant.

It went on for some time. The old man worked his captive
mercilessly, with a measured, almost clinical approach. The nerve
strikes were delivered with a brutal precision, the end of the iron
war fan driving deep into soft tissue, grinding on pain receptors,
until the grunting captive danced in agony. He was bathed in
sweat.

So was the old man, Hatsue noted. There was a rage burning,
seeping out of his very pores. It did not seem to her that it could
go on as long as it did—certainly either the torturer or the victim
would be consumed in the process—but it was a measure of the
old man's terrible skill that the session stretched out for some time.
Finally, when the overload on the nerve endings acted to dull the

response of the victim and he sagged for longer and longer periods between attacks, the old man stopped. He gestured for the prisoner to be cut down, then wheeled on Hatsue. She shrank back, a jet of fear shooting through her.

"Care for him. As long as he lasts, you last."

The old man turned away. The guards prodded her toward her cell and dragged her new charge behind them.

18

COUNTDOWN

In my dream, Sarah Klein sat on the edge of the bed in the half-light. The sheet had fallen down around her waist to the soft swell of her hips. The shadows played along the muscles in her back. Sarah's dark hair fell down and hid her face, half turned away from me. I stretched out and reached for her, but her head came up in alarm at a noise off in the darkness, and she jerked just out of my reach. I stretched out again, but the bed was too wide, and the pounding sound that had alarmed her now made Sarah jerk farther and farther from my embrace.

Eventually, the banging on the door of my hotel room brought me back from that deep place, and I rolled off the bed, groggy and befuddled with yearning.

Micky pushed a room service cart into the room and Art closed the door. "Geez," my brother said. "Took you long enough." I looked at the two cops and grunted. They started pouring coffee into cups and took the stainless steel tops off various plates of food.

I splashed some water into my face from the bathroom sink and staggered back into the room. It was pretty standard surroundings and if you didn't look out the window, you could have been in almost any generic upscale hotel in the world. A big bed dominated the relatively small space. Directly across from it there was an armoire with a TV crouched inside. A compact writing desk with a straight chair was tucked on the far side of the armoire, almost as an afterthought. A padded easy chair sat in one corner, strategically placed for TV viewing, next to the chair, a floor lamp. Light washed in from the broad bank of windows at one end of the room: when I had gone to bed, I hadn't even drawn the blinds.

My brother and his partner sat on the end of the bed and watched me. Micky jerked a fork at one of the plates. "We're gonna roll soon. Better tank up."

I nodded in agreement but sank to the floor instead and started stretching. I had spent considerable time in the shower before falling asleep at dawn, trying to get clean and hoping that the heat of the water would take away some of the muscle soreness I had from the *eskrima* match. Fat chance.

Eventually, I got up and ate. There wasn't much conversation: this was a fueling exercise, not fine dining. Besides, nobody really wanted to talk about last night. But we knew we needed to.

"Ueda called to say they were workin' on some things," Micky finally said. His tone suggested he was discussing a particularly offensive activity. "When we get the call, we'll probably have to rocket outta here."

Art had been eating steadily. Then he grunted. "For what it's worth, and this may not come as a shock, I don't think that guy Marangan is playing with a full deck." He inspected the remains of his scrambled eggs carefully, and then used a piece of toast to scoop the dregs up and into his mouth. Art looked at me, waiting for a comment.

"I figure he's a man on a mission," I said. "They're always just a little bit off . . . "

"A little!" Micky snorted. "I'm used to usin' all sorts of skeeves as informants, but this guy should be kept on a real short leash."

I shrugged. "I got a whiff of it at his *eskrima* school."

"Yeah," Micky broke in, "I meant to ask you about that. What gives? You're all in a sweat to get here and track Yamashita down, but you take the time to dick around with Marangan's students."

"I've learned some things, Mick. One of them is that you shouldn't trust many people."

"A sad yet true thing," Art commented.

"The other is that you can tell a lot about people by fighting with them. They say the real masters can do it just by touching their sword to yours." Micky jerked his head and looked at me skeptically. "It's true," I told him.

"So what'd you learn?" my brother asked.

"Marangan's a pretty angry guy. He's skilled and so was the student I fought, but there was something really . . . I don't know . . . out-of-balance there." It was a difficult insight to verbalize. There was a spiky quality to the energy at Marangan's school: a stew of fury and pain and resentment simmered with something more complex that was still eluding me.

"Come on, Connor," Art said, "you don't think you're reading something into this as a result of the rest of the night?"

"No," I replied. "Remember when he grabbed that guy in the alley? I knew something bad was going to happen."

Micky sat on the edge of his seat, elbows on his knees and his head hanging down. "Man," he said, "the alley was just the warm-up."

"We don't have much choice but to use him," Art said. "Marangan seems to be pretty wired in and we need the info if we're ever going to find Yamashita."

No one said anything for a while. Micky got up and looked out the window, brushing the flimsy curtains aside to get a better view. "You know, this whole thing is weird . . . the rhythm of it."

"How so?" I asked.

"It moves in fits and starts," Art explained. They had obviously been hashing ideas over before they came to my room. "First, the girl is kidnapped and the ransom demand is made. Okay, so far so good. But then they ask for Yamashita to be the bagman. It slows things down for a few days."

"We're assuming that getting Yamashita is a big piece of this" I reminded him.

"Yeah, okay. But then they *do* get him, and what happens?" Art looked at Micky, then at me.

"Well, not much until we got here . . . " I started.

"Right!" he said in triumph. "We arrive and Mori gets taken out. Then we get to go crawling through the slime with Marangan all night trying to run leads down. It's like someone's playing this thing. On. Off. On. Off. Do you get it?"

"And," Micky picked up the thread, "what's with the snatch of Yamashita, anyway? I mean, why do they want him in the first place? If it's for ransom, we haven't heard a word. That's unusual."

"Maybe they wanted him for other reasons," I said.

"Like what?" Micky pressed.

I shrugged. "Someone like Yamashita's probably pissed off lots of people in his life . . . "

"Anyone in the Philippines?" Art asked. It was the obvious question.

"Not that I know of." But my statement wasn't very confident. There are large swaths of Yamashita's life that are closed to me. "The person who probably knew the most about him was Mori."

"Now, of course, he's not talking," Micky said.

"The guy was always a disappointment," Art agreed.

"That could be why Mori got killed in the first place," I suggested. "If someone in this country wanted to kidnap Yamashita, Mori might know enough to be able to figure out who it was. So he was a threat to be eliminated . . . "

My brother turned away from the window. "Okay, but why wait? Why take him out when they did?" None of us had a suggestion, so Micky continued. "So now who's the next most likely person to have some information on this for us?"

"Why," Art said smiling broadly, "Mori's right-hand man, Mr. Ueda, our jolly tour guide to midnight Manila."

I was beginning to follow their line of thought. "Sure! If he knows so much, why send for us in the first place?" I asked. "If he knew who the kidnappers were, he could have told the police and solved his problem."

Micky was walking slowly around the room, absently opening drawers and inspecting the furniture while he thought. He sat down on the bed and looked in the night table. There was a Bible in there. The Gideons, it seems, are everywhere. Then Micky got up, folded his arms across his chest, leaned against the wall, and smirked.

"I'll tell you why, because he *is* Mori's right-hand man. And last time we ran into Mori, he was . . . " He let the question trail off to encourage a response from me.

"He was cleaning up a mess in New York," I said, the answer slowly becoming clear in my mind. Mori had tracked down a killer, a Japanese national stalking martial arts masters across America. It was a sensational enough crime spree without the added revelation that the Japanese government had trained the murderer. So Mori had operated outside normal police channels, hoping to prevent a public embarrassment for the Japanese government. And that's the way it ultimately turned out.

"Follow along," my brother told us. "Mori's niece is kidnapped as a way to get Yamashita here. That's the whole point. Whoever's doing this knows that Mori can manipulate Yamashita into serving as the go-between for the ransom delivery. And Mori knows that they know, but figures he can use Yamashita, rescue the girl, and ultimately outmaneuver them . . . "

"The man was way too smart for his own good," Art said.

"Sure," Micky agreed. "But you know there's more . . . "

Art nodded. "I'm with you, Mick. Mori knew who was behind this and he did not want the Filipinos getting anywhere near it." Art looked at me. "Why do you think that is, Connor?" Art's eyes are a washed out blue-gray, and he seems easygoing most of the time. But now the eyes bore into me.

"Whoever's behind this is connected somehow to the Japanese," I concluded. "And they don't want anyone to know. They've got this thing about 'face' and all that. Plus, there's still bad blood between them and most of the countries they occupied in World War Two . . . . The Japanese know who's ultimately behind this," I concluded, "not the people who did the snatch or the shooting. They were just hired guns."

"It's why Marangan offed the triggerman last night," Art said. "And why Ueda let him. Once they got whatever information the shooter had, he wasn't really important—just a loose end."

"Revealing the identity of whoever's behind this is way too problematical for the Japanese," I continued. "They tried to solve this problem on their own, through Mori, and it went bad."

"So now the Filipinos are even more mad at them," Micky said.

"And it's not like there was lots of love lost between them before," Art added.

"Mori was getting kicked out of the country when we arrived," I said. "The Japanese were probably running out of assets except for Ueda and that lunatic Marangan. So I guess Mori figured he'd use us to help him out. We're American, for one thing."

"And we've done it before," Micky added with a dry laugh.

"There's probably more to it than that," Art said quietly. "I was watching Mori when you grilled him in the car, Connor. The guy was really concerned for Yamashita. And deep down, he knew he screwed up. Was he trying to manipulate us? Sure. But I think he was also genuinely scrambling for a way to bail out your teacher. Think about it. We're not seeing much evidence of Japanese governmental involvement, are we? Okay, we got some plane tickets and hotel rooms, but mostly all we see is Ueda. My bet is that Mori knew he had his ass in a crack and was running around like crazy trying to figure out a way to salvage the whole mess. And most of it was probably not done with the knowledge of the home office."

"So it was a rogue operation?" I asked.

Art lifted one shoulder and cocked his head toward it. "Probably started out legit in some ways. But guys in Mori's end of things always operate on the edge."

"Makes it easier to deny you knew what was happening in case things get screwed up," Micky said.

"Like now," I told them.

The phone came alive on the table by the bed. I noted just before I picked up the receiver that the phone had a red light that flashed when it rang. It was like a small, subtle warning signal. But by now, that was old news.

"Dr. Burke?" Ueda asked on the other end of the line.

There was a simultaneous knock on the door. Micky looked through the peephole and then opened up. Inspector Reyes moved his bulk into the room, his face grim and severe.

"I'll need to call back," I told Ueda, and hung up.

"Is that your friend from the Japanese Embassy?" Reyes asked. "I'm hoping to have a conversation with him sometime soon." Poor Ueda; it would not be a pleasant chat. The Inspector moved near the room service cart, silently inspecting the remains of breakfast. He walked to the window and peered out in much the same way Micky had.

"We have heard from the kidnappers," he said. "They claim to have your Mr. Yamashita and have announced their terms for his release."

I felt a surge of excitement. Reyes came back to the breakfast dishes. He carefully selected an unused cup and poured himself some coffee. He added cream and sugar, and then stirred the cup for a moment. He looked up.

"Your teacher is being held by a splinter group related to Abu Sayeff, Dr. Burke. They call themselves . . . well it hardly matters, does it? The Moslem insurgents in my country have a penchant for melodramatic names." Reyes sat down in the easy chair in the corner of the room and sipped carefully at his coffee.

"What do they want?" I asked. My throat felt raspy. "How much?"

Reyes grimaced. "I'm afraid it's more complicated than that."

"Come on, Reyes," Micky said. "Enough with the dramatics."

The Inspector sat forward and put the cup down. "They have demanded the release of a number of terrorism suspects who were recently captured in a raid in Mindanao. And that it must be accomplished within seventy-two hours."

"Shit," Art said under his breath.

"That's not likely to happen, is it?" I asked the policeman. He didn't have to answer. I knew as well as anyone in that room that governments rarely agree to the release of terrorists, and the prospect of the Filipino government caving in to ransom two Japanese nationals was not a good one.

"So what's the plan, Reyes?" my brother asked. "Play for time? I assume your people are negotiating."

The Inspector pursed his lips as if tasting something unpleasant. "We are trying to make contact. At this point, we are following up on leads to see whether there is any way we can determine the location of the hostages."

"Do you have an idea?" I said.

"The girl was taken in the mountains of Mindanao. The group claiming to have Yamashita is known to operate there as well. It has been a few days since he was taken. It's possible that he is now there with her. These groups like to operate from safe havens. My government has assets down there that are trying to locate them."

"That's it?" I asked. "You don't have any more than that?"

Reyes' eyes flashed briefly with anger, but he got it under control. "I wonder whether *you* have any information that you would like to share with me, Dr. Burke?"

I looked from Micky to Art. They were deadpan. "What do you mean?"

"I think you know very well what I mean. You," he gestured at the three of us, "come to this country uninvited and begin activities that can only be described as questionable, if not illegal."

"Come on, Reyes," my brother began.

"Interference with the conduct of a criminal investigation," the Inspector said.

"Reyes . . . " Art tried to break in, but the Inspector was working up a head of steam.

"Withholding of information," the Filipino continued. He seemed to swell with indignation. "Assault."

"Reyes . . . " Art tried again, without success.

"And I am still pursuing additional, more serious charges." He glared around the room at us, his thick face swelling with anger. He seemed like he was waiting for someone to respond. Micky did.

"Gimme a break, Reyes," he said. "If you wanted to burn us, we'd be in lockup by now. Or even if you didn't have enough on us for a real prosecution, you could pull a few strings and get us deported." The Inspector sat there, stone-faced.

"Know what I think, Mick?" Art said.

"What?"

"I think the Inspector here has a pretty good idea what we've been up to." Art eyed Reyes for a reaction as he spoke. "And, since he knows that someone like Ueda can probably cut some corners that he can't, I'll bet he let us run just to see what we could come up with."

"Sure," Micky nodded. "That's what I'd do. And when I figured we had something, I'd come in and get all angry and threaten us with all sorts of horrible things."

"The neck swelling thing was very impressive," Art commented.

Reyes leaned forward and tipped the coffee pot forward to fill his cup, but it was empty. He gave a little sigh and sat back, regarding us stonily.

"I see we understand each other," the Inspector said. "But please make no mistake. Your ability to come and go here is directly related to your usefulness in this investigation."

"So what do you want to know?" I asked him.

"Your friend Ueda and his associate, Marangan," Reyes spoke the name with distain, "must by this time have found some information as a result of their . . . activities. I need to know what it is."

"The only thing we got that's concrete is the feeling that the Japs are not telling us very much about what they know," Micky answered. "We're thinking that the real goal of the Abe kidnapping wasn't the ransom money, but to get Yamashita. Why Yamashita, we don't know."

"We don't quite get the link between the Japanese and this terrorist group," Art said. "Although it's got to be there. It all seems too well planned to just be coincidence. And we think the fact that Yamashita was taken and Mori killed means that there's way more to this than we understand."

Reyes grunted and reached into his jacket pocket. He unfolded a paper. "The link between the Moros and the Japanese is, I agree, unclear. But we, too, are increasingly convinced it is real." He set the paper down on the bed so we could see it. "This was delivered along with the ransom demand for Yamashita. It's a copy of what we believe to be an old woodblock print. And the small characters in the corner are Japanese, are they not?" He looked at me while I examined the sheet.

He was right. It looked like an old woodblock illustration. The black and white figure in it had a birdlike head and long nose. Dressed in a kimono, the creature held a sword in both hands. Wings jutted from his back.

"It's a *tengu*," I told Reyes. "A mountain goblin. From Japanese mythology."

"A myth?" Reyes asked. "What was the significance?"

I shrugged. "Mothers use them to scare children. You know, 'If you don't behave, the *tengu* will get you.' That kind of stuff."

"Is that all?"

"They figure sometimes in stories about the martial arts. *Tengu* were master swordsmen who sometimes could be coaxed into teaching aspiring warriors the secrets of their art."

Reyes picked up the picture and folded it away. "Just so. My intelligence people told me the same thing. Can you think of any reason why a group of Philippine terrorists would use such a symbol?"

I shook my head.

"Nor can we," the Inspector answered. "But it is significant that a similar picture was left at the site of a double homicide not too long ago. Two of your own embassy guards were beaten to death. Our informants tell us that this action has been attributed to an Islamic group as well."

I looked up sharply, remembering the images on the video that Baker had shown me. Reyes was watching me keenly, a large, seemingly sluggish man with bright eyes. "Does that mean anything to you, Dr. Burke?"

I swallowed. "I . . . know something about that incident but had no idea that they could be connected." I was still almost breathless trying to digest the implications.

Reyes levered himself up and out of the chair. He moved to the door, but before he left he looked at each of us. "I suggest that this is an extremely complex case, gentlemen. Our chances of solving it would be much greater if we could work together." He patted his pocket. "I'm taking this to the Japanese Embassy to see what I can learn. Who knows? Perhaps your Mr. Ueda can shed some light on things. If you think of anything, call immediately. The clock is ticking on your Mr. Yamashita."

As he turned to go, I stopped him. "Reyes." He turned his bulk in the doorway and looked back. "If the government doesn't release the prisoners, what will happen? To Yamashita?"

The Inspector looked at the carpet for a moment. Then he looked up at me. "They will behead your friend. I am sorry."

The door clicked closed.

19

KEIKO

When they had dragged him in that first day, Yamashita was groggy, and old looking. Hatsue thought that he looked like one of her older relatives: befuddled by the drag of time and gravity.

"Were you really sent to rescue me?" She had asked, barely holding back her hysteria.

Yamashita looked at her for a moment before answering. His head swiveled about slowly, taking in the surroundings and struggling to record them through the fog of the drugs. But his eyes slowly grew brighter as focus crept in.

"*Honto*," he told her. Truly. He was on the floor of the cell where the guards had dumped him. He gradually drew himself up and sat in the old traditional way, legs tucked under him. With an effort, he straightened his torso and faced her. His words came out thickly, slowed by whatever drug they had given him. "Your Uncle Mori and I . . . he was *oyabun* to me. You understand the word?"

She nodded. In Japan, close personal relations were typically structured as those between two parties of unequal status. The *oyabun* was the senior member and was expected to act with the care and authority of a parent. The *kobun* was the junior, who stood in the same relation as a child to that parent, with the same complex mix of emotions and obligations.

Yamashita took in a long, jagged breath. He rolled his head around, his thick neck stretching with the motions and the muscles under the skin straining with the action. He fixed his gaze upon Hatsue. "When he told me that you were kidnapped and asked for my help, I . . . came," he continued. A Westerner would have shrugged to indicate the complete and simple logic of the action. Yamashita merely sat there in the approaching darkness, his stillness an expression of certainty.

Hatsue felt a number of things: the sickening internal plunge of hopes dashed, bewilderment, and above all, anger. What had her family been thinking, to make this old man responsible for her release? She wanted to scream, to beat her fists against him in frustration. She looked at the man, sitting as rigidly as he could, yet unaware that he was in fact swaying and trembling slightly.

Hatsue swallowed her first impulsive words. She saw Yamashita peering about in the gloom and licking his lips. She got up and brought him the water jug they provided her with. He took it in both hands and bowed slightly, then drank for a while. She said nothing.

"Please excuse me," he said, wiping his mouth. His lips were wet from drinking. Hatsue wanted to laugh at the incongruous formality of such a statement. Instead, she drew once again from the strength of her ancestry and calmed herself, knowing that on the other side of that laughter lay madness. *Funny*, she thought to herself, *I have always scoffed at the old ways and now I find they are what keep me sane.*

The man gathered himself. "I am Yamashita Rinsuke, *sensei* of the Yamashita-ha Itto Ryu. I worked with your Uncle Mori in the Kunaicho. Do you know what that is?" Hatsue nodded silently. Her family spoke little of her Uncle Mori and his activities on behalf of the Imperial family. But they spoke enough for her to know what this entailed.

Yamashita sipped more slowly at the water. "I am not without experience in matters of this sort. Your uncle sought your safe return and a trusted assistant to help him. I came, but . . . " He bowed formally to her. "I have failed you and your family. This matter was more complex than I imagined." His head turned slowly to face toward the hut of their captor, as if he could see through the walls.

"That's it?" she blurted out in protest. "You've failed? That's all? There's got to be more," she insisted. "What's the next step? The backup plan." Her words lashed into Yamashita, her empathy smothered in frustration.

He closed his eyes and he swayed slightly. She could hear his breath being forced in and out in an odd, deep rhythm. He held up a hand. "I do not know. When I was taken . . . I was drugged. I cannot know for sure what your uncle is doing now."

Hatsue moved closer to him to follow-up, but a motion at the barred door caught her attention. The guards brought the evening meal, a slop of rice and vegetables in a pail, accompanied by an old bleach bottle filled with water. The guards opened the door, one man shoving the food in and another standing vigil with a Kalashnikov assault rifle. *The weapon is new*, she noted. *Perhaps there is more to this man than I thought.*

When they left, she offered Yamashita some food. "You should eat," she told him.

He shook his head. "*Ie*," No. "Water is what I need. The drugs are still with me . . . . " She gave him the new water jug and he sipped at it as they continued their conversation.

"I am sorry, Hatsue-san. The man who met me . . . the *Nihonjin*. Do you know him?"

She shook her head in confusion. The *Nihonjin*—the horrible old Japanese man. She tried not to think about him at all. It was a protective response to his energy.

"I know him," Yamashita told her. "When he first came down the steps of the hut, I thought that perhaps the drugs were making me dream . . . " He smiled tightly as he moved his shoulders.

Hatsue could tell that the motion pained him. "My body tells me that this is no dream."

Her voice almost failed her. She had lain awake in this dark cage for so long, trying to discern a reason for her kidnapping, to impose some rational pattern on events. "Who is he?" she croaked.

"He wields the *tessen*," Yamashita answered. "The iron war fan of the old lords. He, too, is a *sensei*." The Japanese word for teacher could refer to many things and Yamashita saw her perplexed look. "He is a master of the *bugei*," he explained.

"The martial arts?" she asked disbelievingly. Here in the mountains of Mindanao, fighting was done with assault rifles and high explosives. The old fighting systems of Japan had always seemed anachronisms to her; more so now. "What can this have to do . . . "

For the first time since bowing, Yamashita moved from his sitting posture. He reached out and laid a hand on her arm. "He is highly skilled in his art and men, certain men, seek his tutelage." He gazed off into a corner of the room, gripped in the power of personal memory. Once again, he straightened himself with a conscious effort. "I thought that he was diverted from his path but now I fear he trains others."

"Why?" she asked.

"Hatred has many reasons. Some we can understand. Others . . . " He closed his eyes briefly.

Hatsue sat near Yamashita, watching him. His breathing was deep and forced, his stomach expanding and contracting with effort. She knew that some martial artists stressed the role of *kokyu*, or breath, in training. She felt sure that Yamashita was engaged in such an exercise, probably related to throwing off the last effects of the drugs. She was confused. The *bugei*. Two *sensei* amidst an armed camp of Islamic insurgents. The old ways embedded in the jumble of a modern struggle.

"Why?" she asked again.

Yamashita spoke slowly, his eyes still closed, an oracle seeing shapes in the dark. "Hatred can warp the best of men. It creates an insatiable hunger. They struggle to master techniques that will feed this hunger. They seek . . . control . . . and dominance." His eyes flickered open and regarded Hatsue in the gloom. "They crave possession. To take from us the things that we value . . . "

"Why?" she whispered, almost afraid to hear the answer.

Yamashita took a deep, sighing breath. "It would take great wisdom to know that. We are left only to know what is the outcome. A person such as this . . . is incomplete. He has no *kokoro*."

She nodded in understanding. *Kokoro* meant heart, or essence. When she had first looked into the eyes of the old man with the war fan, they seemed to her to open onto a vast, dark, and empty space.

Yamashita saw the knowledge reflected in her face. He continued. "And his life is spent taking from others what he himself cannot have. He struggles to capture something that always eludes him. And so his actions become more savage as time goes on. He seeks now not only to possess, but to inflict pain in the process."

The *sensei* sat quietly for a time. He was still shaky, and the act of explanation seemed to drain him. Hatsue said nothing. Outside the cell, distant voices could be heard as the camp prepared for nightfall. The room they sat in grew dark. Around the camp, small fires glowed bright against the darkened tree line, their embers like the eyes of hungry animals. Finally, Yamashita stirred. Light played on the wet surface of his eyes.

"You ask why he brought you here," he told her. "He brought you here . . . to lure me closer." Yamashita sighed sadly. "You have suffered for this, and I am sorry. He has taken much from you. Your freedom and . . . more, I sense?"

Hatsue looked down in shame, the darkness hiding the tears

that slipped from her eyes. She felt his broad hand reach out and rest on her arm. It was rough feeling and hot to the touch. She flinched, but Yamashita did not break the contact. His hand stayed there while he spoke.

"He will work to take whatever we have, whatever we value." His voice was quiet, and oddly soothing, despite the despairing message. "Slowly, one by one, these things will be stripped from us. I see it now . . . "

"What do we do?" she pleaded in a rasping whisper.

"We must . . . surrender these things. Surely. We are in his control. But at each step, we retreat farther and farther back. Into the core that he cannot touch . . . the *kokoro*."

"I don't understand," she admitted tearfully.

For the first time, she heard an indulgent smile in his voice. "I have a student who tells me that often." Again, a sigh. "No matter, I will teach you."

"Teach me what?" Hatsue pleaded.

"Do you know *keiko*?" he asked, avoiding her question. "The word for training in the martial arts? It literally means to reflect on the ways of old." Yamashita felt her stir with impatience, and his hand pressed down on her even more firmly. "There is much there to learn. True lessons. Important lessons."

Then he sagged slightly, clearly exhausted. Hatsue made a space for him and Yamashita lay down. After a time, his breathing deepened even further. In the dark, Hatsue could hear the rustle of his clothing as Yamashita's body jerked spasmodically from the aftereffects of the drugs and the beating.

She lay down as well, eyes wide, listening to the night. Men's voices, faint and faraway, sounded from the camp. Insects whirred. From deep in the jungle, an animal howled—fury? fear?—it was difficult to tell. The sound made her shiver and she held herself tightly, no longer alone, but bereft of comfort.

20

PALADIN

If they were dogs, the hair on the back of their necks would have been standing up. As it was, I think I saw some fangs showing. Ueda and Reyes looked at each other, faces immobile and eyes threatening.

I got them together in an upscale restaurant on Roxas Boulevard that had a great view of the long line of Manila Bay. It came highly recommended by the hotel and I figured there'd be less chance of them throwing things at each other in a public place. We sat at a large round table, tucked away in the far corner of the room, away from the windows. The hotel concierge would have been disappointed in me. The table had a nice, crisply pressed linen tablecloth, and glassware sat, sparkling and ready for use. The cutlery was a standard setting and I was relieved there were no really pointy knives available.

I sat between the two men. Micky and Art watched carefully as I continued talking. I tried to project a calm I didn't really feel— time was slipping away. But I needed these two men to help me, so I smoothed out the tension in my voice.

"What's done is done," I told them. "What I want you both to focus on now is the best way to resolve this situation . . . . *Please.*"

"This is unbelievable," Reyes growled. The Inspector had learned a little more about Ueda's activities with Marangan. He welcomed the intelligence, but the idea that the man from the

Japanese Embassy had crossed some fairly clear legal lines continued to outrage him. Ueda sat stone-faced. In some ways I could sympathize with him: like any good samurai, he'd done his master's bidding. But he wasn't a samurai; he was a government official living in the twenty-first century. He knew what he'd done. Both men came from cultures where dignity was prized and an affront of public standing was intolerable. For Reyes, his sense of *hiya*, the Filipino equivalent of face, had been violated. And Ueda had done the violating. But he wasn't about to admit to anything: getting caught was humiliation enough.

I held up my hand to try to bottle up Reyes. "I'm not excusing it. It's just the way it is." A waiter saw the movement and began to move hopefully toward us. I shook my head, no.

"I will ensure that an official protest is made at the highest level," Reyes continued, but Art cut him off.

"Reyes, you've got to let it go for now," Art said. "It's not helping and the clock's ticking."

"Once we get Yamashita and the girl, you can sputter all you want," my brother added. He looked balefully at Ueda. The memory of last night still haunted Micky as well.

The cultural attaché looked back at my brother. "And what . . . inducement is there for me to cooperate, Detective?"

"Look," I said, breaking in, "we're here to get the victims back, right? Both of them, right?"

Ueda nodded slowly as if admitting a minor point. You could see him thinking. "That is a consideration, yes."

"The Abe family is not going to like losing their two million dollars," Art reminded him.

"Tokyo's got to want you to get the people responsible for killing Mori," I said. It was a carefully crafted statement. Ueda and Marangan had already found the man who pulled the trigger. That wasn't the essential point. "The real people behind all this," I added pointedly. The attaché looked at me carefully. His hands had been resting on the tabletop, palms down and fingers lightly touching. As I said this, one hand began to move slightly, as if Ueda were trying to sense the texture of the table beneath the cloth, to feel the subtle reality that was being masked.

My brother sat up a little straighter. "We want to get to the bottom of this, just like you do, Ueda," he said. The attaché remained silent, so Micky gestured at Reyes. "Am I right?" The Filipino nodded slightly, but didn't seem too encouraging.

"It's in all our best interests," Art said soothingly. "I'm sure that your people," he was looking at Ueda, "want whoever's behind this. So does the Philippine government. And we can probably all agree that it should be done with a minimum of fuss and publicity, right, Inspector? We get the kidnap victims back, we get the terrorists. There's no mention of . . . anything else," he paused for a minute, trying to figure out how to put it, then gave up. "The bottom line is that the Manila cops get the credit for busting this thing right open. Okay?" Reyes closed his eyes and acquiesced.

Ueda's eyes were focused on the table in front of him as he prepared to speak. He didn't look at any of us. For the Japanese, the most important things are often said when they're not looking directly at you. Ueda was a long way from the Old Country, but some cultural habits are deeply ingrained.

"In a hypothetical situation," he began, "if I were able to be of some service in this search, what could I expect . . . "

"In return?" I finished the question for him and went on. "Your chances are much better of finding whoever's behind this by working with the police than without them. Which would mean the mess that Mori made could possibly be cleaned up. Which could be very good for you."

"Of course," Micky said, "you could always decide not to cooperate. But that would be messy."

Ueda smiled tightly. "How so, Detective?"

"Probably make a big ugly splash if word got out that the Japanese government was running amok in Manila."

"Amok," Art commented happily, "I like it."

"And how would this happen?" Ueda inquired quietly.

"I'm sure someone would be willing to testify about your activities in return for immunity," Micky answered. "The government would be interested in something like that, right Reyes?"

The big man stirred slightly. "Undoubtedly," the Inspector brightened up, looking at Ueda like he wanted to kill him.

"And who would testify?" Ueda asked. "Marangan? He's hardly a creditable witness." You could see the calculations whirring behind his eyes.

Micky waved the suggestion away. "Him? Nah. I'm thinking about someone else."

"Us," I told Ueda. And I looked right at him while I continued, even though my words were directed at Reyes. "But that's not going to get Yamashita back, so here's the plan: We'll tell you what we know, Inspector, but the deal is that we get to come with you when you track these people down." The big Filipino opened his mouth as if about to protest, but I kept talking. "You get the information you need to solve the case. We get the kidnap victims back. And Ueda makes sure that his loose ends get tied up." This was the clincher for Ueda—he would want to be there to wipe out the Japanese connection: the Tengu.

"Deal?" Art prompted.

Reyes was shaking his head. "I don't know if I can go this far."

"Sure you can, Inspector," Micky told him. "Chalk it up to international cooperation in the war on terrorism. You'll be a freakin' hero."

"It's also the best way for you to keep tabs on us," I added to Reyes.

"We can be somewhat unruly," Art reminded him.

The Inspector looked at Ueda, who straightened up and bowed tightly. Reyes bowed slightly in return.

Nobody spoke for a moment or so. Then I licked my lips and asked Ueda quietly, "What can you tell us about the *Tengu?*"

It hadn't taken Ueda long to tell us what he knew. It changed everything. We had three hours before the plane left for Davao, the largest city on Mindanao. Reyes churned off to grease official wheels, and Ueda took us shopping.

My gut felt like it was filled with acid. The knowledge of what we faced had rocked me. I was a man surging into a maelstrom, in a tearing hurry to get going and yet dreading where he would end up.

The Australian, on the other hand, acted like we had all the time in the world.

"Going into the bush?" he asked us happily, nodding at the prospect. "Getcha everything you need, right here."

It was a big run-down building, hidden behind a marine repair shop in a part of the waterfront that tourists didn't see much of. Crates were stacked up haphazardly along the rutted drive that led up to the wide warehouse doors, and machine parts rusted silently in the scrubby grass. You could smell oil and dust and rotting things in the mud that ringed the bay. But the Australian didn't seem to mind. He was big and square, with a shaved head that glistened. He seemed pleased with the world in general and, once he had recognized Ueda, immensely glad to see us.

The attaché nodded at him. "Gentlemen, Mr. Tom Horowitz. He is an . . . outfitter."

Horowitz grinned tightly. "That's right. Tom Horowitz, Sydney branch of the Diaspora. Supplier of . . . " his mouth opened a bit wider in mirth, displaying teeth that were as square and wide as he was, " . . . well most anything you need, gents." He was wiping his hands with a rag, working the skin vigorously. He peered critically at the results for a minute, squinted into the sun, and finally looked at us, almost as if he'd forgotten we were there. He shook his head slightly. "Come on in outta the sun. Ramonito!" he called at the top of his lungs, and walked through the double doors into the gloom. We followed.

"We will need standard equipment for backcountry travel," Ueda began, handing him a list.

Horowitz nodded as he read. "Clothes, boots . . . "

"Gloves," Art added. I looked a question at him. "You go into the jungle, everything's got stickers, Connor."

Horowitz looked up at Ueda and wagged his eyebrows. "Topo maps for south Mindanao? We're off on an adventure, eh?" A small Filipino emerged from the back of the building. "Ramonito," the Australian said, "let's get these gents kitted out." He lumbered over to an old refrigerator, cracked it open and pulled out a bottle of San Miguel beer, and held it up. "Anyone?"

We shook our heads no. I looked at Ueda impatiently. "We are on a very tight schedule, Mr. Horowitz," he reminded him.

"Gotcha, mate," Horowitz answered. He screwed off the cap, tossed it into a corner, and gulped down half of the bottle in one, long pull. "I'll have to drink a little faster, won't I?" He winked at us.

"For Christ's sake, Ueda," I said, "we're wasting time with this joker." I started to move toward Horowitz, but he held up his hand, and he no longer looked as friendly. "Easy now, sonny," he told me. "No need to get your dick in a knot." He set the bottle down and, as he stretched out his arm, the short sleeve of his shirt rolled up and you could just see the tattoo: a winged dagger with a three-word motto: *Who Dares Wins.*

"Calm down, boys," Horowitz said to us all. "Give him your boot sizes and Ramonito'll get your kit worked up. And while he does that," he finished his beer and licked his lips in satisfaction, "we'll get the toys together." Horowitz looked at me and cackled. Then he beckoned and we went further into the warehouse.

"You think this guy knows what he's doin'?" Micky asked in a murmur.

Art nodded. "Probably. Did you see the tattoo? Special Air Service." But he didn't say it very loudly.

Ahead of us, Horowitz was talking on. "Don't need to know where you're going, Ueda, just what you'll be up against," he said over his shoulder.

"Small arms, perhaps some RPGs and light machineguns," Ueda answered him.

We got to a locked door and Horowitz fished a key out of his pants. He unlocked the door, heaved the heavy slab sideways, and threw on the lights. The room was perhaps twenty-five feet square, windowless, and the jumping light of ceiling fluorescents pulsed over tables piled high with armaments of every conceivable type.

Micky whistled.

"It's like Ali Baba's cave," Art said.

Horowitz stalked into the room and began handling weapons with a careful precision that spoke of experienced formality. He looked at us without expression for a moment, and then asked Ueda, "What type of weapons' competence do your people have?" The Aussie accent was still there, but the words had a clipped focus that had been absent from his earlier speech.

"Two are policemen," Ueda answered and Horowitz frowned at the news. "The other one has . . . more specialized skills."

"Really?" Horowitz replied with a smile that got wider. "Really." Then he began selecting various items from his stock. "You'll want side-arms. Certain. I've got some nice nine-millimeter Berettas. You mates familiar with nines?"

Micky nodded. "We use Glocks."

Horowitz nodded back. "Nice. Berettas do you, though?"

"Sure," Art told him.

Horowitz moved along a table. "Anyone see military service?"

"Marines," Micky told him.

"Army," Art added, "Tenth SFG."

"All right, mate," Horowitz smiled. "We can work with that. Let's go with the tried and true, eh? I can give you either the M-16 or the M-4. A variety of sight options . . . "

My brother and Art walked over and examined the rifles in question. Micky looked at his partner. "I'm thinking we go with the A-2 with the mounted grenade launcher . . . "

Art nodded in agreement. "More bang for the buck." He faced Horowitz. "It's been a while. How about a laser sight? I'd like to hit what I'm aiming at if it comes to that."

"Roger that, mate. I can set it up, no worries," he told Art. Then he turned my way. "What about him?"

"Keep it simple," Art suggested. "A standard M-4 will do fine. Firepower is not his thing."

Again the smile from Horowitz. "What is your style, mate?"

I shrugged, not in the mood for conversation or explanation. "You got any knives?"

It took perhaps twenty minutes to assemble the gear. Ramonito worked quietly from a list, packing gear into black duffel bags as Ueda looked on, occasionally glancing at his watch. Horowitz packed the weapons, humming happily to himself.

"If you're headin' south, ya don't want to come up short on ammunition," he told us.

"That," Art agreed in a judicious tone, "would be bad."

Horowitz's half grin disappeared and his eyes got that strange bright look again. "Bad? You don't know the half of it. You Yanks were here in the Philippines about a hundred years ago, fighting the Moros. The standard sidearm then was a .38. The Army adopted the .45 when they were down here. Know why? Ya could pump .38s into an attacking Moro all day and he just kept comin'. Not enough stopping power, ya see. They needed a bigger slug. And even then . . . " Horowitz paused while he stepped back into a memory, and it was obviously not a good one. Finally, he stirred, looked around him, and got back to packing. "I've added some extra magazines . . . " his comment trailed off. He was still in that unwanted past. Art looked at Micky and raised his eyebrows. My brother shrugged, but kept silent.

Horowitz's assistant Ramonito didn't have much to say. He had wet brown eyes and watched us slyly and smiled a bit, which told you nothing about what he was thinking; most Filipinos, with the exception of Reyes, smiled as a matter of habit. It was only as he finished tallying the supply items and zipped up the duffels that he grew momentarily somber.

"If you would load these bags, I'll settle up with Mr. Horowitz," Ueda said to us. We each grabbed something and headed for the door.

But Ramonito put a restraining hand on my arm. His voice was very soft, almost a whisper. "If you fight the Moros, you will need more than this," he said, nodding at the equipment. He pressed something into my palm. It was hard and cold. "Go with God," he said simply, then ghosted off into the shadows of the warehouse.

I came out into the brightness of the day, squinting a little, and looking at what I held in my hand. It was a small, copper colored medal of some sort with a small loop that could be used to attach a chain.

"What gives?" Micky asked. "St. Christopher's medal?"

I shook my head. The engraving on the medal was vaguely religious—a picture of a human figure carrying a cross in one hand and a spear in the other—but it was no saint that I was familiar with. A few words in Latin were engraved under the figure: *Deus noster refugium.*

"It's a charm," I told them, as its significance sunk in. "A talisman. The Filipinos call them *anting-anting*."

"For good luck?" Art asked hopefully.

"Sure. But in the old days, their warriors used to believe that wearing this amulet made you invulnerable."

"So this is a pre-.45 sort of thing," Micky responded sarcastically.

"What's the inscription?" Art asked.

"*Deus noster refugium*, God is our refuge and our strength," I translated.

"Well, Him and the M203 grenade launcher," my brother added.

I thought about the inscription for a minute and laughed. "It's probably more appropriate than you think, Mick. It's the opening line from Psalm 46, 'God is our refuge and our strength, a very present help in trouble.' Or something like that."

"Connor, my boy," Art told me, "for all your heathen ramblings you're still a good Catholic boy at heart."

"Yeah," my brother broke in, "but remind me to explain to you how to shoot a gun." It was a welcome bit of sarcasm. Micky hardly ever let anyone see that things were bothering him. Art, either. Today they both had grown quieter and tenser as things unfolded. It only added to my alarm. I was relieved by their banter.

"Oh, there's more," I told them, reluctant to let the moment go. What lay ahead was too frightening. "You guys'll like it. See if you recognize this . . . " I closed my eyes to see if I could remember the quote correctly and tried to use the appropriate accent: "He maketh wars to cease unto the ends of the earth. He breaketh the bow and snappeth the spear asunder . . . I will be exalted among the heathen, I will be exalted in the earth . . . '"

"Hey!" Micky exclaimed with a grin. "Color Sergeant Bourne!" He looked at Art, whose face had also lit up in recognition. "It's 'from *Zulu*!"

"I thought you'd get it," I said with satisfaction. In the course of a long career cooped up in cars together, Art and Micky have become inveterate movie freaks. They discuss directors and scenes and recycle old dialogue relentlessly. Now, in this strange place, came a reminder of something familiar, a link to a '60's era motion picture they knew and loved.

"Great flick," Art commented. He held up a questioning finger. "And introducing who in his first starring role?"

"Michael Caine," Micky answered with satisfaction. "And don't forget his co-star . . . "

"Stanley Baker," Art replied. "Ah. A fine actor. Unappreciated, really. Career cut short. Gone too soon . . . "

"He was also in *The Guns of Navarrone*," I added helpfully. But they both looked at me like they were offended that I had broken into their little game. The moment was gone.

"You gonna wear it, Connor?" Micky asked, gesturing at the *anting-anting*.

I shrugged. "I'm watching Horowitz load all that gear and I'm thinking I could use all the help possible." They said nothing in response to that, growing somber again. We loaded the SUV in silence and waited for Ueda. The day was clear and pleasant, the sun warm but not too warm. Aside from the smell of the water, it would have been nice to lean against the side of the vehicle, eyes closed, and pretend that all was right with the world. But time was short.

"I never really said . . . " I began, but faltered. I started again. "I never really thanked you both . . . for coming." I looked each of them in the eye. I hesitated to say more, struck by the awareness that what Ueda had told us earlier today made the whole enterprise vastly more complex, and potentially more lethal for all of us.

My brother squinted at me, hands on his hips. There's an old picture of my father in just that pose, standing in the desert outside of Las Vegas on some long-forgotten business trip. Children seek to create their own sound in the world, only to discover in part that they are echoes. "Buddy boy," Micky said to me, "since we were kids, you have been nothing but a pain in my ass." But there was a smile playing on his lips.

"Like you're any better, Mick," Art retorted. "Connor, I could tell you stories that would curl your hair . . . "

"Well, I just want you to know . . . " I began lamely, but then my voice petered out. It wasn't just that I was unsure of how to explain things; there was a funny tight sensation in the back of my throat.

Art smiled tightly. We were all trying to keep it light. "This is what we do, Connor. You, too, I suppose . . . "

"In your own, really weird way," Micky added.

Ueda emerged from the warehouse and Art opened the door to the SUV. The black duffels were stacked neatly in the back. He reached in and patted one. The armament inside gave a little dull clink in response.

"Have gun, will travel," he told me, and winked.

21

TARGET

"Run this by me again," Cooke said in exasperation. The new arrivals sat across the briefing table looking tense, their faces washed out in the fluorescent light of the briefing room, their expressions ludicrously serious. "I mean you have got to be kidding!" The noise of helicopters cycling up over the steel mesh landing pad robbed his tone of some of its intensity.

The alert had come in late that morning: a cryptic radio message to Aguilar from Brigade to suit up and prepare for a mission. Details were sketchy. *They always are*, Cooke thought—other than the team could go at any time, there were multiple hostages involved and it would be what was politely termed "a contested insertion." But someone had neglected to tell them where. Cooke looked at his Filipino counterpart and they both rolled their eyes and got to work. Aguilar and his troopers always had a go-pack ready for short-alerts like this. They drew ammunition, water, and rations, checked their rucksacks, and settled down for one of the truly difficult things in professional soldiering: the enervating experience of waiting.

Cooke watched the soldiers go about their duties. He noted that his people—*Aguilar's people*, he corrected himself—moved quickly, but didn't rush. There was a certain underlying excitement among the troops, but no real tension that he could see. As the day wore on, the soldiers talked quietly or slept, propped up against their rucksacks in the shade. Cooke grunted in satisfaction: they had become real soldiers. He wished that Barnes and Abruzessi could have seen this, but they had been redeployed to work with other teams.

Aguilar said that someone from Manila would be down to give them the briefing. Cooke snorted at that: *Manila.* He hoped that their intel was up-to-date; he'd been dropped into more empty places because of old intelligence than he cared to think about. What was worse than that was landing in a hot zone when you hadn't expected it. The insertion could play either way. Nobody down here had a high opinion of the counter-terrorist people in the capital. When the strings were being pulled in Manila, the operational end of things was always made more perilous. They weren't in real good touch with things on the ground down here. The old joke was that you needed a passport to travel from Manila to Mindanao—they were in the same country but a world apart.

That was bad, but Cooke also sweated the local angle. Operational security was always a problem. It was hard for the locals not to get a fix on what was going on at the base. Like their American allies, the Filipino military had outsourced many of the non-combat functions to contractors. The place was alive with civilians —truck drivers, cooks, maintenance people—and it leaked like a sieve. Cooke hated to bring it up to Aguilar—the Filipino officer took it personally—but it was a fact.

On top of all these concerns, when the briefing party arrived from Manila, they had turned out to be a grab-bag group of comedians spinning him a story that was so convoluted he could barely believe it. But their identities had been verified, and the information they brought tallied up just enough with what he knew already to make it all seem possible. Just barely.

He sighed, tapped the topographical map spread out in front of them, and compared the GPS notations on the satellite imagery they'd brought with them. "This stuff is how old?" he asked the Filipino.

"Two days," the Inspector told Cooke. Reyes looked to him like someone who once had known his stuff but had grown thick and slow behind a desk somewhere and now resented having his considerable girth yanked out from behind it. He might have been one of those people who was generally pissed at the world. One thing was for sure, however: he was really pissed now.

"What makes you think this is where the hostages are being held," Cooke pressed. "We've been humping a ruck all over these hills for months. There's more of these little camps than you can count. You scrub one and two more pop up within days." He looked skeptically at the cop from Manila.

"We know the general location where the woman—the first victim—was taken," Reyes explained, "here in Mindanao. We," his eyes flickered at the guy from the Jap consulate, and Cooke noted the tension between the two men, even as the Inspector continued. "We have traced the links between the ransom go-betweens in Manila and the terrorists holding them."

"How'd you manage that?" Cooke asked. He didn't think much of the Philippine cops. He'd seen too much corruption down here. Then again, he hadn't thought much of Aguilar and his men when he first started to work with them. Maybe Reyes had something.

The cop from up north drew his chin back into his neck and took a deep breath through his nose. He seemed like he either didn't want to explain or he couldn't.

The Jap leaned toward Cooke. "We were able to utilize some . . . assets I had in place, Sergeant," he said smoothly. "The details are not as important as the fact that we've established a chain of association that provides actionable intelligence for you. I believe that the Lieutenant's brigade commanders have confirmed this for you? And you have been asked to cooperate, yes?"

Cooke didn't much care for the Jap. He was a little too smooth and a little too sure of his standing. Cooke had seen guys like this fly in from various places at different duty stations, all laptop computers and models and certainty. They were all too smug for Cooke's taste. *No one's dropping you into a hot LZ any time soon, I'll bet.* But he looked at the Jap impassively; he was an old hand at hiding his feelings.

Cooke shook his head and continued. "Not enough. How'd you come up with this particular location? There are scores of these camps. Probably five more within a fifty klick radius."

Again, Cooke noted the hostile glances that darted between Reyes and the Jap. *These guys are working together, but clearly not by choice.* He sat up a little straighter, squared his wide shoulders, and looked around. The guys from the States were not saying much. Cooke shook his head and eyed Aguilar, who was sitting with him. "I wouldn't authorize anything until I get a better explanation. Your men are too valuable to waste on some wild goose chase, Lieutenant."

The Philippine lieutenant nodded. He looked at Reyes for an explanation. The Inspector was still glaring at the Jap.

Two of them were cops: Art Pedersen and Micky Burke. But it was the other Burke named Connor who spoke.

"Tell him, Ueda," the American said.

The Jap named Ueda lifted his eyebrows a little and smirked. "When the original ransom drop was arranged, we were . . . " He paused and looked at the Americans. Cooke thought he saw a shadow of something—guilt? —flit across his eyes.

Ueda paused, then began anew. "The ransom bag was fitted with a small GPS unit and transmitter. Since there might be a possibility that the money could be separated from the person carrying it, we surgically implanted a similar device under his skin. The device is the size of a grain of rice. It is highly unlikely that it would be discovered."

The smaller American cop with the white patch in his hair commented acidly, "Figures. Now I know how you ran down that guy so quick."

Ueda looked at him without expression.

"What happened?" Cooke's voice was flat, his expression stolid. He didn't have an emotional investment in the question: he was just looking for information.

"The transmitter has a limited range—perhaps twenty kilometers," Ueda explained. "The . . . " he paused and looked at Inspector Reyes, "complications at the ransom delivery permitted them to abduct our representative. By the time we were able to begin tracking, he was out of range."

"So?" Cooke was not letting up.

The Inspector leaned forward and interjected with some acid in his voice, "With our recent discoveries—provided almost too late by our friends at the Japanese consulate, I may add—we were able to request a low-level flight over suspected areas in this vicinity. As a result, we now have a fix on their location." He nodded at Aguilar in reassurance.

"Look," Connor Burke broke in, "the important thing is that we're running against a seventy-two hour deadline, and we're already . . . " he looked at his watch, but one of the cops—he had the same last name and they looked like they were related—beat him to it.

"We've already burned twenty hours, Connor," the cop said.

The man named Connor nodded and looked at Cooke. "We've got about two days to get the hostages back. So can we save the explanations for later?" There was strident urgency in his voice. Too much emotion for Cooke's liking. Personal involvement was not an asset in his line of work.

The big sergeant looked at the map again. He pursed his lips.

"This is cutting it close." He looked at Aguilar, who nodded in agreement. Cooke turned to Inspector Reyes. "Are we sure they're not moving them around?"

Ueda started to answer, but Reyes overrode him. "Our best information suggests that they are remaining in this location. They consider it very secure."

Cooke examined the map closely. "This is Indian Country, all right. Other side of Mount Apo, here." His big index finger touched a site. The fingernail was discolored by a recent injury. "Twenty-eight hundred klick peaks. A few logging roads for access, but this is roller-coaster land. You're gonna slog up one ridge only to slog down another. Then start all over." He scrutinized contours on the map and details from the satellite imagery. "The site they've got is hard up along the coastline. Narrow band of rocks and beach with the mountains jumping right up. Makes it hard to take from the water." He traced a road. "Even here, you've got maybe ten klicks . . ."

"What's a click?" the one named Connor asked.

"Kilometer," the bigger American cop, Art, told him quietly.

"Ten klicks of mountain to negotiate," Cooke continued. "It means we should be at this point no later than noon tomorrow if we want to reach the camp by dawn the next day."

"That's cutting it too close," Connor exclaimed. "Can't we just use the helicopters?"

Cooke looked up at him. "You ever do this kind of thing before, Mister?" His eyes were hard. "Ever rappel down ninety feet of rope from a swaying chopper carrying eighty pounds of gear, hopin' no one shoots your balls off before you get to the ground? Huh?" The American looked down and Cooke continued. "I didn't think so."

"They'll hear us coming, Connor," Art explained. He saw Cooke's expression and answered the unspoken question. "I've done this before, Sergeant."

The Special Forces trooper wasn't mollified. He looked around at the group. "Then you should know better. We gotta get a few things straight, gentlemen. You need help and we can give it. But it's going to have to be on our terms. Because we're the best chance you've got of salvaging even a piece of what is one of the most truly fucked up situations I have ever encountered."

"Okay, Cooke, we're clear," the smaller cop said, simultaneously laying a restraining hand on Connor's arm.

The soldier pushed himself up and jerked his head to Aguilar, who followed him from the briefing table. The two men conferred in a corner of the room. Then Aguilar left, calling to a corporal, while Cooke approached the table once more.

"Okay. First things first. We'll insert tomorrow morning at this point along this logging road." The men at the table stood to get a better view of the details on the map. "We move inland toward the site. With any luck, we'll be in place before nightfall. Optimum time for a strike is around three a.m. Backup plan is for dawn. Either way, we're in for some hard soldiering. We can probably get you people to a forward ops base at the insertion point to monitor . . . "

"Sergeant Cooke," Ueda interrupted. The soldier looked right at him. "The security issues are such that we are authorized to accompany you."

"Bullshit!"

Ueda smiled. "Perhaps so. But this is essentially a Filipino operation and the arrangements have been approved. Perhaps you should check with the Lieutenant . . . "

Cooke stomped off and returned some twenty minutes later. He seemed bigger and blacker and more intense than he had before. He shot them all a look of pure disgust. "You people are baggage. Understand? You fall off or fall behind, I'm not stopping to come back for you." He glared around the table. "You got weapons?"

They nodded. It hardly seemed to mollify him. "Any experience with air assault tactics?"

Ueda nodded.

"Where?" Cooke demanded.

"Hostage Rescue Training at Quantico. Two years ago."

Cooke looked around for new victims. "How about you," he asked the big American named Art, who nodded. "How long ago?"

Art looked sheepish. "Too long," he admitted.

"Too long—what's that mean?" Cooke snapped. "You're workin' on stuff twenty years old if it's a day. And you?" he said, turning on Connor.

"None."

Cooke got right up into Connor's face. "None? What makes you so all-fire eager to do this then? You special? Or just stupid."

Cooke was hot and he had long experience in using the force of his personality to dominate soldiers. But this man didn't back down. He didn't even blink. Cooke noted it dispassionately even as he tried to cow the man. Once again he got a curious sense of something invisible pushing against him from the American. It was a subtle force, yet it made him pause.

The younger American named Connor looked at him with a hard expression, a brief flare of intensity. Then it subsided and he shrugged. "They have my teacher," he said. "I'm going to get him back." And the bleak simplicity of the assertion, combined with Cooke's vague sense of a deep and odd power, made him back off.

The day was spent with Cooke in tense discussion with Aguilar and his sergeants. The troopers were told to stand down until dawn. A normal camp pattern reasserted itself. Eventually, the Filipino Special Forces team gathered in the mess hall for supper. The visitors from Manila sat at a separate table, all but ignored, to talk among themselves.

"Lotta chopper activity," Connor said. Periodically, the building was rocked by the rotor wash and intense noise of military helicopters. He was watching through a screened door at the latest takeoff. The landing lights on the helicopters were beginning to glow more brightly as evening approached. "But I don't get it. They're empty."

Art came up behind him. "I overheard Cooke and the Filipino lieutenant talking. They're worried about security. Probably didn't help that we arrived here with a police escort."

"Reyes was taking no chances, I guess."

"Maybe, but now they're worried that maybe someone's watching. So they're probably spinning up a lot of activity and sending decoy helicopters all over the place in the hopes of distracting anyone who's watching." Art looked across the camp to the fenced-in perimeter and the wall of mountain and jungle that leapt up right outside the camp. He shrugged. "Better than nothing."

They turned at the sound of raised voices. A sergeant was rousting the troops. They left their meals at the table and quickly filed out of the room.

"Hey, c'mon," Micky said, jerking his thumb at the departing soldiers. "Looks like we're on the move."

Cooke was going over radio frequencies and map coordinates for one last time with the team leaders. He looked up as the Americans approached. They were clearly confused.

Cooke smiled. "Saddle up, gentlemen. We're airborne in fifteen minutes."

"I thought the insertion was for tomorrow morning," Connor said.

"Maybe it is," Cooke replied. "Maybe it isn't. Lots of eyes watchin' this place. Lots of locals workin' here. You people come blowin' into town with some government escort. You think that's not noticed? So I scrambled some aircraft to keep 'em guessing, and stood the troopers down in case someone's got ears inside the camp, if you follow. They see the mess hall gear up and figure we're buttoned down for the night." He winked. "Gives us maybe a little edge. I'll take all we can get."

"The samurai say that the difference between living and dying is often a matter of inches," the younger American said.

Cooke eyed him suspiciously and thought, *I gotta take a philosopher into a free fire zone!* But he said nothing in reply, just used both hands in a scooping motion to encourage them to get their gear. "You have ten minutes, gentlemen. Collect your gear. I'll send someone for you when the Blackhawks are ready."

Four Blackhawk helicopters swept down out of the darkening sky. One peeled off from the group, maintaining a security station some five hundred meters away. The remaining craft plunged down toward the ground, flaring up slightly at the last moment to soften the landing. Their strobe lights pulsed insistently, as if encouraging haste. The noise was tremendous. Men fought through the wash of the propellers, lumbering across the landing pad, heavy with gear. Non-coms shouted as the troops formed up in small clusters near individual choppers. Aguilar and Cooke stood at a distance, heads moving quickly from point to point, noting progress. At a nod from the lieutenant, a soldier led the visitors from Manila out to the landing zone. They staggered a little, lugging unfamiliar gear and reacting to the force of the helicopters as the first two pushed off, loaded with troops.

Cooke beckoned impatiently at the visitors, leading them to the third chopper. He was bellowing, but even so they could barely make it out. "Gear first! Make sure those weapons are secured and safeties are on!" They made their awkward way to the Blackhawk's side. A crewman gave them a hand and they slowly loaded.

Above them, the two other troopships rose to a hover and waited, in formation at a station just off-center from the landing zone, for the third craft to join them. It was dark on the ground, though the pilots in the airborne craft could see a narrowing line of light along the hills on the western horizon. Cooke was urging the visitors into the last Blackhawk, focused on the urgency of the task, when something on the periphery of his vision caught his eye.

He saw the streak of light as it arched out from the dark perimeter of the camp. Cooke's body reacted before his conscious mind did, and he yanked one of the Americans back out of the doorway, shouting at the top of his lungs at the pilot, and craning his head up to check the sky above them.

The rocket shot across the night sky. A second trailed it by less than fifty meters. *Two of them*, he thought pointlessly. *There are two people firing.*

The first rocket engulfed the troopship in a blaze of orange. The second pilot, who had perhaps seen the incoming ordinance, jerked his craft out of hover, seeking altitude and distance. The security gunship vectored in to the source of the rockets, firing into the bush. But the second rocket had already locked on. It blew off the tail section of the second helicopter, and trailing smoke, the aircraft began to cycle violently, spiraling away for a time as the pilots struggled for a semblance of control. But the spin was too much, the various hydraulic systems failing almost simultaneously. The cockpit was flashing with warnings and failure alarms, the pilots felt the shoulder harnesses tighten against them as they struggled against the G forces being exerted in the spin. The second chopper slammed into the ground with a huge, rending crash of metal, its giant main rotor beating itself into lethal pieces against the ground.

Cooke was still screaming, dragging people out of the last chopper. He hunched his shoulders against the burning debris that was raining down on the landing area. Somewhere, a siren had started up and the crash vehicles were starting to arrive. Aguilar had already bolted for the crash sites, ashen faced.

The first Blackhawk burned, thick oily smoke disappearing into the night sky, its presence marked only by the heat and the smell. It was mostly the scent of fuel and oil, but underlying it was the stench of bodies burning. Cooke had smelled this before; it was something you never forgot. Soldiers were setting down foam to suppress the blaze, but he held no delusions about the outcome.

Men were running toward the other crashed helicopter. Here, there was little fire. But Cooke had seen it go down. He knew what a landing like that did. The pilots were strapped in. Their seats had springs in the base to mitigate the crushing impact that a crash had on the human skeletal system. Even so, Cooke doubted they would walk away from this one. For the troops riding in back, he knew that the results would be catastrophic.

"My God," the Inspector from Manila breathed. They were grouped around Cooke, frozen into immobility.

Cooke flagged down a humvee heading for the crash. He jumped into the back. "Get back to the briefing room! All of you." He sped away, toward the disaster.

In the darkness, the men looked at each other, silent amid the carnage.

22

FINAL THINGS

She didn't know how much more Yamashita could take. The beatings were systematic and prolonged. It was as if it were part of some bizarre training regimen at the camp. Each day, the guards would drag the *sensei* out and string him up between the posts on the practice field. Then the old man with the fan would emerge from the hut, his retinue of Arabs around him, alert to his every command, tense and yet eager. They were like children trying to please a stern parent. The others—the Filipinos who guarded the camp and lugged supplies in and out—would sometimes watch from a distance. Hatsue watched as well, wincing, her stomach muscles jolting tight in empathy, as Yamashita was beaten.

The old man would lecture his students, gesturing in a pantomime of technique, then indicate points on Yamashita's body to be struck. He touched his victim lightly with his fan, cruelly teasing his victim with the knowledge of where the next strike would land. Hatsue watched how the old man moved around Yamashita, the set of his body, and the slight hint of tension in his movements. And after a time it struck her, *the old one is afraid of Yamashita.*

This gave the beatings a deeper savagery, a greater significance. The attacks were painful to see, but she set herself to it. *If Yamashita can endure it, I can watch it,* she thought, her witness a silent act of solidarity.

After each session the guards dragged the *sensei* back to the cell.

They smiled cruelly at her as they dumped him to the ground. Hatsue hadn't been molested in any way since she came to the camp, yet the feral set of the guards' teeth made her shiver. She tried to hide the reaction, hoping that the small acts of solicitude for Yamashita would prove a shield from fear and a ritual of protection.

As the beatings wore on over the course of days, it took longer and longer for Yamashita to recover. Invariably, he would drop to the floor of the cell, and curl up as if he were still trying to protect his stomach. Often, she could barely tell whether he were fully conscious. His eyelids almost closed, the whites moist, his mind gone a long distance into some other reality. She wondered sometimes whether he would ever return and felt a faint surge of panic at the idea of being once more alone with these men. She had come to rely on Yamashita's presence.

But he always did return, eventually pulling in a ragged breath that seemed to draw him upright. More than not, Hatsue felt herself draw in her own breath in emulation and relief. She would gently sponge his face as he sat, quietly exploring the new damage the beatings had done. Occasionally, Yamashita would grunt or hiss as his thick fingers probed his torso, but that was the only overt sign he gave of suffering once he sat up.

"How can you stand it?" she asked in a whisper after the latest session.

The *sensei* probed thoughtfully around his mouth with his tongue. He silently took the jug of water she held to his mouth, rinsed it and spit carefully in the corner: a bloody wash of thick saliva. This latest beating had closed his left eye. The skin on one side of his face was bruised and shiny. His lips had been cut early on—whether from blows or biting them to keep silent, she couldn't tell—and it was growing more difficult for him to speak.

Yamashita cocked his head to bring his good eye to bear on her. "Unhh," he said, then cleared his throat to continue. "It is a skill of long development." He looked down at his hands. When he had first arrived, they were strong and capable looking. Now they were merely swollen things on the ends of arms that rested heavily in his lap, capable of only limited movement. "When I was young, I thought my time in the *dojo* was used to develop skill with weapons. Now I see that it was merely prelude . . . to this."

"To what?" she prodded.

He tried to smile, but it was obvious that the movement of his lips pained him. "You have heard the phrase, *gambatte?*"

"Hold out?" she said.

Yamashita nodded, a slight motion that was part of the economy of pain. "So. It was what our teachers would tell us—*gambatte* —when training grew difficult. Perhaps . . . " he closed has eyes and leaned forward slightly. Hatsue could see the skin tighten at his temples as the force of the pain gripped him. After a time, he let out a faint "soooooo," then continued. "Perhaps it was not an exhortation after all, but the true goal of our training. To endure."

"But why?"

He ignored the question for a moment, his attention drawn to something else. "Listen," Yamashita told her. "Something is happening."

The *sensei* was one of the most observant people she had ever met. It was a judgment made by someone schooled in watching. Hatsue marveled at the acute level of Yamashita's sensitivity, even now. She got up and peered out the window. The structure was made of stone and old timber, and her captors had placed ill-fitting shutters across the windows in place of bars. The gaps were wide enough to see through if you craned your head just right. The light was fading and objects in the distance seemed lightly veiled in a thickening blue mist, but she could still see well enough.

"There's something happening by the communications hut," she told Yamashita. Hatsue watched the men cluster around the building, heard the excited sound of their voices, and saw their congratulatory gestures. One of the Arabs ran to the old man's hut to share whatever news had set the camp abuzz.

Soon there was more activity—an armed group formed, were given instructions, and then set off down the mountain path, flashlights bobbing through the trees until they were swallowed up by foliage and darkness. Others still in camp began to pack supplies.

"What is happening?" the *sensei* hissed.

"They have sent a group of armed men down the trail," she told him. "They seem very excited."

"Do they seem frightened?"

She glanced back at his hunched form. "No," she told him, then thought for a minute, "they seem . . . excited."

"Which trail did they take?"

The camp was sited on a small clearing just shy of the top of the hill—the military crest, Yamashita had told her. They could smell the sea not too far away, and there was an infrequently used trail that led in that direction; occasionally supplies would come in along this path. But most activity was oriented toward the trail that twisted down slope into the jungle trail that led to the highway where she had been delivered what seemed like a lifetime ago.

"The jungle trail," she told him. "Is that important?"

Yamashita ignored the question. "How many men?"

"Perhaps twenty."

"Have you ever noticed that many men leaving at one time before?"

"No," she said.

"But they appeared excited? Not anxious? Were they in a rush?"

Hatsue dreaded the direction his questions were leading. "No," she answered flatly. "No rush. They seemed . . . eager."

"Eager," he sighed. "And the old one?" They both knew to whom he was referring.

"An Arab went to his hut. But he hasn't come out." As she said it, she caught movement on the veranda of the old man's hut. He emerged from the shadows like a ghost. He stepped into the dim light cast by the kerosene lantern that flickered just inside a window. The light played on his face, making his eyes seem like sightless blobs that moved restlessly in place, dark, liquid organisms restless for escape. The old one turned to face in their direction and Hatsue jerked back away from the gap in the window.

"He is . . . there," she said, and swallowed. "Watching."

Again, Hatsue heard the hiss of air escaping from Yamashita. He sagged, then straightened once more. "Perhaps we can talk of other things," he said quietly. "A lesson in . . . distraction."

"I don't want lessons!" Hatsue pleaded, her voice tightening with tears. She could feel the cold force of the old man's gaze on them, as if he could sense their thoughts. It unnerved her. "I want help! To escape! Don't you understand?"

Yamashita reached out and tried to hold her small hands between his. They were like paws, clumsy with only the skin's warmth to make them feel alive. "I understand," he said soothingly. "But that is not possible now. I have failed. All I can offer is another lesson. It is perhaps the only one worth learning."

He said nothing for a long time. He listened to her weep and felt her body jerk with sobs. After a time, they subsided.

"Come, child," he whispered in the blackness. His voice was sad, yet calm. "I will teach you to die well. It is the only gift I have left."

23

MA-AI

The pills left a funny taste in my mouth and made me feel as if my eyes were stretched way too wide. Micky said they had called them "go pills" years ago when he was in the Marines.

"They're amphetamines," I protested. "They can't be good for you."

The dashboard threw a dim light into the interior of the jeep and I could just make out his sardonic expression. "Connor. You moron. We're heading toward a camp of armed terrorists and kidnappers. A little chemical enhancement is going to be the least of your problems." So I had gulped them down dry and now I sat, restless and wired, as we bounced through the night.

In the aftermath of the chopper attacks, Ueda had made us drag our gear back into the ready room. People were rushing around like mad and nobody was paying any attention to us. Cooke was off caring for what was left of the strike force and Reyes was in another room, phoning in to his superiors. He had looked green as he prepared to report on another debacle in this case. Only Ueda seemed untouched by the chaos at the camp, and strangely unworried.

The cultural attaché glanced at his watch and looked at us significantly.

"We're screwed, right?" Micky said to him. "No way to get another raid mounted in time." He sounded pretty sure.

"Maybe they can get another team assembled . . . " I started to protest hopefully, but Art put a big hand on my arm to stop me from saying any more stupid things.

"It's not gonna happen, Connor," he told me quietly. A truck raced by outside, its motor screaming through the gears. "They're gonna button-down and try to figure out why they got hit and how they got so vulnerable. Even if they had another team they could put on alert, the powers that be probably wouldn't want to put them in harm's way until they figured out whether there was a security breach down here."

I sagged down onto a bench, knowing that he was right. I looked around me in the harsh light of the briefing room, as if the battered table and maps were going to provide me with an answer. Ueda was examining the planning map that Cooke had pinned to a board when he briefed the troops earlier for the raid. He traced the route from our current location at the camp to the insertion point.

"How far?" Micky asked him. His voice was tired and not very hopeful sounding.

Ueda shrugged. "One hundred kilometers or so by air. On the road, perhaps twice that."

"How good are the local roads?" Art said quietly.

"A mix. Some highway. Then dirt tracks. The insertion point was along an old logging route . . . "

"Driving would average, what," my brother said, thinking out loud, "thirty kilometers an hour?" Ueda nodded in agreement.

"Be tight, but we could make it," Art concluded. "If we decided that was the only option . . . " He looked at me.

I stood up and approached the map board. Ueda moved aside and watched me. I traced the route with a finger. "If we drive all night, we could be at the planned insertion point by morning," I told them. "That would give us the day to hike in to the vicinity of the camp."

"It's a long shot," Micky agreed, "but it's probably the only option we've got left."

Art was thinking as well. "We got our gear. We know the GPS coordinates of the camp, right?" Ueda nodded. "Only thing I can think of is that it would be nice to have a local to make sure we take the right roads. And maybe another vehicle as a backup."

Ueda smiled and took out a small satellite phone.

"You dog," Art said. "Why didn't you let Reyes know you had one?"

Ueda punched in a number and held the phone to his ear. While he waited for a connection, he told us, "I do not always tell Inspector Reyes everything. It preserves . . . options."

Ueda had a hurried, low conversation on the phone. He kept one eye on the door in case Reyes returned. Ueda finished talking, listened for a minute, and grunted. Then he cut the connection. "Take the map," he told me, getting Micky and Art's attention and nodding toward the door with his chin. "Hurry," he hissed.

We tossed our gear into the mud-spattered jeep that had brought us to the camp and then piled in. The place was still in some confusion, lights flashing and people running all over creation. The fact that we had arrived earlier at the camp with a police escort let Ueda fabricate some plausible explanation for the guard at the gate to let us leave. Once we were a decent interval from the camp entrance, Ueda floored it. The jeep was cramped and Art and I would have bounced around inside the back of it, but with all the gear we were wedged in pretty tight. The headlights flashed along a wall of green as we sped down the road. Moths flickered brightly in our high beams, and the occasional insect splattered against the windshield. Ueda was at the wheel and Micky was next to him with the map in his lap, using a small flashlight to read it.

"We head west along the coast road, then pick up this northern artery after about forty klicks," my brother said. The jeep lurched slightly as Ueda downshifted and then gunned us up a slope. "Hang a right when you get to the main intersection."

Art was looking out the back window to see whether anyone was following. "So far, so good," he commented.

"It will only be a matter of time before they realize we're gone," Ueda said. "The Inspector will not be pleased." He didn't sound particularly upset about it.

"What're the chances they'll send someone after us?" I asked.

"I believe that nothing will happen until morning," Ueda answered me. "I told the guard at the gate we were heading into the city. Perhaps that may throw them off a bit. By the time they realize we went the other way, if all goes well, we'll be too far ahead of them to be stopped." Ueda barely touched the brakes as we sailed onto the coast highway. He shot a quick look to his left to check for oncoming traffic, and then swung us onto the road. The force of the turn pulled us up against the left hand side of the vehicle. Crammed against the duffels, I could feel the hard edges of weaponry. When the jeep had steadied and our speed had inched up to about seventy, Ueda glanced over at Micky.

"There will be a small town indicated at a point just beyond where we pick up the northern route," he said.

My brother peered at the map, moving the flashlight around its surface. "I got it," he said.

"We pick up the second vehicle there," Ueda said.

Micky shot a glance sideways, but said nothing. Art leaned forward. "How'd you pull that off?"

"Marangan," I guessed out loud. I saw Ueda smile tightly and knew I was right. The old *eskrima* expert had dropped out of sight once Reyes was back in the picture.

"The *batikan* has many useful contacts among various factions here in Mindanao," Ueda explained. "When I knew we were, indeed, to travel here, I took the precaution of sending him down ahead of us . . . "

"You're a piece of work, Ueda," Micky said. "He's been shadowing us all the time we've been here?"

Ueda leaned back into a more comfortable driving position. The road was well maintained and the tires hummed in the darkness, their sound made rhythmic by the regular *thunk* as they hit the seams on the highway's surface. He checked the rearview mirror and seemed to relax.

"In my line of work, I have found it useful to always have a variety of plans and assets to fall back on. And I was not always sure that the Inspector's intelligence was accurate. So Marangan has been useful in getting independent confirmation. You saw tonight that the security of the Philippine forces leaves something to be desired." In my mind's eye, I saw the rocket streaking again toward the helicopter and the churning black and orange ball of the explosion. "The *batikan* warned me of this. And I have been able to relay information on the GPS coordinates so he could scout out alternate access routes."

"He's meeting us at the village?" Micky asked.

"Yes. He has an approach mapped out to the area that is slightly different from the one Cooke developed. It provides us with a little more cushion in terms of time . . . "

"And also ensures that Reyes won't know exactly where we are," Micky concluded. "Slick." But his voice didn't sound pleased. I glanced at Art, sitting next to me in the back of the jeep, and I didn't like the look on his face.

After twenty minutes, Ueda called on his satellite phone to alert Marangan that our arrival was imminent. We slowed and made a right turn onto a two-lane road. We passed a fenced-in field where some animals stood in the darkness. At first you just saw their eyes glowing, but as the jeep got closer, you could pick them out, carabao standing motionless, hulking dark sentries waiting on the dawn.

Some small houses with tin sheets for roofing were clustered around a wide dirt plaza. It was dark and there was no sign of life. As we approached, Ueda shut off the vehicle's lights, pulled to one side, and coasted to a stop. He flicked his lights on and off in a pre-arranged signal. From up the road, headlights flashed in another pattern. Ueda nodded, got back on the road, and drove forward. A small, battered pickup truck was idling in the darkness. The interior lights flashed on briefly and we could see Marangan's craggy face. Ueda flashed our lights as well to show him the occupants of the jeep.

Ueda braked just short of the pickup. "I will go with the *batikan*. You follow closely." He checked his watch. "We should be there before dawn," he told us and started to get out of the jeep.

"Ueda," I said, and reached out to grab him. In the dark, his face was even more contained looking than usual. "Leave us the phone."

"Why?" He was suspicious.

"Marangan has one. It'll be easier to talk with each other using the phones rather than stopping every time we need to confer or you need to give us directions," I explained. "I don't want to waste any time. We're running pretty close to the edge here." I put some of the urgency I felt into my voice.

He shrugged. "Good. The *batikan's* number is saved. Press memory one." He left without saying anything else and Micky took the wheel. The pickup pulled out and we followed them.

"Good thinking, Connor," Art told me. Micky was feeling his way through the jeep's unfamiliar gearbox, muttering under his breath.

The rest of the journey wore on, accompanied by the whine and growl of the jeep's engine. Following another vehicle along the winding mountain roads was a challenge—the jungle closed in on both sides of the road and the night sky served as a lid to our long and twisting tunnel. Bugs flickered across the beam of the head-lights and occasionally the surreal glow of floating eyes punctuated the darkness. But mostly, we were fixated on following the two red lights of the truck ahead of us. We didn't want to get too close because the changing road conditions meant that we were con-stantly braking and speeding up, but we didn't want to let Ueda and Marangan get too far ahead. We had a map, but in case they needed to take an alternative route, we wanted to stick close to our guides. The effort of keeping those lights in sight, rubies that bounced and swayed in the tropical blackness, created an almost hypnotic experience.

By dawn, we had all had a turn at the wheel. My eyes burned and felt gritty. Deep down, I knew I was tired, but the pills forced that feeling way below the surface. I was anxious and itchy, eager for the hint of gray that would announce the arrival of morning. Yet, at the same time, I was worried that the hours were slipping away from us, that we weren't going to be able to reach Yamashita in time.

The roads had gotten rougher. We jounced along the track, climbing up switchbacks. The holes and ruts set your teeth on edge. Nobody was talking much. We conferred periodically with Ueda by phone and traced our progress on the map, but that was about it. One really bad jolt in the road spurred Art into conversation.

"Thank God we didn't take that lunatic Horowitz up on his offer of explosives. Some of that stuff looked old and unstable. We'd be blown sky high by now."

Micky shot a look over his shoulder from his position behind the wheel. "We've still got enough ordinance in here to make a pretty good bang." He's always got a cheery word. After some more silence—he twisted the wheel and wrestled the jeep's stick shift into a lower gear to match the latest sudden twist in the road—Micky spoke up again.

"Art, why don't you get the rifles and stuff out."

His partner sat up a little and peered out into the jungle. We were beginning to be able to note some detail among the trees in the coming light, but not much. In some ways, it was worse than not being able to see at all. "You see something, Mick?"

My brother shrugged. "Nah. But we've been driving farther and farther into Indian Country here. And I got no clue where Marangan's takin' us."

"The guy gives me the creeps," Art agreed.

"Yeah. I just hope we can count on his gun if things get hairy," Micky reminded him. "Anyway, let's be ready. Just in case."

Art began rummaging around in the duffels. He checked out the rifles and pistols, and then set Micky's weapons up front where he could reach them. I set mine down on the floorboards.

"What do you think our chances are?" I asked quietly.

Neither Art nor Micky said anything. Art fiddled with the laser-sighting device on his rifle. Micky drove.

"That good?" I prompted.

Micky took a breath. "If we can get to the location undetected and find out where Yamashita and the girl are, we might have a chance. Sneak in sometime during the night and grab 'em. Then scoot and hope they don't come pounding down the trail after us."

"That's the best plan," Art confirmed. "Sneak, snatch, and scoot."

"What if we get spotted?" I asked. "Or we don't get away clean and they come after us?"

"Not many good options," Micky admitted. "You move quick and put out as many rounds as possible. Hope for the best."

It was quiet for a time. The pace of events had been so fast, that I'd been carried along without having too much time to think about what was going to happen when we reached the target. All the preparation, the weapons from Horowitz, had seemed like worst-case scenario stuff. In the end, I'd been banking a great deal on the ability of Cooke and Aguilar and their troopers to pull off a successful raid. Now it was just us.

Art looked at me and grinned slightly. "Don't think about it too much, Connor. You'll drive yourself crazy. We'll do the best we can. Think about it this way: If we don't get in there, what are Yamashita's chances of living?"

"Slim to none," I admitted.

"Right. At least now, he's got a chance."

"God help him," Micky muttered.

At this point, it was really a matter of time and distance. We were going to be cutting it close. We all felt the pressure. The trip into the rugged hills had been slower than estimated. We were jerking the jeep around another hairpin turn as Marangan's vehicle led us deeper and deeper into the backcountry. By this time, it was fully light, and my body was vibrating with tension. It may have been the pills, but I didn't think so.

In the *dojo*, the distance between you and your opponent is a carefully calibrated thing. You can see the weapon in someone's hands. You evaluate their size and fitness to gauge their speed, and you adjust accordingly. Too far away, and neither of you can land a blow. Too close, and you place yourself in danger. *Ma-ai*, combat distance, is something you work to get a feel for, skirting the edge of safety and danger on the basis of what you know of you and of your opponent.

But here, I didn't have a good feel for any of the elements in the equation. Art was cradling his rifle and both he and Micky had put on their web harnesses with the extra ammo. Their heads moved constantly, scanning the road and the jungle, trying to peer into the shadows. But we were boxed into the jeep and it made us feel like a target as the road narrowed and climbed higher and higher.

We knew what these people were capable of. They had viciously executed two embassy guards. They had proven adept at kidnapping. They had no regard for life. Could they be out there, silently watching as our two vehicles climbed up the road?

In the *dojo*, you can see your opponent's approach. Here, we could usually keep Marangan and Ueda's truck in sight, despite the switchbacks, but there were areas where we could barely see beyond the hood of the jeep, the trail had become that narrow and twisted. I picked up my pistol and made sure that the magazine was full, handling it nervously. But it didn't offer much comfort.

"Make sure the safety's on and put it in your holster," Micky said quietly. His usual sarcastic tone was gone. He was reserved and quiet. Matter-of-fact and almost kind. It's how I knew that we were in danger.

Ahead, the truck's brake lights flashed and we came to a halt. Marangan and Ueda got out and made their way to us. The Filipino had a map in his hand, all creased and marked up. For once, he looked apprehensive. The reptilian stillness was still there on the surface, but I noticed him surreptitiously scanning the underbrush, as if he, too, sensed that we were being watched. It was eerily quiet with the truck engines off. There was a faint breeze making the leaves rustle high up in the tree canopy. Birds called from deep within the trees.

Ueda spread the contour map open on the hood of the jeep. "We are approximately here," he indicated, touching the spot with his index finger. He looked up the trail, which ran in a relatively straight line for a hundred yards or so. "The *batikan* says that there is a side trail that branches off on the left-hand side, very near a clearing." He craned his neck. "I believe I can see the grass of the clearing from here."

I looked and saw a change in the color of the foliage in a spot along the trail—a splash of lighter green and yellow, which was the overgrowth typical of old, abandoned highland farm plots.

"The side trail is narrow," Marangan said. "We will take our trucks up as far as we can, but soon we will have to leave the vehicles behind." He explained that the side trail was so narrow that we would have to pull in toward it, back into the clearing on the other side, and then straighten out to be able to drive straight up it. "It is very rough," he cautioned. "Go slowly so you do not break an axle."

We got back into the jeep and crept forward. Marangan's truck swerved toward the side trail, backed up into the high grasses of the old clearing, then straightened out and jerked up the trail. He was probably going five miles an hour, but you could see the pickup bounce on the uneven track even so.

Micky pulled up cautiously and repeated the maneuver. He inched forward, the motor racing as he worked the standard transmission to keep the jeep's speed steady, but low. "We do this too long, we're gonna burn the clutch out," he murmured.

Marangan's vehicle bounced to a halt again. Ueda got out and motioned to me.

"The track is rougher than we expected," he told me. "Marangan says that you should walk in between the trucks, watch us, and guide your brother accordingly."

I shrugged. "Okay." We were moving at a snail's pace and it would be no problem keeping up. Besides, my body was racing, and I didn't think I could stand any more time cooped up in the jeep.

We started forward again. The foliage was thick along the trail, and what wind there was, was high up in the trees and didn't reach us. In the time between the monsoons, the weather in the Philippines was generally pleasant, but the humidity of the jungle and the tension made me sweat. I followed Marangan slowly, watching him lurch around rocks, and then waving Micky on with advisory hand signals. My eyes were supposed to be focused on the ground, but they kept darting up into the trees. It was good to be moving, but you could hear a lot more on foot. Deep in the undergrowth, things rustled around. Birds squawked and odd-sounding bugs whirred. On the best of days, it would have given me the creeps. Now, it fed the spiky unease that was slowly spreading along the backs of my arms, up and over my shoulders to the base of my neck. I closed my eyes and rubbed my hands across my face. My skin felt greasy and slack. *Easy*, I thought. *Breathe. Focus.*

The pickup truck negotiated a deep series of ruts and bounced forward. I walked in its wake and cautiously signaled Micky to follow. I heard the squeal of his brakes as Marangan stopped suddenly. I looked up ahead and saw that a tree had fallen, blocking the trail.

End of the line.

Marangan and Ueda were out of the truck by now, looking at the map. Micky stuck his head out of the jeep window, with the same action I had seen countless grid-locked motorists use on a car-jammed Manhattan street. "What gives?"

Marangan had turned his engine off; I could hear the motor pinging in the quiet.

Quiet.

I closed my eyes to concentrate. The jungle had gone still. The birds were silent.

"No birds," I murmured.

Micky was looking quizzically at me.

"No birds," I said more urgently.

"Wha'?" my brother said.

"The birds," I said with mounting conviction. "No birds, Mick!" I looked around the sides of the trail, trying to pierce the veil of foliage, to see what hid there. Something *was* there. I could feel it in the same way I could sense the moment when a moving swordsman crossed the invisible line into my attack zone.

I picked up something on the periphery of sight—a shadow flitting between trees. Then another.

I stepped closer toward the jeep. "Get out!" I hissed.

But Micky still wasn't getting it. What was going on with Marangan and Ueda? Surely they must have sensed something. I cast a glance toward them and, simultaneously, the jungle exploded with fire and noise.

"Go Mick!" I yelled. I saw something crease the jeep's hood and pieces of dirt and rock fragments jump into the air. My brother slammed the jeep into reverse with a grinding noise and began to jounce backward. I saw the windshield shatter and the jeep rocked back and forth in the narrow confines of the trail in an attempt at throwing off the aim of the ambushers.

I threw myself down into a rut to get out of the line of fire. Ahead of me, Marangan's truck was being riddled with bullets. I could see the *eskrimador* and Ueda, taking shelter on the far side of the tree that lay across the trail. I fumbled for my pistol, looking for a target.

The firing near me seemed to have slackened. I raised my head again as men began to pour out of the jungle and onto the trail. I was in a bad position and had to roll on my side to get the pistol out. It was too late. An attacker slammed a rifle butt into the side of my head and another kicked the pistol out of my grip. I rolled away from the blow, but the side of my head felt like it was on fire. I got to my knees and someone kicked me hard in the side.

The blood was roaring in my ears, but even so I could hear the increased rate of weapon fire down the track. I tried to lift my head high enough to see. My eyes weren't focusing too well. I got a glimpse of the jeep, swerving backward down a hairpin turn and out of sight. Men raced after it, pouring bullets down the trail. "Mick," I grunted thickly.

A man with an RPG on his shoulder ran to the bend in the trail and let fire. *Mick.* The whoosh of the rocket was swallowed up a split second later by the *crump* of the explosion. A moment later, there was a second, larger detonation. Flames bloomed through the trees.

"Mick!" I gasped and tried to crawl down the trail. Someone kicked me again. The force of it lifted me up and turned me over. The shooting had stopped, but down the trail ammunition was cooking off inside the fireball that had been the jeep.

I looked groggily around, part of me sure that this couldn't be real. I retched into the dirt and tried to get up again. I peered toward the pickup, now riddled with holes. Marangan and Ueda slowly stood up, ringed by armed men.

They only hit me one more time, and just before I slipped down into that dark world where pain closes off everything else, I saw Marangan reach out and, with a feral elegance, cut Ueda's throat.

24

KAISHAKU

The hike beat me up more than my captors did. They put a hood over my head and, while it didn't block out all the light, I couldn't see where we were going. I stumbled awkwardly along in their wake, hands bound before me, as they yanked me upslope and around the obstacles that studded the jungle trail.

In the enclosed world of the hood, I could smell the must of old burlap and my own saliva. I was wrapped in shadows and buffeted by unseen things. It was disorienting, but I was glad that they had shut some part of the world away from me; the last thing I could remember was the oily scent from the fire that consumed the jeep and the sickening awareness that my brother and his partner were now part of the flames.

I stumbled, but they urged me forward without respite, dragging me along on my knees as I tried to get to my feet. The going was steep and my arms were stretched out before me. They hadn't tied them behind my back. It was a break of sorts, since it provided some possibilities for action. *They're going to regret it*, I promised myself.

I tested my captors cautiously, slowing myself down and pulling back slightly on the tether to see how sensitive they were to slack and tension, how good they would be about anticipating any moves on my part. Whoever was holding the rope had two basic responses to any slowdown: pull and, if that wasn't effective, pull harder. It's a classic error, based on the assumption that the person you're pulling will always pull back and fight by going in the opposite direction of the tug forward. But what if you go with the force of the pull? Then you've essentially tricked your opponent into aiding the velocity of your attack. It told me that these guys were not of the same caliber as the men on the video who had fought with the embassy guards. *Maybe there's some hope yet*, I thought. But then I remembered Micky and Art, imagined the smoldering stick figures that would be left after the fire had burned off, and I felt angry and disgusted with myself for even entertaining the thought.

It's funny how the organism takes over. No matter what happens, the body fights for survival. Despair doesn't stop the urge, it just makes us feel guilty about it. But guilt wasn't a particularly useful emotion right now; it turns energy inward at a time when I needed to be alive to the swirl of elements all around me—people, rocks, even the moist air of the jungle. Despite the hood and the haunting memory of Micky and Art, my path led me on and away from those things. Toward an uncertain end, it was true, but Yamashita had taught me that the measure of a person is, in part, discovered in the manner of the journey. I slogged on, hoping only that my journey would bring me to a place where I could avenge my brother.

We walked for hours, in a manner of speaking. I assume my captors walked; I sprawled, skidded, and staggered in their wake. At one point, they stopped and the lower part of the hood was pushed up enough to allow a water bottle to be forced between my lips. I gulped the lukewarm liquid, the organism responding gratefully. *Gotta stay hydrated*, I reminded myself. *Get every edge you can*. I tried for more, but they took the bottle away and yanked the hood down again. The trail leveled out for some time—we must have started to travel across the slope—then we began to head downhill. I was briefly relieved, but soon discovered that I was equally good at falling in this direction. *Gravity is a wily opponent.* I snickered to myself at the thought—Micky would have appreciated the insight—then felt my throat tighten with grief. The trail seemed to wind on forever.

I couldn't hear much as we traveled—either the hood blocked it out or they had very good noise discipline. But finally, I could pick up the beginning of various conversations from the people around me. They sounded confident and excited. They dragged me to a halt and there was shouting ahead of us. Then gunshots.

This is how fickle resolve can be; despite myself, when the shots rang out, my heart leapt with yearning for escape. *Oh please.*

Someone tore the hood off and I stood, blinking in the light of a clearing. The people around me were smiling grimly and a few were shooting their rifles into the air in celebration. They forced me to my knees—at least this time I could reach out and see enough to break the fall. I looked around at the circle of men. Filipinos mostly, but some others who looked Middle Eastern. They were all armed to the teeth.

I looked up into the sky. It was still daylight, perhaps late afternoon. I was confused. If they were bringing me to their camp, the journey should have been longer. Had I been taken by another group? Cooke said that they were all over these hills. Or were they delivering me to a different location? I felt an odd sort of panic, a superfluous jet of fear from a person already trussed like a chicken and delivered to his enemies. I felt ashamed. The only comfort I had left was that in one way or another I was going to reach Yamashita. Now had I failed even in that?

The crowd was milling around and I could see glimpses here and there of shelters and tents in the tree line. The clearing was irregular and the long grass looked recently trampled, like these people had arrived only recently. I eyed the men around me. Their clothes were stained with sweat and dirt, their boots showing evidence of recent travel. These were people who had been on the move.

"Where . . . " I could barely make a sound. I tried to work up some spit. Swallowed. "Where am I?" I finally croaked. Some of the Filipinos laughed.

Then there was movement at the back of the crowd, and the smiles disappeared. The men gave way before he got too close, as if they were afraid that a mere touch was dangerous. They needn't have bothered. The old man wove through the crowd with unconscious fluidity, the product of decades of intense training. You see someone move like that, you know you're in the presence of a master. I recognized that, even as I knelt there openmouthed in astonishment.

He was old and short, with a round head. His skin was shiny and slightly flushed across the cheekbones, and it made the glittering slits of his eyes even more frightening. When he opened his mouth, I saw teeth jagged and irregular, like those of an animal, and I could sense his power washing over me, leaving a thousand tiny needles pricking my skin.

It was unexpected, this wash of *ki* here in a mountain field thousands of miles from my *dojo*. So was his unsettling, almost demonic appearance. But what struck me most of all was that he was immaculately garbed in a dark gray kimono with an old war fan stuck in the belt, surrounded by grimy soldiers armed for battle in an era that had long turned its back on the sensibilities of traditional Japan.

"Dr. Burke," he said in a heavily accented English. "We were beginning to think that you would never arrive." He cackled at that, and the fang-like teeth flashed briefly. He drew the folded fan from the wide *obi* that belted his robe and lifted my chin with it. He pushed my head so that he could examine each side. It was like being sized up by a stockman. He stepped back a pace and regarded me. "So," he concluded, "the damage is minimal. I am pleased." I noticed that some of the guards were fidgeting nervously during his inspection. They seemed to relax a bit with his pronouncement. If the old man noticed, he ignored it.

"Where am I?" I asked again.

"Where?" he smiled grimly. "Where I wished you to be."

"Wha'?" He was such a freak. An old Japanese guy with a fan. *Man with a fan. Fan man.* The pills had worn off: I was tired and thoughts were getting jumbled. I blinked and tried to clear my head. I was having a hard time following him.

He stood there and looked at me with a curious expression of satisfaction. I noticed that he stood out of the range of my arms, alive to the possibility of an attack. "At times, I worried that the plan was too elaborate," he confided in me. "The way of strategy is complex, *neh*? Surely your *sensei* must have taught you something of *heiho*?" I said nothing. His expression told me that he hadn't really expected a reply. He grunted to himself finally. "It is a subtlety probably lost to Westerners."

"*Wakarimasen*," I told him in Japanese. I don't understand.

His eyes narrowed. "Please. We will use English. There is no need to submit the language of the Yamato to butchery by a *gaijin*."

Gaijin simply means "foreigner." But the Japanese use it to describe Them. Barbarians. The Other. It's a description loaded with condescension. For years, this same attitude on the part of some of the old-time *sensei* had bugged me. I was way beyond it now. But the odd, out-of-place comment from the old man before me gave a slight clue to the workings of the mind that spun behind the remote eyes. He may have hated me for something I had done; I couldn't be sure. And it didn't matter, since on a more fundamental level he hated me merely for what I was. There was no rationality in those eyes, and no mercy.

He glared at me for a time. "You wish to know where you are?" Again, that odd, angry cackle. "Why, you are where you wished to be." And with that, he stood aside. The crowd parted with him, and I could see a crumpled form in the distance, tethered to a post in the earth, as if they feared his spirit could still rise up and do battle.

They let me run to him. I sank beside the wrecked form that had once dominated the *dojo* with its sheer sense of power. Yamashita's eyes were closed at first—his face was swollen and bruised, and even if he wanted to, it would have been an effort to get the lids parted much. But I whispered his name, and one eye cracked open. He sighed.

"So," my teacher said. "You *have* come." His voice sounded like dry wind forced out over a field of broken stones. He took a sudden sip of breath, gripped by a spasm.

I meant to smile, although it probably looked like a grimace. My eyes were taking in a silent inventory of the damage. Yamashita was sprawled there in the grass, legs stretched out in front of him. They looked swollen and lifeless. His left shoulder was slumped down, his arm cradled in his lap. Only his right arm appeared to be intact, although the hand was discolored with deep bruises.

"Ah, Professor," Yamashita told me when the pain that gripped him had faded, "you have a true talent for getting into bad situations."

I felt a catch in my throat. *You will not let these people see you cry*, I insisted with a sudden, silent ferocity. I got ahold of myself and tried to smile a little wider at him.

"I have a good teacher," I rasped in response.

"It is a subtle pleasure," the old man said contentedly, "to sip warm *sake* as the evening grows cooler. Is it not, Yamashita-san?"

They had brought over a small low table, and he sat with us, arranging a heated ceramic jug of rice wine and its two small white cups on the table. The guards brought over the pawn in the play, Hatsue Abe. I recognized her from her photo. She gazed at me as if trying to read some significance in the look on my face, then sat quietly by Yamashita's side. She never raised her head, as if afraid to look into the old man's eyes.

Our captor settled himself and withdrew the long iron-ribbed war fan from his sash. They had tied my lead rope to Yamashita's post. The table had been set down near it. *If he puts the fan on the table, I might be able to get ahold of it*, I thought. I could feel my muscles tense in minute rehearsal of the killing lunge I would make at his throat. I thought that there was just enough slack in the rope. The old man stopped his motion in midair and looked at me curiously. "*So desu ne*," he murmured. Then he carefully placed the fan on the ground next to him, away from my reach.

The old freak gestured with a hand at the woman. "Dr. Burke. Abe Hatsue."

I looked at her carefully, remembering the formal portrait that I had been shown in a faraway place a lifetime ago. Her hair was cropped short now, her skin was dirt-smudged, and fatigue lined her face. The ordeal had marked her. She bowed slightly and sniffed, but didn't say a word to me. The old man gestured at the cups and Hatsue carefully filled them. He reached for his and held it expectantly.

"*Dozo*," he gestured, encouraging Yamashita to drink.

Sensei lifted his battered right hand. "I am afraid that my fingers will not work well enough for this honor tonight."

The old man bowed slightly. "I regret it extremely. My men had specific orders to spare the right side . . . "

"It is nothing," Yamashita said, clearing his throat to make the statement sound stronger. "A temporary thing."

Hatsue reached across and silently lifted Yamashita's cup to his lips. He sipped gently, eyes closed. Then he nodded. "*Domo*," he told her and she set the cup down. She sat, rigid in formal elegance.

"Perhaps Hatsue-chan may be excused?" Yamashita asked. "She finds this . . . a strain."

"*Ie, Sensei,* I wish to remain with you," she whispered. She kept her face down and impassive, but you could see the trembling of her features as she struggled for control.

The old man snorted in contempt. "The generations after the war have deteriorated. A woman of an old samurai family should be stronger." But he gestured to a guard, who led the poor woman away.

Yamashita watched our enemy impassively. Since the old man's approach, he hadn't given any indication of discomfort or weakness. His voice was raspy and his words came out as if he were carefully forming them, but his appearance aside, only someone intimately familiar with him would have noticed anything wrong. I marveled at the performance.

Yamashita looked along the tree line to the west. A line of light sky lingered there, the hue sliding from red and gold to green to blue to black as you brought your eyes up to the vault of the heavens. He looked at me, then down at his battered form. "There is beauty in the strangest places, Burke. It is a matter of how you look."

"Yes, *Sensei*," I bowed. I looked at the old man. *Red and gold like fire. Black like smoke.* I remembered the burning and looked at the Tengu. *I'm going to get you, you old freak.* I was stoking my ferocity—it was all I had left.

"The capacity to see true beauty in the oddest places is a truly Japanese sensibility," the old man was saying. He poured the last of the *sake* into his cup, shaking the bottle gently. Then he finished his drink and licked his wet lips. "We will see how well your pupil has learned this lesson tomorrow, Yamashita-san."

He rose, his retinue of guards followed after him, and we were alone.

"Tomorrow?" I prompted.

"*Hai*," Yamashita answered simply. He saw that I was not completely getting it. He settled back against the post, wincing slightly. "Have you forgotten the deadline? We are to be executed tomorrow at dawn."

I swallowed at the matter-of-fact finality in his statement. "Why?"

Yamashita smiled tightly. "This is one of the things I like about you, Professor. Always the urge to know more."

We leaned against the pole, my left shoulder touching his right, our heads close together, and Yamashita rasped out the story.

"The old one is a master of *gekken*, the old-style swordsmanship. And other arts as well: nerve points and the body's power meridians, the darker means of harnessing power through *mudra* and *kuji-no-in*. His skill is legendary. It was said he learned the hidden arts from mountain goblins. His name . . . well, now he is simply called the Tengu. He has become a demon himself.

"He mourns the passing of Imperial Japan. Its culture. He labored hard to preserve it in some way, through passing on his art to a worthy successor . . . "

"Did he succeed?" I whispered.

"Oh yes. The will of someone like the Tengu is not easily denied. He labored long and hard to find a fitting heir. He trained him, hoping to see this part of old Japan live on. And, truly, the pupil he chose was remarkable. But he was unable to control him . . . "

"What happened?"

"His pupil answered to . . . other demons. He left the Tengu to pursue his own destiny." I nodded in silent encouragement. Yamashita could feel the movement of my head. "The Tengu's pupil . . . is not unknown to you, Burke. His name was Tomita."

I sat upright at the name, my stiff muscles protesting at the sudden movement. *Tomita!* I thought back to that night years ago when I first learned the terrible implications of walking the martial path. Tomita had left a string of bodies in his wake as he made his way to New York, desperate to wreak revenge on Yamashita for something my teacher could not control. In the end, I had stopped Tomita. It wasn't something I was proud of, but when the fight was over, I lurched away and left him dead on the floor.

And now this. Was it some sort of karmic revenge? I was breathless. "And all this . . . " I gasped.

"Has been to bring us here and into his power," Yamashita answered with certainty.

"No!" I protested.

"Yes. He is an evil man, but a gifted strategist. Consider. He used the two most powerful motivators to draw us here: duty and sentiment."

Giri and *ninjo* are often thought by the Japanese to struggle in the human heart. For the Japanese, *giri*, or duty, usually triumphs. The Tengu had used Yamashita's sense of duty to get him to help Mori rescue a kidnapped relative, and I had rushed headlong to the aid of my teacher, blind to everything but my concern for him. I had even lured Micky and Art to their deaths with my stupidity.

I sighed sadly. I now knew enough. But habits die hard. "What's the connection with the Moros?"

"I cannot say. For some reason, the Tengu sought out a neutral location to trap us. To do that, he needed assistance. It would not be hard for a man like that to sell his services for a price." Yamashita thought a moment more. "And they have this in common with him; they hate the West and its culture. Perhaps it was enough."

I sat there and looked up at the night sky. The stars were emerging, brighter with every passing moment. They were beautiful in a way, yet cold. Some cultures think that they're the spirits of dead ancestors watching over the living down below. I squinted up at them. *Sorry guys*, I told Micky and Art. Even Ueda. I had a vivid image of Sarah Klein, of home and my family. I felt a spasm of deep grief. It held me for a moment, then I set it aside. I shivered.

"What was your plan in coming here?" my teacher asked, more to keep the conversation going than anything else. I told him. All three options.

"It would appear that this will not be," Yamashita concluded.

"We can hope until dawn," I told him. I left the rest unfinished.

So my teacher told me his plan. I shook with denial.

"I can't!" I protested in a hiss.

"You must," he said quietly.

"But *Sensei* . . . " I pleaded. He cut me off.

"Think!" the force of his urging made him cough. He spat thickly into the darkness. "This is our last chance to gain some small victory here, Burke. If we can do this little thing, there will be some measure of victory."

"But it's too horrible," I whispered. "No one should have to do this."

"We have to, Burke," he said.

"I can't," I told him.

Yamashita sighed in the darkness. "Burke of course you can. You are my pupil. And I have taught you well."

In the end, he wore me out and I knew he was right. The path we were on was the path we were on. All you could do was walk it. The night was alive with the restless noise of the jungle at night. I looked up at the stars. Distant. At peace. My eyes slowly closed, then flickered open again for one last glimpse of a night sky. *Might be nice to be up there.*

And I sank into a troubled half-sleep, restless with the certainty that at dawn, *giri* would once again triumph over *ninjo*.

25

FLASH

The human body is a strange, frail vessel that can withstand unbelievable amounts of agony. The spirit is even stronger. The old samurai knew it and Hatsue learned it as well. She blanched when she learned of the bargain that Yamashita planned on striking, but nodded in resignation.

The stars had kept watch over us long enough and now fled with the sun's return. The guards came, bearing gifts: a bucket of warmed water, some cloth, and a clean kimono. I sponged Yamashita carefully, since he could not do it himself, and I knew that he would wish to conform to the ritual requirements for purity. In the half-light, it was almost possible to imagine my teacher as he once was: unmarked and whole. I dressed him silently, the hush of morning broken only by the muffled sounds of camp life and Yamashita's occasional gasps when the pain of movement grew overwhelming.

The Tengu had savored the idea of Yamashita's demise for some time. He had lived in the details of it with self indulgent delight, but when Yamashita proposed a new twist to his scenario, it clearly intrigued our captor.

"Think of it," Yamashita urged. "I only ask that she be given one small chance. And in return . . . so much for so little." I saw the Tengu's nostrils flair slightly; his checks seemed to redden, although it was difficult to be sure in the poor light.

I sat there like a stone, the implications heavy within me. To stop a human body, you can break the support structure of bone, overload the nerve circuits with pain, damage important muscles, or cut off the flow of oxygen to the brain. These things usually take a while—all that Hollywood stuff about the hero sneaking up, delivering a quick chop to the neck, and dropping someone is mostly fiction. Anyone who really fights people knows that it usually takes a while to bludgeon them into insensibility, or to set up the killing technique.

And killing was on my mind. But it's hard to do without a weapon. I would be relieved if I could have one in my hand again. I eyed the men around me wistfully, dreaming of targets. But it was a fantasy, really. I knew that Yamashita and I would be on the receiving end of things this day.

Seppuku, commonly known as *hara-kiri*, is a Japanese form of ritual disembowelment. It inflicts horrendous pain. The first stabbing incision takes place low on the left side of the gut. The blade then slices horizontally across the body, severing the stomach muscles. At the end of its traverse, the blade is turned upward for a final, tearing cut, to expose the peritoneal cavity and its contents. It provides much on the list of bad things that can happen to a body: pain, muscle damage, bleeding, and organ disruption in a fixed sequence.

Unfortunately, it doesn't kill you immediately. And it's designed that way. It is an action of atonement, or a demonstration of honor and fidelity. The white hot blasts of pain shoot through the victim, and in the experience of endurance his inner nature is thought to be revealed, much as the physical act itself exposes the center of the human body to the elements.

That's the theory, at least. In reality, you can live a relatively long time like this, and the Japanese evolved a way out. When someone commits *seppuku*, another person is honored with the role of *kaishaku*. The *kaishaku* stands behind and to one side of the victim, sword poised. When he judges that the victim can stand no more, the *kaishaku* severs the victim's head and ends his suffering.

I was Yamashita's *kaishaku*, simultaneously honored and appalled. But it got worse.

Yamashita's proposed bargain was that the Tengu should let Hatsue go free. He wasn't naïve enough to suppose that the old demon would agree to an act of mercy, so he proposed just before the ritual of *seppuku* began, that she be untied and permitted to flee. The Tengu would restrain his men for as long as Yamashita could endure the knife; once his head was off, they were free to pursue her. It was a straightforward swap: his personal agony for another's shot at freedom. The longer he could last, the greater her chance to escape.

He didn't bother to negotiate on my behalf. We both knew that was futile, that the elaborate series of events strung together by that crazy old man were designed to bring us to our end. Hatsue, on the other hand, was merely a pawn. Yamashita was hoping to eke out one, tiny victory before we died.

What was in it for the Tengu? Seeing Yamashita suffer. And I'd suffer along with him, knowing that as *kaishaku* I could end his agony, but that in doing so I would thwart my teacher's last wish and ensure that Hatsue's innocent life would be lost as well.

You could see the calculations flitting in the Tengu's eyes, restless shadows cast by inner thoughts. Finally he spoke. "You have such faith in your *gaijin* pupil?" Yamashita nodded, and the old man cackled, removing the war fan in his sash and opening it with a flourish. "I do not share your confidence," the Tengu concluded, "but it will be an interesting game."

"It's not a game!" Hatsue protested in a small, brave voice.

The Tengu ignored her. "You seek to save a life by your suffering," Then he looked at me with contempt. "You seek to spare your master and obey him at the same time." He whirled to face Hatsue.

"And you wish to escape."

He mulled it over, looking around the silent circle of men who had formed in the clearing. "I like it," he finally concluded. "If Yamashita-san succumbs to pain, he fails. If he endures, then his *kaishaku* has failed. And long time or short, the woman will be caught." He nodded to himself. "None of you can win."

"We must try," Yamashita said quietly.

The war fan snapped closed and Tengu bowed mockingly at him. "I honor you for the attempt and will rejoice in your humiliation." He straightened and looked at me. "All of you."

Hatsue shook her head. "No," she protested.

Our *sensei* looked into the eyes of his new pupil and merely said "*keiko.*" I watched as Hatsue struggled to master her agitation, and then settle under its heavy weight. She bowed deeply and accepted her fate.

Yamashita was standing, unsteady on his feet. He took a deeper breath and seemed to swell with some of his old power. "I would ask a moment with my pupils," he told the Tengu. "This one," he gestured at me, "must be clear on his role."

The Tengu nodded, and Yamashita sank down to the grass. The motion was smooth, but quick, as if it were an effort to maintain control and he wished to hurry through the ordeal.

She had tears in her eyes when Yamashita addressed her, but Hatsue nodded her understanding. "You must start out on the main trail," Yamashita instructed her, "and cover as much distance as possible. But then swing to the west, toward the coast. We know that most of their men and equipment move through the jungle. The coast may hold a better chance for you to escape."

I added my encouragement. "You've got to move quickly. Maybe you can flag down a fishing boat." The advice sounded lame, even to me.

"The time will be short," Yamashita urged her. "Do not look

back. Do not hesitate. Do you understand?"

"*Hai!*" Hatsue whispered.

"And you, Professor," Yamashita asked, "are you ready?"

I swallowed and nodded, but I didn't feel too confident. Yamashita smiled one of his rare smiles, reached forward, and touched me gently. "Have you heard the traditional saying, Burke? Duty is heavier than a mountain . . . "

"But death is lighter than a feather," I sighed in response. It was from the old Imperial Rescript for Soldiers and Sailors. Was it true? I guessed we were going to find out. I started to speak, but a half shudder, half sob shot through me and I had to master it before continuing. "*Yoi,*" I told him. Ready.

The men in the camp were restless. They had relocated from their previous base to meet us, but they still had to worry about the capacity of the Filipinos to mount another raid. You could see the split in the camp between the Middle Easterners who followed the Tengu and the hard-core Moros. The Tengu's people watched him for a sign; the others watched the tree line, nervous about what was to take place, and anxious with the need to be moving.

The Tengu gave no sign of noticing, but he too was impatient for blood. "Enough!" he called. "The sun is rising and it is time."

I helped Yamashita up and led him to the place they had prepared. There was a straw mat placed upon the earth, and I lowered him down into the formal sitting position. It was hard with his legs in the shape they were in; I wondered that he could stand it. But other than a slight hissing noise, he was silent as he sank into finality. My teacher faced the dawn, the sun awakening the hills to the east and lighting the edge of the trees.

Before him there was a short sword—the *wakizashi*—as well as a white piece of paper. A bucket of water waited to one side. The Tengu and his attendants stood to Yamashita's right, about twenty feet away. You'd think that it was a sign of respect not to get too close. In reality, they probably just wanted to stay out of the way of flying blood. The rest of the camp arranged themselves around the clearing, watching the proceedings with morbid fascination.

I knelt down beside Yamashita and helped him slip his arms out of the kimono. I tucked the freed sleeves of the garment under his legs. It's the sort of grisly aesthetic that is the constant companion of the martial artist. The action not only makes things look neat and tidy but is also designed to minimize the indignity of the death throes once the cutting begins.

"Is your arm up to this?" I asked quietly. It seemed so odd and matter-of-fact a question, but all through the night we had both begun traveling to a place where the sights and sounds of this world are muted. It made for a peculiar calm. When you've run out of options, what path do you take? The only one left.

He rotated his right shoulder slightly. "Yes. They were careful to leave this side intact." Yamashita clenched and opened his fist. "The fingers are stiff, but they should obey my will for a little while yet." He paused for a breath. "As will you, I hope, Professor."

I sat up straight and then bowed formally to him. No words were necessary and I don't think I could have spoken anyway.

Two of the Tengu's men walked over. They were both armed with AK-47s, but one carried a *katana* as well. The long sword of the samurai was the weapon wielded by the *kaishaku*. One handed it to me, clearly unfamiliar with sword etiquette: You are supposed to proffer a sword with two hands. Did it matter? Probably to Yamashita. I grasped it with both my hands and bowed. They looked at me like I was a visitor from another planet. Then the guards moved away slightly and stood behind Yamashita, fingering their weapons. I eyed them.

"Take another two steps!" the Tengu commanded. "You are within his killing range." I was sizing things up to see what kind of damage I could make in my last moments. The Tengu sensed it.

"The girl," Yamashita called. One of my guards grabbed her roughly and sliced through the ropes that bound her hands. She knelt down and hugged Yamashita. Hatsue was crying. *"Domo arigato goziemashita, Yamashita-san,"* she said, thanking him.

He slowly pulled her arms away. *"Keiko,"* he said gruffly in response, and gently pushed her away.

Hatsue looked at me, bewildered for a second by her emotions. "Run, you fool!" I ordered. The tone in my voice galvanized her and she leapt across the clearing and down the trail. I watched her go, and then looked across at the Tengu and his people.

I grasped the sheathed sword in my left hand and swung the blade free with my right: a silvery arc of brightness flashed in the morning sun. I threw the scabbard away and focused on the Tengu. The symbolism of throwing away a scabbard is that you're going to fight to the death. The Tengu knew this but the guards did not. I could sense that some of our captors were unsettled and I wanted to encourage that. If they weren't afraid, they were going to be.

I pointed the sword straight out at the Tengu. "Prepare, old man. I am coming for you." My voice was a low growl and I projected all my vengeance across that clearing to push against the Tengu. Did he feel it? Probably. But he was skilled enough not to show it.

"Enough!" he called, and gestured with his fan toward Yamashita.

I stepped over to the bucket and drew out water with a small ladle left there for that purpose. I held out the sword and let the clean water trickle down the blade, one side, then the other, in a ritual act of purification. I set myself in position, working on controlling my breathing, focusing on the task at hand.

Yamashita swiveled painfully and bowed toward the Tengu. Then he faced the knife. He settled back for a moment, seeming almost comfortable, and looked out over the horizon. The morning was washing across the sky in bands of subtle color. I could smell the wetness of dew, feel the cool of the sword handle against my hot hands.

My teacher swiveled toward me and regarded me with the brown eyes that had watched me critically for so many years. There was a calm in them now that I had never really seen before. Yamashita's head moved to take in the unfolding morning.

"Beauty in the most unlikely places, Burke."

"*Hai*," I replied in a choked voice.

"I am glad we are going together," my *sensei* told me. "The world would be . . . diminished without you." And he turned away toward the knife.

I raised the sword over my right shoulder in the *hasso* stance. I adjusted my angle in relation to Yamashita and began to breathe deeply. Lights were flashing in front of my eyes. *Focus!*

"Please tell me when you are ready, Burke," Yamashita said quietly.

I hesitated, trying to make sure I was ready. *Calm. Focus. See the beauty of the sky. Feel the sword's handle. Listen to the birdsong.* I wished that light would stop flashing.

It was pulsing, just out of the corner of my right eye. I could see it dance on the fingers of my right fist, wrapped around the *katana*. It was a small distraction, but I wanted everything to be right. I wanted my focus to be pure. And that light was throwing me off.

Look at the sky. Ignore the flashing light. Listen to the birds.

The birds. I realized with a start that the birdsongs had ceased. The world was silent as if waiting for Yamashita's end. But the flashing light persisted on my fist.

Flaaash. Flashflashflash. Flaaash. Flashflashflash. I thought it was related to my heartbeat, but it wasn't. *Flaaash. Flashflashflash.*

"*Nan ja?*" I heard the Tengu ask impatiently.

I watched the light. *Flaaash. Flashflashflash.* I saw Yamashita begin to turn.

"It's alright," I told him. And I began to believe it was. "Gimme a minute."

The Tengu cackled. "I knew that the *gaijin* was weak!" He gestured at some men and they started across the clearing for Hatsue.

"Wait!" Yamashita called. They hesitated and the Tengu watched us expectantly. Then my teacher urged me, "Burke, do not fail me."

Flaaash. Flashflashflash. I focused. Dash-dot-dot-dot. The Morse code for the letter B. A small point of light on my hand. Like something from a laser pointer. And with a thrill, I knew: *B is for Burke.*

"I won't fail you," I told him, and my voice sounded like my own for the first time that morning. I shouldered the sword and I saw the Tengu lean forward in anticipation. I knew this was going to be close. I took a deep breath and called "Ready!" so all the world could hear.

Then I moved forward and all hell broke loose.

26

FLIGHT

Hatsue ran from that place of death, seeking life. Her breath sawed in and out, ragged with emotion. Terror gripped her even as her heart thrilled with the idea that she might now be free. Free! She wanted to fly down the jungle trail, like a bird, but her body's movements were earth-bound, jerky, and tense. Yamashita had warned her that she must keep her strength up for the time when escape might be possible, but she could never understand him—he spoke in almost the same breath of ways to meet death and of the need to be able to flee it. Now, she could feel the strain in her calves and thighs, the muscles tight and thin with disuse.

Her throat was tight with effort; she wheezed as she flew along the winding track through the trees. She stumbled but did not stop, throwing herself headlong into the escape. Tears burned in her eyes, but she merely blinked and kept running. They had told her that she was alone now. There was no hope of solace from anyone else. Her escape rested entirely with her—her ability to run hard and fast, to slip away from the hunters that would inevitably follow. She had no time for fear, she realized. Or guilt. All of her had to focus on one thing. Flight. Forget the last sight of Yamashita, his injuries rendering him pathetic and only his spirit keeping him upright. Forget Burke, the hapless student who had followed his master into a deadly trap. Mourn them later. Thank them for this gift by surviving.

Run!

The trail dipped down, away from the clearing, winding in a series of switchbacks to a ridge, where it leveled out for a time before crossing down into the next valley. She ran, not even feeling the tree branches that whipped across her body as she lurched too close to the side of the trail. Rocks stabbed into her feet. She winced, but ran on. Head for the coast, they had reminded her. Use the trail for a time, but head down to the water.

Hatsue plunged into the jungle to her right, winding her way quickly through the trees and thinking of what she knew of the topography. They were not far from the coast. This part of the mountain territory had small valleys that opened steeply to the ocean. There were cliffs of jagged rock bounding the shore, but the runoff from monsoons had carved pathways through the slopes down to the sea. The trees here were tall, a climax forest with little in the way of undergrowth except for a carpet of branches and leaves from the ancient trees. It was easier on her feet, and she moved quickly, leaving the ridgeline to follow a gully that seemed to lead in a promising direction.

Her excitement grew as she scrambled through the cut in the jungle. The rocky channel grew wider and deeper, a path obviously forged by seasonal water on its way to the ocean. The gully bed was thick with leaves and deadfall, and she continued down it, hoping that it would lead her to the coastline.

Hatsue's ears thudded with her own heartbeat and the rush of her breath. She was sure that her passage was a noisy one, punctuated by snapping twigs, the skitter of small rocks, and the chatter of leaves. But she didn't care, surrendering stealth in the interest of speed, of flight, of escape. She tried to listen for the sounds of pursuit, but she realized that this was a waste, a projection of energy behind her, when everything should be focused forward.

The gully wound down the narrow valley. Hatsue's nostrils

flared. The sea! She could swear that a brief hint of salt water had wafted across her path. It made her redouble her efforts. She threw herself down the dry mountain riverbed.

The course turned where a huge rock outcropping jutted out, redirecting the flow. A huge tree sat on the top of the rock, its ancient roots surrounding the rock like an old, claw-like hand. The thought had barely registered, when Hatsue sensed a movement on the periphery of her vision—a fleeting shadow, nothing more, back in the trees above the riverbed.

She froze in panic. Gasping for calm, her eyes wildly searched for movement, her heart hammering in fright.

As Hatsue looked into the jungle, a massive hand, rough to the touch, reached around her and covered her mouth. It dragged her to the ground, smothering her wail of despair.

27

EDGE

They say that there's a zone where time appears to slow down, the rush of events thickens to a crawl, and light seems more intense. You dance within the fleeting space in time, once so brief, that now stretches out to surround you.

Maybe that's the kind of description people create in retrospect. It sounds so beautiful. Peaceful. Memory often works to soften life's rough edges.

Not mine, though.

I was moving in front of Yamashita even as my ears registered the *bloop* of the grenade launchers. My teacher was still focused on an inner reality and reaching slowly toward the blade that he would use to disembowel himself. I knocked him over with a brutal nudge—I heard him grunt in pain—simultaneously kicking the *wakizashi* away and out of his reach.

The grenades went off. The explosions were life changing. The whole camp froze for just a moment. It was what I needed.

The two armed guards behind Yamashita were my first concern. They were closest to him and had to be taken out. As I rose up before them, one turned his head in my direction, trying to tear his attention away from the explosions. My sword arced down: a classic *kesa-giri* cut, the angle designed to slice through the neck and across the torso. I put everything I had into it, focusing on using my hips to draw the blade through the muscle and tissue. To cut through a living thing is a fearsome, complex task. I pulled the *katana* in toward me, using the curvature of the blade to guide it through and out of his body. A gout of arterial blood shot out of the guard's neck. I was already turning on his companion when the blood hit the left side of my head, a spray of thick warmth.

A few more explosions went off somewhere behind me and people had started shooting. The surviving guard's eyes were still wide with surprise, but he managed to bring his AK to bear on me. I swiveled to present a smaller profile, realizing I had to force the weapon up and away from Yamashita, who was still lying on the ground behind me. But there wasn't time. I swear I could see the slow tensing of the guard's right hand as he prepared to squeeze off a burst with the assault rifle.

I cut down, a short chop to his forearm. But my form was off and the blade didn't slice cleanly through the arm. He shrieked and tried to twist away from the bite of the sword. The action dragged the sword with him. I tried to wrench it free, but it was stuck in the bone. Then, with a snap, the blade broke. A sword like this, so razor sharp, is also brittle. Even as my hand came away with the jagged remains of the weapon, I was working out my next step. I lunged at the man, pushing the assault rifle up and across his body and plunging the stump of the sword into his throat. I heard the tearing sound it made as I drove it home. His eyes rolled up into his head and we both went over. I can still hear him gurgling in my ear as we thudded into the grass.

There was a storm of shots. Out of the side of my eye I could see the Filipinos in the clearing scrambling for cover, emptying weapons at a rapid rate, furious bursts aimed at unseen opponents. There were occasional muzzle flashes from different spots along the clearing's perimeter, but it was obvious that the attackers had limited firepower. As that awareness grew, the Tengu's men became more aggressive and began to put out more rounds.

High velocity ammunition makes a *crack* when it comes close to you. Things were starting to snap and zip through the air in our direction. Some of the Filipinos were directing their guns at me. I turned to get Yamashita out of the line of fire.

"Head for the trees!" a hoarse, distant voice screamed.

I was covered in blood and had just killed two men. But God help me, when I heard that voice, my heart leapt and I smiled.

Yamashita was stunned and I dragged him by his good right arm into the undergrowth. Our path went right through the pool of blood left by one of his guards. It couldn't be avoided; there was going to be blood everywhere before much longer.

I got Yamashita behind a fallen tree trunk that offered some shelter from the gunfire. I wanted to pause for a minute and think my options through. *You've got to move! Don't think! Go!*

In the rush, I must have registered the look of fury on the Tengu's face, his orders to the Arabs around him as they faded back into the jungle. They'd be coming for us. I had to go meet them, but I wasn't sure how well Yamashita would do in a fight.

I crawled out into the clearing. One of the guards was still spasming slightly. I stripped him of a pistol and a knife: I thought that in the trees most of the work would be done up close. I also grabbed the AK, slick with his blood.

"Stay here," I urged Yamashita, pushing the assault rifle into his arms. His eyes crossed and struggled to find focus. My teacher had been on the threshold to another existence—so far removed from this world that it was hard for him to pull back into the here and now. I realized he wouldn't be able to use the rifle in the shape he was in. I handed him the pistol instead, wrapping his fingers around the butt, and took the rifle. "Wait. Stay down. I'll be back," I hissed. I looked in his eyes to see whether he was tracking, but it was hard to tell.

Rifle fire still exploded across the clearing. The attackers were slowing their rates of fire and moving occasionally to avoid the concentrated volleys from the Filipinos. Most of the terrorists had faded back into the tree line and I could hear them calling to each other occasionally. In the lull, they were regrouping. It was becoming obvious that the attackers were few in number. Time was short. I made my way toward the spot where I had last seen the Tengu.

In the brush, I tried not to focus on individual elements in the vegetation. You look instead for patterns, the shifting of visual fields that telegraph movement. There was still too much sporadic gunfire to hear the sound of anyone approaching. In some sense, I didn't need the help: I could *feel* them moving toward me.

Even so, when someone exploded out of the brush, it caught me off-guard. I was scanning around me in a 180-degree arc and he waited for my head to turn away from him. Someone had trained him well, but his energy pushed out in an invisible arc that led him by a pace or two. I felt it and spun toward him. He was carrying one of those broad-bladed swords I had seen on the wall at Marangan's training hall. His mouth was wide open as he swung at me, the skin around his eyes taut with excitement and effort. I followed the momentum of my turn toward the attack and threw myself down in an effort to get under the swipe of the sword. I tracked him with the AK, pointing in midair, and pulled off a short burst that took him in the groin. He collapsed, writhing as his blood soaked the front of his pants and began its osmotic climb up his shirtfront. The sword spilled from his grasp. I took it and hacked down at him. It wasn't an act of mercy, just part of the brutal calculus of a fight: You never leave anyone alive behind you.

Then I dove into the underbrush, trying to get away, trying to make myself a moving target. I peered around, trying to read the hidden intent that could be contained in the green foliage and darker shadows of the mountain jungle. If the terrain were more open, they could rush me in a group or make better use of their firepower. But the trees broke up lines of attack and fields of fire. They were here, somewhere just out of sight—a pack of wolves roaming in slowly tightening circles, waiting for an opportunity.

The air exploded suddenly with the renewed sound of gunfire. It was off to my left in the direction of the clearing, and had a volume and intensity that was entirely different from the earlier start of the firefight. Grenades crumped and projectiles clipped through the undergrowth near me. I ducked down instinctively.

Off in the distance, someone defiantly shouted *Allahu akbar*, and the gunfire pulsed in response. There was a disciplined, methodical sound to the mayhem. Whoever was out there knew what they were doing. And they were moving closer—something tore a gash in the tree I was crouched by, the bark blown away to reveal the white of the inner wood.

It was the growing volume of fire that flushed them. I caught the shadow of movement in a few spots as the Tengu and his men began to pull back, away from the new attack. I crawled in the same direction, watching. A ray of sunlight drilled down through the forest canopy up ahead and I thought I caught the flash of a gray kimono—just a hint—moving through the bright beam of light and then back into the shadows of the trees.

Oh no. You're not getting away. I knew that the Tengu was too dangerous, too crazy, to let escape. If he somehow slipped through the trees to freedom, I knew he'd be back. I didn't think *Sensei* could survive another attack.

I checked the AK I was carrying. I removed the magazine to check on what ammo I had left. But what do I know about guns? I could see a few rounds in the top of the magazine, but had no way of knowing how many were below them. And I wasn't about to take them out—I had a mental image of me dropping the bright-jacketed bullets and then scrambling around in the undergrowth trying to find them. So I left the rifle and crawled over to the body of the man with the sword. He had a sidearm and an extra magazine on his belt. I took them. *Shoulda used the gun, pal,* I thought. *But you probably wanted to prove something to your teacher, didn't you?* I knew the feeling. It was a beginner's mistake.

I scrambled away from the approaching gunfire, deeper into the jungle, trying to keep the Tengu and his people in sight. They had pushed through some brush and left a trace, a hole in the greenery. I plunged through the gap, eyes scanning for motion ahead and on each side, all the while moving forward.

They were headed west, downslope toward the coast. For a while, huge trees, their shoulder-high roots standing like buttresses against the trunks, dominated the forest. The going was easier here, but the trail they left was harder to see. I had to watch for the odd boot print or patch of disturbed leaves. It slowed me down and made the effort of tracking even more nerve-wracking—I had to stay hard on their heels, but at the same time was worried that the huge trees could harbor an ambush.

I was lucky, I thought. They seemed more interested in escaping than they were in getting me. But luck just means that the odds are in abeyance; it doesn't mean that they won't catch up with you later.

I led with the pistol, pointing it as I jerked around trees, alert to attackers who were never there.

After the gloom of the forest, the bamboo grove was bright with light. The shafts swayed gently, thick rows of plants that stretched out all around me. I could see the path that the Tengu and his men had trampled through the stand of giant grass and I was relieved to be on a definite trail again. I sped up.

They had to push through the bamboo stalks to get to me. The stand was so dense that they had hidden not ten feet off both sides of the trail. The sudden clatter of movement gave them away. Here, finally, was the ambush. Three of them.

They had knives, probably because you avoid guns in a multiple attacker scenario—bullets are idiot servants, a danger to friend and foe alike. And probably also because they were afraid that gunfire would draw attention to the direction of their escape route. They drove in on me in a classic pincer technique—one to attack and distract, a second to slice in on my blind side, the third to hang back and exploit any opening that develops.

The first Arab lunged at me, exploding through the bamboo on my right. I could hear the other two off to my left. They would expect me to jerk away from the initial attack, into the waiting blades of the other two.

I moved in toward the knife instead. I had the pistol in my right hand and tried to get my left up to parry the thrust of the attacker. But the interval was too tight. I had moved into the initial flow of a *kote gaeshi* wrist immobilization, but the bamboo inhibited my movement. My technique was off: I couldn't get around to control his wrist. The knife blade sliced across my hand, laying it open at the base of the thumb. I pushed anyway, then brought the pistol up.

When dealing with multiple attackers, it is unwise to stay in one position too long so I slid to the right side of my attacker, turning to face the men behind me. My gun hand had stayed to track the first assailant, and I put two quick shots into him while pushing backward into the bamboo.

The second man's knife lunged in after me. His momentum carried him in and he was on top of me before I could get the pistol to bear. I felt the knife tip prick my gut and I yanked my hips to the right to pull away. His knife caught my pelvic bone—I could feel the metal knifepoint grinding in through the electric jolt of pain. I clamped down on his knife hand. *Immobilize it! Don't let him move the blade or he'll gut you.* Then I backhanded him with the pistol, whipping the gun around in a vicious blow that caught him across the temple and cheekbone. He grunted and sagged, and we tumbled backwards together in slow motion as the young bamboo gradually gave way beneath our weight.

I was on my back, the second guy sprawled out and draped over me. It was the only thing that saved me. The third guy had his pistol out and was trying to get a clear shot—the cat was out of the bag and one more report wasn't going to change things any. I reached around the stunned man on top of me and shot the third guy. He sat down, looking stunned, and I shot him again.

By this time, the man laying on me had started to move. He reached up for my gun hand, forgetting the knife. I waved the pistol around, struggling to keep him focused on it. My left hand was slick with blood as I groped around for the knife. He realized what I was up to at the last moment and felt the shift in effort as he reached around, struggling to find the knife as well.

But I got to it first. His eyes changed; the fierce light of fury faded and his body grew limp and heavy. His last breath sighed out of him, a soft, hot puff against my face. I rolled over onto my knees, checking my stomach and hip. Blood, but I didn't think he got the blade into any organs. I was more worried about my left hand.

I heard some voices back in the forest, faint calls, but couldn't make them out. *Could be help. Could be more of these guys.* I tore a strip off one of the dead men's shirt and bound my left hand. Then I went after the Tengu.

I slid and stumbled down through the grove of bamboo. The cut on my hip had probably done some muscle damage and I moved in a bent-over shuffle. My one leg wasn't working too well and the slope was growing steeper. The trail was clear until the bamboo petered out and the denser jungle took over. I slid down an embankment, wincing at the impact, and noting that someone had done the same before me: the earth was slick with another's passage. I ended up in a shallow ravine where water trickled in the direction of the sea. In the monsoon season, it must have been a greater flow: there were pieces of trees wedged along either side of the depression. I scanned around the steep walls and saw no sign of recent passage. I decided to follow the stream. The Tengu was heading to the sea and this seemed the shortest possible route.

I took stock as I went. The ragged bandage on my hand had soaked through and blood dripped off into the shallow water. I had dropped the knife somewhere back in the bamboo and now only had the pistol. I tried to remember how many times I had pulled the trigger. Four times? Six? How many slugs did this thing hold? It was the problem with guns; they ran out of bullets at critical junctures. I pulled out the current magazine and rammed the second one home. Better to start full. Reloading was difficult—none of that manly ramming of a new magazine home and looking around, steely jawed as I pulled the receiver back. The truth was, the dark, blood-soaked bandage on my left hand meant I fumbled around for a while.

But I got it done and continued to make my way down the ravine toward the brightness. The streambed twisted slightly here and there, studded with rocks and old branches, but never so much that you lost sight of the hint of sunshine at the end. Light at the end of a tunnel.

The streambed broadened out in a shallow fan and the foliage overhead gave way. A huge old tree had toppled backward from the edge of the water, its roots ripped up to face the air like so many frozen snakes, or fingers clenched in a final spasm of struggle. I stood for a moment, stunned by the suddenness of sun and the immensity of blue ocean that stretched out, far below the cliff I stood on. I gave a quick peek over the edge. Water trickled down, silver drops that seemed to drift briefly until gravity's inexorable force dragged them downward to shatter on the rocky coast some seventy-five feet below. It may have been the blood loss, but I got a sudden surge of vertigo and jerked back from the edge, my heart jumping.

It was then that he struck. The weighted chain shot out, wrapped around my hand, and yanked the pistol free. I turned in alarm, and he came at me, swarming from among the roots, a gnarled thing emerging from earth and darkness like a troll. I braced for the impact, but wasn't prepared for the force with which he hit me.

The Tengu flailed at me with his chain, whipping it across my face and laying open my brow and cheekbone. At the same time, his left fist slammed into my clavicle like a hammer and I felt the bone give way. Then I was struck with the full force of his body. We went flying backwards, locked together. *The cliff!* I thought, twisting and trying to keep away from the edge. I went down hard in the rocky streambed. Something caught me in the small of my back and the wind went out of me in a paralyzing *whoosh*. The water was shallow here, just enough to make the surface slick and to soak my back. My mind was making pointless observations as a futile defense mechanism. *At least you won't drown.*

But he had me. The Tengu was much stronger than he appeared—the insane always are. He didn't say a word, didn't make a sound except for a faint grunt when we hit the ground together. And, even as I struggled to recover my breath, to move, to do *something*, he was methodically moving to pin my shoulders back, hitching his body forward so that his weight sat on my chest.

Once he got there, it was going to be all over. I looked into the gaping, wet mouth, studded with crooked, angled teeth. His eyes burned at me, like something through a mask. For a moment, I could swear that they glowed red, like a demon. My hands scrabbled around in the wet, seeking purchase, looking for a weapon—the helpless spasm of the doomed. Because once he had me pinned, this *thing* was going to snuff my life out.

I tried to escape his grasp and only inched myself closer to the edge of the cliff. My left shoulder was now actually hanging over the precipice. It made it harder for him to immobilize me, but also meant he could probably just keep working me right over the edge. *You go, make sure he goes with you.* But I had to keep struggling. He had immobilized my right hand—not much good with the clavicle snapped anyway—but my left slipped away from him—maybe the blood and water made me too slick to hold. In desperation, I struck at him, but the blows were ineffective—the angle was bad and my hand was too beat up.

I was grunting with effort, my breath finally coming back, moving, trying everything, *anything* I knew in an effort to escape. My left hand brushed against a hard shaft in the Tengu's belt—the iron war fan stuck in his *obi*. I yanked it free and drove the *tessen's* point into his armpit—there's a nerve plexus in there and if you get it right, you can shock the heart enough to kill. But I didn't drive deep enough.

He hissed at my attack, and his eyes only glowed more furiously. I pulled back the fan and rammed upward in desperation, this time catching him in the soft spot under the chin. He reared back in a snorting gurgle and the motion was enough. I grabbed his collar, the fan still in my left hand, pulled and simultaneously hiked my body up to dislodge him a little. My freed right hand pushed him in the direction of the edge. It was feeble, but it was enough.

The Tengu tumbled off me and went spinning over the cliff, into space. Finally, he made a sound. It was a shriek, not of terror, but of rage, a final assault enduring until the impact on the rocks below drove it out of him for good.

I spun awkwardly around onto my belly to see: I had to be finally reassured that it was over. Bad move. Because our struggle had weakened the edge and the rocks were shifting. I felt the hard line of earth under me begin to crumble. I was too close to the edge and could feel the momentum of the slide begin. I threw my arms back frantically, trying to recover. As I flailed around, a piece of the cliff tumbled off, spinning down and out to crash onto the rocks that waited to greet me as they had the Tengu.

My center of gravity was sliding over the edge. My right arm was useless and the left hand kept gouging itself into the streambed, coming up with pebbles and mud and little else. I tried to *will* the toes of my boots to dig in and stop the fall, but I found that there was nothing for it. I looked down below, toward the rocks and the crashing waves. Maybe I should have resigned myself to death like a good samurai, but my mind fought it. *To have come so far*, I thought in protest.

The edge began to disintegrate beneath me, and I stopped breathing for a second. I looked, wide-eyed, at the sea foam washing the rocks and felt the final slide begin.

Someone grabbed me hard by an ankle and I was yanked back from the brink. And whoever it was didn't stop for a good ten feet. I got dragged through the stream, rocks and all, feeling the cool scouring of gravel against my belly. It hurt and felt good at the same time.

I rolled over onto my intact left side and looked up. I was ringed by a group of soldiers, lumpy in black jump suits, harnesses, and helmets, submachine guns held across their chests. One of them squatted by my ankles, his face splattered with mud from our trip back from the edge.

I lay there, completely spent, panting. They stared at me, openmouthed. I was covered with blood, my clothes torn and muddy. My left eyelid was twitching and I tried to keep my useless right arm clamped tight to my side so the bones wouldn't grind together. I tried to think of something to say in the silence.

Finally, one of them stirred. "Holy shit, man," he said. Another spoke into a small handheld unit clipped to his battle harness, calling for a medic.

I squinted at them when I heard that. "Army?" I croaked. I had the urge to drink the stream dry.

The guy crouched in the water with me grinned. "Dr. Burke?" I nodded silently in affirmation. "Colonel Baker sends his regards."

There was a commotion among the soldiers standing around me and a ragged figure pushed its way through. He didn't look much better than I did. He was torn and battered; part of the hair on one side of his head had been singed away and the skin on his face looked shiny with burns. He collapsed down next to me, his body touching mine, and said nothing. The mere act of contact was enough.

Micky.

I leaned my head against his. It was good just to feel the heat of him, the strength of bone. The presence. My brother. My eyes burned and I was convulsed by a painful sob. We pressed our heads harder together like two kids, joined in a silent communion, the tears making tracks down the dirt and blood on our faces.

28

HIDDEN

I still think about the events of that last morning in the jungle. They flash into awareness. I grunt as the therapist forces my arm back, stretching it until the fibers scream, and I remember the feel of the attacker collapsing on top of me in the bamboo grove. I stand, sipping a steaming mug of coffee in dawn's half-light, and once again I'm tethered to a post, to watch my last day brighten the sky. It's not an act of will. I don't do this because I want to remember; it happens because I can't forget.

They never found the Tengu's corpse. The sea took it. It's just as well. Maybe waves and tides exist in part to scour the world of our leavings. Enough bodies remained in the jungle to serve as witnesses to what happened there.

I had been in contact with Colonel Baker from Manila once I had learned about the connection between Yamashita's kidnappers and the murder of the two embassy guards. And it turns out that Art had been in contact with Baker from the start. He fed him the GPS coordinates that Ueda eventually got for the camp. Baker had been told to stand down and let the Filipino Special Forces take the lead on the raid. Art said that he could practically hear Baker's teeth grinding over the phone, but the politicos in Manila were steering this and he had to comply. When Aguilar's choppers went down, I made frantic attempts to make contact with Baker again using the satellite phone, but never got through. As we drove up the rutted jungle path behind Ueda and Marangan into an ambush, I had no idea whether Baker was going to be able to help.

And Marangan? He'd been playing both sides. The *eskrimador* had been most interested in who was the highest bidder. He had gotten onto Mindanao ahead of us, and contracted to lead us into the ambush. We had our suspicions that he was doing the Tengu's bidding from the start. The Tengu had access to the Abe ransom money and he could easily afford to outbid Ueda. The ransom, like the kidnapping, was meaningless to that old demon. It was merely a means to an end.

Marangan disappeared right after the ambush. I never saw him at the Tengu's camp. The word on the street was that he'd gone to ground. The cops looked for him. So did the Japanese. And some Special Forces troopers I knew. He eluded them all for a time. But it's hard for people to stay away from their lives, no matter what the threat. And Marangan was someone who believed in his self-proclaimed identity as a *batikan*, a warrior. Eventually, he surfaced trying to make contact with a few associates who could set him up with a new assignment.

They found Marangan floating face-down in Manila Bay with two 9mm slugs in his head. Witnesses said that they had caught a glimpse of him at the docks, getting into a battered fishing boat with a big, thick black man wearing a Hawaiian shirt. An American, the witnesses thought. Probably an off-duty serviceman. The investigating officer, a Tomas Reyes, had shrugged and let the case go cold. Sergeant Cooke was back in Mindanao before anyone knew he was gone.

The guys in the Nomex jump suits that pulled me off the cliff that day were from Delta Force. Baker had done more than grit his teeth when he was told to stand down. He'd alerted a Delta troop that just happened to be participating in covert Malaysian counterterrorist activities. I thought back to the intensity on Baker's face long ago when I'd first seen the video of the execution of the embassy guards and wondered how much he knew about what was going on in the Philippines in the first place, and how many strings he had pulled to have troops on hand and ready to go. I was forever thankful that he did.

The feeling of being on the brink of that cliff, of the earth shifting beneath me and knowing that my hold on life was crumbling away, has never left me. More poignant are the memories of facing death together with my teacher.

But then I remember the almost electric surge of joy when I heard Micky's ragged voice shouting above the gunfire to head for the trees. And when I'm tired from the therapy, drifting in the uneasy half-sleep where things return unbidden, I sometimes give a convulsive sob of deep gratitude for the remembered feel of his head against mine.

They immobilized my arm and put field dressings on me in three different places. The soldiers hauled Micky and me to our feet and we started to make our slow, hobbling way back up the trail.

"Wait," I told them, and went back for something. I gripped it tight in my hand, feeling its hardness even through the padding of the bandages.

There was smoke in the clearing, and more soldiers prowled the edges, dragging out bodies. A group of Filipinos sat disconsolately in a cluster, arms bound behind them with plastic ties. The troopers had brought us back along a slightly different route, and I was disoriented for moment, not knowing where to look. I stumbled into the trampled grass of the clearing, looking left and right with increasing concern. I began to panic, but caught sight of them at last. I hurried over, my feet clumsy and catching on the tufts of grass, my stride jerky and broken as the uneven ground I stumbled across.

He was propped up in the shade against a tree trunk. Yamashita. His eyes were closed. Art sat quietly watching him, a canteen in his hand. He was raising it to his lips when he spotted us. He smiled and drank at the same time, and the clear liquid spilled out of either side of his mouth. Art didn't seem to mind. He stood up carefully and put a finger to his lips, looking at Yamashita and motioning us away.

Art gave both of us a hug. Micky grimaced in embarrassment.

"You got him," Art said to Micky in a pleased yet tired voice.

My brother and I sat down heavily. Art was a bit more graceful. "Took some doing," Micky told his partner.

Art eyed me, trying to assess the damage. He shook his head. "Man, Connor, what'd ya do, jump in a blender?"

I squinted at him and just shook my head. I was trying to watch Yamashita at the same time that I listened to Art.

"I saw you take off down the trail with the Deltas," Art confided to Micky, "I thought I was goin' to pass out. Bad enough that we lost track of Connor; there was no way I was gonna go home and have to face Deirdre without you."

"Yeah, well," my brother agreed "that would be bad." He smiled. "Glad to spare you the experience."

Art nodded in mock relief and looked at me again. "I don't even want to know what you've been up to, you lunatic. You couldn't have stayed put?"

I shrugged and inadvertently moved my right shoulder. *Ow.* But I didn't answer right away.

"I still don't know how you two made it out of the ambush," I finally said.

"Simple," Art began. "The old skills never leave you . . . "

"Sure," Micky interrupted, "basic rule of surviving an ambush. When everyone's shooting at your car . . . "

"Get out . . . " Art concluded.

They had floored the jeep backward in a hail of gunfire. When they whipped around a bend, the two of them jumped and tried to roll clear. Scrambling into the brush, they'd been singed by the explosion caused by an RPG. While the Filipinos poured bullets into the burning hulk, afraid to get too close because of the ammunition that was cooking off, Micky and Art had scurried off through the undergrowth to follow in my wake.

"We got out with our weapons," Art explained.

"And the satellite phone," Micky added with quiet satisfaction. And so they'd used it to update Baker, letting him get his force to within striking distance.

"The girl?" I asked.

"The Deltas almost gave her a stroke when they grabbed her halfway down the mountain," Micky told me.

"They've already taken her down to the landing spot," Art said. I looked at him quizzically. "They came by water, Connor. Choppers would have given them away, remember?" I nodded in response.

Art looked slowly out across the clearing, growing somber at the sight of the dead and wounded, the chewed up foliage, and the odd bits of clothing and equipment that got strewn across the field of battle. "Was there much more?" he asked Micky, quietly gesturing at me. "When you went down after him?"

"Some," Micky answered. "But it was all pretty much over except for the shouting when we got there." Then we were quiet for a time, each caught in our own thoughts—hard shards of memory struck off the different facets of our individual fights.

I saw Yamashita stir and went to him. He had a bandage across his chest and shoulder and a tag taped to him with a record of the initial drugs that had been administered. Art had told me that *Sensei* had taken a stray round in his shoulder but the wound wasn't life threatening. My teacher's eyes fluttered, struggling to come open. I knelt before him and bowed awkwardly.

"Burke." The name came out half whisper, half sigh as he recognized me.

"Yes, *Sensei*." My throat was tight with emotion.

He tried to sit forward. The action made him wince in pain and he sat back, but the sensation seemed to make him more alert.

"The old one?" he asked me urgently.

I held out the *tessen*, the iron war fan I had gripped so tightly all the way back from the cliff. I set it down on the ground between us and bowed again.

My teacher nodded. "So . . . " he sighed and gestured at me. "You have done . . . well." The words were halting and the effort to bring them forth appeared immense. "But," he said slowly, thickly, "At what cost?" Then he drifted away, the drugs taking hold once more.

The damage done to my teacher was extensive. We were evacuated to a ship and eventually to the U.S. Naval Hospital at Okinawa. It's close by Nara, one of the centers of Okinawan karate, but I didn't get to do much sightseeing—I wasn't in great shape, either. When they finally got Yamashita stabilized, they bundled us off to Kadena Air Force Base and back to the States.

There was the usual screaming and yelling by the NYPD when Micky and Art got home. Faced with letters of commendation from the State Department, the Japanese government, and the U.S. Army, the police brass toned it down to a low growl. Eventually, my brother and his partner were transferred to the anti-terrorism task force. It sounded good, but in reality they had been shunted off into a career dead end. They knew it, too.

But it wasn't all bad news. The State Department had rewards posted for a few of the Arabs I had met in the bamboo grove. It was an unexpected windfall that I shared with Micky and Art. They had thought about sticking it out until they had twenty years on the force and could retire. Now they were fantasizing about starting their own security and investigations firm.

At home, winter still held the countryside. Although the season's light was thin and washed out, the sun was beginning to work its magic. I could feel it in the fading heat of sunset as I stood in the fields, letting the red warmth brush my face lightly before the wind scoured it away. And even though my breath steamed in the air and snow clung to crevices beneath the trees, I knew that spring was coming. As the sun went down and the world cooled, winter strengthened its faltering grip on the world. The air grew blue as the light faded, as if to remind me that the season of ice was with us yet.

I meditated on change and continuity. On confronting evil and the toll it takes. I thought about life's harsh struggle that, on my better days, I believe is the forge of the spirit.

The long walks still hurt me, a bone-deep moaning in the body. It waxed and waned, and I was slowly mending, but it persisted like a bad memory. I would have done the walks no matter what. It wasn't just that the rehab people said I needed them. There was comfort in the solitude of the upstate forest and fields, and the circular nature of meandering paths that went nowhere and always led me back to my starting point.

All through the long winter, my teacher struggled as well. It was disorienting for me to see him so vulnerable, to see the master humbled. The soft tissue damage from the Tengu's torture had been devastating, and the physical therapy required would have drained a much younger man. Staying in his apartment above the *dojo* was out of the question. He needed access to therapy and daily support in coping with the littlest things. Yamashita was exhausted by the scope of his injuries and the fight it would take to come back even partially to his old level of fitness. I never underestimated him; he still had more to teach—one thing still brought a fierce glint to his eyes.

"The *dojo*," he told me. "The students have been without us long enough."

"They can wait," I told him. I had spoken with some of the senior students and they were rotating to cover classes.

"*Ie*," he snarled. No. "They have been without a master too long, Professor. Go to them."

"I'll stay with you," I said, but he shook his head even as I spoke. He was thinner now, and you could see the lines of muscle that stretched up his neck.

"No," he ordered. "The *dojo* is yours now . . . "

"It is not!" I protested.

He looked at me sharply. "Do not interrupt me, Burke. This is no time for self-delusion. You will go and teach them. I . . . have other battles to wage." And he crossed his arms across his chest to signal an end to the discussion.

Yamashita settled into the Zen Mountain Community, a Buddhist center a few hours north of Manhattan. The abbot was an old acquaintance who arranged for Yamashita's daily trips to a local hospital for therapy. I spent my weeks in Brooklyn, running the *dojo*, and prowling the empty loft above it, worried about the invisible wounds that afflicted my teacher. I was still not really up to anything challenging—in the training hall, I mostly directed the students and used the senior people to demonstrate—so I could only imagine what Yamashita was going through. On the weekends, I spent the days with him, noting slight signs of improvement, waiting for the old Yamashita to reemerge. I realize now that we had both been inalterably changed by our experiences and that things would never go back to what they were. But change meant that we had endured—*gambatte*.

Often, we rose at dawn and stretched. It was painful to watch Yamashita force his muscles to relearn what they had once known so easily. After a session, his forehead was dappled with sweat. I conferred with the physical therapist on a regular basis to get a sense of how things were going.

"He's got a tremendously high pain threshold," the PT told me. "He can push himself farther than most of my patients . . . "

"I sense a 'but' coming," I told him.

He nodded. "Well . . . look . . . he's old. It takes time for the tissue to regenerate. And some of the elasticity is not going to come back fully. Ever. And he knows it. He's going to push and push and push and ultimately, he's going to improve, but he'll never be the same."

I wanted to argue with the therapist. His verdict was the last thing I wanted to hear. But I saved my breath. My teacher has surprised people before.

Over the months, I saw small signs of progress. *Sensei* still tired easily and took naps late in the afternoon. I let him rest, taking the opportunity for long walks by myself in the woods around the monastery.

His legs were continuing to give him problems and the therapist suggested a cane. I recoiled at the image of my *sensei* tottering along with a rubber tipped monstrosity. I brought him a *bokken*, the wooden sword we use to train with, instead.

Yamashita looked at me and smiled briefly. "Ah. An old friend." He held it gingerly.

"Perhaps it's time you held him again," I said. He said nothing, but carried it with him from then on, using it as a support. I hoped it would serve as a reminder as well.

Every weekend after that, we would go slowly through the motions of sword *kata*—the performance routines used to mold technique. *Sensei* crept through the *kata*, like a man newly blind feeling his way across a once-familiar room. But he made the trip. *Little things*, I thought as we trained in a feeble parody of our old practice. *Tiny steps.*

And now I was the one who pushed, who forced my partner to go further, to accept the pain. One afternoon, near the usual close of our session, I pushed a little too hard.

"Burke," Yamashita said, breathing heavily, "I cannot."

"You can," I insisted, and brought my sword to bear on him in the ready position.

"No," he sighed. "Enough for today."

I stood there, the tip of my sword threatening him. "*Mo ichido*," I demanded. One more time.

"I cannot!"

I inched forward aggressively. "Burke!" he warned. But I didn't back off.

He saw me set myself for an attack and his nostrils flared in anger. "Do not push me," he warned.

I began a short, chopping motion that would slam down into his forearm. He saw it coming and could tell from the set of my body that this was not going to be some gentle slow motion parody. I was going for the real thing. "Burke!" he warned again. "Do not!"

But it was too late—I was committed. His body, worn as it was, acted instinctively and he brought his own *bokken* up and around to slam into my attacking blade. It was a little move, but tight, hard and precisely executed—a flash of the old Yamashita. My sword was beaten down and away, the attack defeated.

He glared at me momentarily, but then a rueful smile played across his face. Yamashita gave a small, quiet snort. "As always, Burke, there is more to you than meets the eye."

"I have a good teacher," I answered.

"As do I," he said gruffly. He bowed slightly and turned away. But I noticed that as he left, he held the sword like a weapon and not like a crutch.

I wondered whether I was worthy to be a teacher. I've mastered some of the way of the sword—the externals, the technique—but deep down I know I'm not the equal of my master. I don't know whether I'll ever think of death as something light as a feather. I wandered the trails around the monastery, feeling a mixture of sadness, hope, and confusion. Maybe I'm a fraud.

I shuffled through the old leaves that the maples had surrendered to earth at the beginning of the winter. And it struck me for all these years, although I had always believed that training in the art was a vehicle for something else, that I had never really grasped what that goal was. It wasn't my ability to wield a sword or my commitment to training that mattered. It had to be something else. In the final analysis, skill fails or fades. All that is left is our spirit, and the willingness to endure in the service of something larger than ourselves. The old masters knew that some things were too precious to abandon, no matter what the cost. People like Baker understood that as well as Yamashita. Life seemed to me too bittersweet to be surrendered lightly. And our connection to each other is too strong to be severed by fear. It was not that our paths are always easy—it is rather that they seem to me to be worth the effort to walk.

And my path is one that flows along next to my teacher. It's different from what it was in the past and perhaps not what I expected, but we are still connected, like two wheels of the same cart—distinct, yet linked together.

As I wandered down the wooded slope and into a clearing, I paused to ease the muscles of my left side. The air smelled clean and I caught the scent of earth and water. The sun was working the ground, softening the frost's grip. I probed aimlessly in the mast at the foot of a dormant maple tree, and the matted leaves humped up to reveal the dark wetness that lay underneath. There, just uncoiling and whitely translucent, was the first tentative shoot of new growth.

I made my way back to the monastery. It was time to work again with my teacher, to coax him along a hard road and back to his life. I thought of the effort it took for him just to move, and the pain and weariness that etched his face. He had changed. So had I. But I could still see the feeble spark of spirit in his eyes, and I would work hard to feed it. In the end, it didn't matter whether this frail old man returned to his former self. What mattered was the fact that we would totter along this new path together.

Beauty in the most unexpected of places.

About the Author

John Donohue is a nationally known expert on the culture and practice of the martial arts and has been banging around the dojo for more than 30 years. He has trained in the martial disciplines of aikido, iaido, judo, karatedo, kendo, and taiji. He has dan (black belt) ranks in both karatedo and kendo.

John has a Ph.D. in Anthropology from the State University of New York at Stony Brook. His doctoral dissertation on the cultural aspects of the Japanese martial arts formed the basis for his first book, *The Forge of the Spirit*. Fiction became a way to combine his interests and *Sensei*, the first Connor Burke thriller was published in 2003. John Donohue resides in New Haven, CT.